ISBN Number: 978-1-291-54678-1

Editing / proofreading by Sam Szanto: http://www.samszanto.co.uk
Cover design by Leanne Phillips: http://www.leannephillips.co.uk
Photograph – 'NightLea' by Kriss Lee: http://www.500px.com/CLipiCs

Casey's info:

http://www.caseykelleher.co.uk

www.facebook.com/officialcaseykelleher

Twitter: @caseykelleher

In loving memory of Grandad Clark

One of the brightest stars in the sky

x

'The laughter of a man is more terrible than his tears, and takes more forms. Hollow, heartless, mirthless and maniacal.'

~ James Thurber

Prologue

The custody van made its way through the wrought-iron gates and down the long winding driveway. Although it was dark, the glowing yellow light poured out from the building's windows, casting shadows into the courtyard, creating an eerie silhouette. The high barbed-wire fence surrounding the perimeter was a stark reminder of the old boarding school that used to be there.

Rain pelted down, hitting the van's roof, the droplets bouncing off the metal making the noise of the downpour even louder. A burly prison officer jumped out from the passenger side and ran to the back of the van, opening the door to release the prisoners.

The three girls who got out of the van had endured a cramped and claustrophobic two-hour journey, and despite what was ahead of them they were happy to be able to stand and stretch their legs.

"Come on, move it," the officer ordered, as she led the girls across the gravel driveway. The girls followed, trudging through deep puddles as they went towards the bleak-looking building.

Once inside, the girls huddled together in the doorway; they were grateful for the shelter from the pouring rain but nervous of their new surroundings. Their clothes were soaked, raindrops dripping from their hair and running down their faces. They squinted; the harsh glare of the strip lights that filled the room was a stark contrast to the darkness they had endured in the back of the van.

Looking around the windowless reception, the tallest of the girls took in her new surroundings. The room was bare, with nothing but a desk where two prison officers stood as they waited to check in their new arrivals. The girl scanned the room, noticing two more officers that were standing behind them next to a doorway; the officers' expressions looked blank as they returned the girl's stare and remained in their continued silence. The girl watched them, noting to herself that not only did the officers wear matching uniforms, but judging by the bored expressions on their faces they seemed to have the same attitude; not an ounce of sympathy or compassion graced their features. It was clear that this was just another day's work for them.

"Nishay Gibson?" A stocky female officer directed the question at the chunky dark-skinned girl who stood confidently in front of the other two nervous-looking inmates; filling out a form on her clipboard she barely even glanced up at Nishay as she spoke.

"That's me," the big girl replied, before adding, "you lot can't keep me away. Makes me laugh... call this place a punishment? I get to sit on my arse watching telly all day, with no agro from me old dear. This is a fucking holiday!"

Nishay was fifteen years old but looked older than her years and she oozed confidence: she was scared of no-one.

"I can think of nicer places to go on holiday than here, let me tell you," the officer replied sarcastically.

"I guess. Might be nice to have some gorgeous buff man greeting me with a cocktail on a beach somewhere, rather than be greeted by you lots' ugly mugs! What a bunch of miserable cunts," Nishay said.

The officer rolled her eyes and ignored the girl's comments. Pursing her mouth tightly she was determined not to bite back, remaining unfazed; she had seen this sort of behaviour time and time again by other inmates that had been in this girl's position: the ones that were familiar with the system and had grown comfortable with the institute's surroundings. She wasn't in the mood for this one's feeble attempt at trying to goad her into any form of discussion: she didn't have the time or energy for it. Like her fellow officers, she just wanted to check this lot in and get on with the evening shift.

"Today's date is the second of December 1998." The officer filled out the booking sheet as she continued: "Your name is Nishay Gibson. What is your date of birth?"

"I was born on my birthday." Nishay looked around the room, grinning at her wit. She didn't get the reaction she had been hoping for. She was funny, she knew it, but this lot were a bunch of stuck-up tossers. Not even the other two girls who were waiting to be checked in behind her had given so much as a chuckle at what she had said. Fucking pussies, she thought, as she sneered at the two girls, sucking her teeth in distaste in their direction. A right pair of snobby little bitches. Turning back to the officer she saw that she was still staring blankly at her, waiting for an answer to her question.

"Fuck me, youse lot need to get a fucking sense of humour. What, you on the blob or something?" Nishay looked the female officer up and down. The woman was a state. Judging by the lines around her eyes, she reckoned the woman was in her mid-forties; her manly build made her resemble a tranny.

Nishay stroked her chin mockingly as she jibed the officer. "You been growing that beard long?"

Nishay liked to think she had a knack for intimidating people. She had a way of making them feel wary. However, the officer just ignored Nishay's comments and her attempts to get a rise from her. She returned the cocky girl's stare with a look of contempt as she continued to wait for her to answer her earlier question.

4

"Second of February 1983," Nishay said finally. This woman was a right hard-nosed bitch, she thought, miffed that she seemed to be dismissing her.

"Right, Gibson, you're having a strip search with Officer Cook and Officer Williams. Mind that you don't get too cold," the officer said smugly, as she nodded in her colleagues' direction. Two women stepped forward.

"Nah, I've been searched already. You two nonces just wanna see a young pair of tits that ain't swinging down past a pair of knees for once. Well, you can fuck off." Without warning Nishay struck out with her fists, catching Officer Cook unaware with a punch to the face that launched her across the room.

Then, all hell broke loose.

Nishay swept all of the documents which had been on the desk onto the floor. She was enjoying the disruption that she was causing.

Realising that the girl was out of control and capable of doing a lot of damage, Officer Williams jumped on top of Nishay to try and restrain her, pushing her onto the ground.

Nishay's nose hit the cold tiled floor and pain exploded in her head. A warm trickle of blood dripped from her nostrils, splattering the bright white tiles with dark red droplets. Imagining her nose was broken Nishay lost the plot. Kicking her legs and using her entire strength to manoeuvre herself, she fought against the officer with all her might. But it was no use: Officer Williams was stronger. Lifting her head, Nishay tried to snap her neck backwards so that she could butt the officer in the face. However the officer was one step ahead, and had predicted Nishay's next move, ducking out of the way just in time; she pressed the girl's face into the floor, using all her force to restrain the writhing girl, pinning her down again. She was aware that Officer Monroe had pressed the alarm and three more members of the team had come running to assist her. Nishay was strong, she would give her that, and she didn't know how much longer she would be able to restrain her on her own.

"Do as you are told or you are going to be in a whole world of shit before you have even been allocated a bed!" one of the officers shouted in Nishay's ear.

Nishay could taste the blood as it ran down the back of her throat. She spat a mouthful of it at the officer, which only reached the ankles of her tights. The officer grimaced in disgust.

"I don't get paid enough to put up with shit like this, now behave."

Realising she was outnumbered, Nishay went limp. She knew that ultimately the little performance wouldn't get her anywhere. This was the third time she had been sent to this young offenders' institute and she probably knew the drill better than the officers themselves. It was standard procedure that all the inmates were strip-searched and given clean clothes before they were interviewed, but why should she play nicely? There was no fun in that. These fuckers could earn their wages, as far as she was concerned. Lying quietly now against the cold tiled floor she smiled to herself, satisfied that she had managed to cause a commotion.

The officers dragged Nishay back up onto her feet and escorted her into a side room to be searched while Officer Monroe gathered all the paperwork from the floor as a first step to regaining normality. She turned her attention to the girl who was next in line to be checked in.

"Name and date of birth?" she asked.

The tall skinny girl knew her expression wasn't masking her horror at what she had just witnessed. She was going to be locked up with real criminals like that girl. There was no way she would survive.

"I said: name and date of birth?" the irritated officer repeated.

Tears stung the girl's eyes as she answered.

"It's Sophia O'Hagan. Please... I shouldn't be here. There's been a mistake." It was all she managed to say before she threw up the contents of her stomach all over the officer's desk.

Chapter One

The grinding noise of the key repeatedly scraping the lock told Kaitlin how drunk her husband was this evening. He had been struggling with the door for a good few minutes, unable to find the keyhole, and then rattling the door angrily. Kaitlin had remained sitting in the lounge, dreading his homecoming as she cursed herself for not going up to bed sooner. Jamesie would do nothing but rant and rave if he was as drunk as she was guessing that he was. Turning up the volume on the TV, she pretended to be so engrossed in her programme that she couldn't hear him. She would only be able to hold him off for another few minutes, but she certainly wasn't in any hurry to help him in. Checking the clock on the mantelpiece, Kaitlin hoped that Sophia had dropped off to sleep already, praying that the girl wouldn't have to listen to another slurred outburst from her intoxicated father. Being called every name under the sun Kaitlin could handle, the putdowns and the swearing were par for the course. Jamesie didn't communicate any other way anymore. But Kaitlin wouldn't allow poor Sophia to listen to it. The girl was getting older, almost sixteen, and Kaitlin could see the hurt in her eyes every time another bruise or mark appeared on her mother's skin.

Finally the door opened, crashing noisily off the wall as it was flung open. The sound of her husband's feet stomping through the hallway got louder as he neared, and Kaitlin gulped as she prepared herself for Jamesie's inebriated state; it seemed to worsen every time he had a skinful of alcohol.

"You lazy mare." Jamesie slurred as he staggered into the lounge. He stank of alcohol.

Kaitlin turned up the volume on the TV, hoping to drown out Jamesie's voice. She could tell that he was in his 'poor me' frame of mind, although he often felt hard done by, as though life had deliberately dropped a heavy load on him from a great height, and his wife was always the one to blame for it. Since the factory had laid him off, he had become even more difficult. His stress and worry had quickly turned to anger and aggression and, fuelled by constant drinking, his fiery temper was rapidly started to spiral out of control.

"You could've opened the door for me; don't make out like you didn't know I was out there. You're a lazy bitch, Kaitlin, sitting on your bony fucking arse ignoring me. Don't you ever, ever, fucking ignore me, do you understand?" Jamesie pointed an unsteady finger at his wife.

Kaitlin nodded, desperate to try and calm Jamesie down. She didn't have the energy for the drama tonight; once Jamesie got himself riled up he wouldn't let it go. He was so argumentative that he could start a fight with his own shadow if the mood took him and the sad thing was there was never a real reason for it, he was just bitter about life in general.

"I made you some dinner, fish pie. Shall I heat it up?" Kaitlin asked softly, as Jamesie slumped down in his armchair.

"I'm not hungry," Jamesie said, as he stared at his wife. His vision was blurred due to the amount of drink he had downed earlier but even in his drunken state he could tell that his wife felt timid, that his presence made her feel nervous.

"Here, come over here to me." He motioned for Kaitlin to come over to his chair.

Praying that her husband's mood was improving, Kaitlin stood beside him, trying not to breathe in the fumes of whiskey and cigarettes.

Standing in front of her husband, her arms hung down awkwardly at her sides and she tightly clasped her hands. She felt a wave of unease as Jamesie leered at her. She knew what was coming: he had that nasty glint in his eyes.

Jamesie gripped his wife's breast; he squeezed it and she flinched in pain.

"Take your skirt off."

Kaitlin didn't have the strength for this. But knowing that it was another of Jamesie's tests and that she had no choice but to do as he said, she did as she was told. He would make up the rules and she would play along like a good girl: if she didn't, he would only force her.

"Jamesie, Sophia's only just gone up. She probably isn't asleep yet. Let's just go upstairs to bed, yeah?" But she knew that he wasn't listening. This was another part of his game; he knew Kaitlin would be mortified if their daughter walked in on what he subjected her to. She would have to do what Jamesie told her, or she would only anger him. Even in sex Jamesie was violent, especially lately. He wanted to hurt her, take out his anger out on her. Kaitlin had no choice but to go along with his demands, and he now forced himself upon her on almost a daily basis. If Kaitlin didn't respond to his needs willingly he got his pleasure from making her.

"I said, take off your skirt." Jamesie's glare told her that he didn't intend on going anywhere. Right here was good enough for him.

Unzipping her long skirt and letting it fall to the floor, Kaitlin glanced over to the door.

"And the rest." He indicated his wife's knickers and jumper.

Taking off her jumper over her head, she unclipped her bra and pulled her knickers down, Kaitlin stood before him naked, her exposed body leaving her completely vulnerable to her husband's scrutiny. His eyes wandered up and down her body. Kaitlin just wanted him to get on with what he planned to do; there was no point in trying to stop him.

Kaitlin no longer got physical pleasure from her husband, and he no longer offered it: he was too concerned about himself for that. Sex for him was all about power now; all about showing his wife who was the boss.

He nodded as he sat back in the armchair. "Go on; get on all fours."

Kaitlin knelt on the thin carpet in front of him, shame and humiliation washing over her. The only sound in the room other than his raspy breathing was the ticking clock.

"Look at the state of you," Jamesie said, as his eyes roamed her body. Her frame was so tiny that her ribs and spine stuck out. Kneeling before him, naked and bent over, she reminded him of an old knackered greyhound.

Kaitlin didn't respond. The best thing to do was to let him get on with his rants and abuse. The more she resisted the worse he would be, so she remained silent.

It was always the same, his game. First he belittled her and humiliated her. That was his foreplay if you like. Once Jamesie was satisfied that he had made Kaitlin feel small and powerless, he then forced himself onto her. He knew that he disgusted his wife: he could see it in her eyes. So when he entered her roughly, knowing it was against her will, he made no disguise of the fact that he enjoyed the sound of her pain. Every thrust was harder and harder, as he punished her with his body. He would squeeze her breasts so tightly that she would be left bruised for days afterwards. Often he would pull fistfuls of her hair too.

Until lately it had always been when Sophia was out, but the last few times the girl had been in the house. Jamesie knew that it was the one thing that Kaitlin worried about the most; and he enjoyed tormenting her with it. Kaitlin would never forgive herself if Sophia saw them, and for that reason alone she didn't fight back; she just let him get on with the ordeal without making a sound, hoping that it would be over quickly. Sophia was her sweet and innocent daughter and Kaitlin had fought to keep the reality of her family life from her, but it was getting harder to pretend that this wasn't happening. Sophia had already seen too much. The bruises, the shouting... hiding them from her was near on impossible, especially with Jamesie no longer seeming to care who knew about his violent outbursts. He drank more and more and seemed angrier each day.

Kaitlin knew from experience that any protest from her and Jamesie would hurt her even more. He would do whatever it took to overpower her. Controlling her turned him on. He had told her once that he could only release himself inside of her once he was satisfied that she had earned it.

Kaitlin waited for Jamesie to begin. She was unsure how much more of this abuse she could endure. She wasn't eating properly; she wasn't sleeping well. She felt like a nervous wreck most of the time. She was almost at breaking point.

She fought to control her shaking arms, knowing the enjoyment he got from seeing how frightened she was.

After a minute of waiting, her head hanging down in expectation, her body cold, she looked up. Jamesie was standing over her, staring.

"Look at the fucking state of you. What a fucking disgrace. You're a weak, pathetic excuse for a woman." It was his mantra these days, and Kaitlin was starting to believe it. Weak was what she had become. "Who would want to fuck you? I'm going up to bed."

Jamesie walked out of the room, leaving Kaitlin on her hands and knees, relieved but mortified. She grabbed her clothes, and with hot tears in her eyes, struggled to pull them on.

Slowly making her way to the sofa, Kaitlin threw herself down onto it and curled into a ball, burying her head into a cushion as she desperately tried to stifle the noise of the huge sobs that escaped from her mouth.

How had her life come to this?

Chapter Two

Jonathan tilted the video camera, angling the lens so that it focused on the small box on the grass. The camera was his pride and joy and had been very expensive; it had taken numerous arguments with his parents before they had agreed to buy it for him, he had even had to agree to share it with his brother but luckily Tommy had no interest in using it, so it was all Jonathan's.

Crouching down on the grass, Jonathan peered inside the box and saw the tiny sparrow that he had captured earlier that day. Jonathan knew that it was a sparrow because his dad had done nothing but bore the arse off him harping on about birds ever since he had caught Jonathan with a box containing the three he had captured a week previously. Jonathan had said he was trying to make a nest for them. His dad had taken this as a sign that his son and he could share a new-found hobby and he had tried to encourage Jonathan to bird-watch with him ever since.

Jonathan couldn't think of anything more boring than him and his dad, who rarely had much to say to each other, sitting together in the shed peeping out of the windows. And despite his dad's insistence on buying Jonathan a pair of binoculars and installing a bird-table in their garden, Jonathan had rejected his offers of joining him, to the point that he had now given up trying.

Jonathan pressed the record button, and then the night light. The unnatural green light in the videos added a darker atmosphere to his movies, he found. Jonathan shook the box, enjoying tormenting the little bird, before tipping it out onto the grass. It was starting to look weak and Jonathan guessed that it was close to death. He had snapped its legs earlier, and pulled off one of its wings. He had been surprised and impressed that the bird hadn't squawked more whilst he inflicted the pain upon it. He wished that he had filmed that bit, but he had had no time: he had to be quick while there was no one about.

The bird lay limp on the grass; the only sign it was alive was its brown eyes darting in panic, as if it knew what was coming next.

Jonathan dragged another box from behind the shed and carefully picked off the edges of the masking tape that he had used to seal it earlier. Then he opened the box, freeing the neighbour's cat. He had been worried that his dad would find the box that he had so thoughtfully punctured air holes into and stashed behind some old planks of MDF behind the shed. Luckily for him, however, his dad had been playing golf for most of the afternoon so hopefully no-one had heard the cat meowing inside its prison.

Hearing his mum calling him from the back door, Jonathan crouched down lower so that he was out of sight behind the shed. He hoped that the cat would be hungry enough to quickly take its prey. The last thing he needed was for his mum to sneak up on him and spoil his hard work and careful planning.

She didn't call again. Jonathan sat back against the shed and relaxed as he watched the cat stretch, clearly relieved to be out of the box it had been confined to. It strolled over to where the injured bird lay, prodding it with a claw before rolling it over as if it was a prize toy. Then, realising the bird was his for the taking the cat started to eat it, feasting first on the head. The bird's body twitched as it met its fate. Jonathan zoomed in for a close-up.

The bird lay decapitated on the grass as the cat chewed on its neck. It looked as though it were savouring every bite. Finally, just a few brown feathers strewn on the grass were all that remained as evidence that the sparrow had once been there.

Licking his lips, and then cleaning his fur, the cat seemed pleased. Jonathan wasn't so happy. The killing hadn't left him as satisfied as he had expected. He hadn't captured the moment of death. He needed its exact moment. As he packed away his camera, he considered what it may be like to set a bird on fire. He might try that next time.

Jonathan placed his camera inside its padded bag and zipped it up. His belly rumbled: the cat wasn't the only one that needed feeding.

***

"You've called him twice now, Bernie; he'll be in any second." Stanley was growing tired of listening to his wife's exaggerated sighs as she glanced up at the clock and waited for their son to come inside for dinner. Bernie was trying to create a drama when it wasn't necessary. "He's fifteen; we don't need to wrap him up in cotton wool. He's only in the garden, for God's sake, it's not like he's gone AWOL."

Stanley knew his words had fallen on deaf ears. Bernie did nothing but fuss over their children; it drove both Stanley and his sons stir-crazy. Stanley wondered if Bernie was aware of how much her constant nit-picking irritated their kids.

"Go on, Tommy, you may as well make a start on your dinner, no use in all of our meals going cold just because Jonathan can't be bothered to join us," Bernie said sulkily to her other son, after rolling her eyes at her husband's flippancy.

Bernie continued to prod her meal in silence, pushing it around the plate; her bad moods caused her to have stomach aches and so her desire to eat had vanished.

Hearing the back door slam, Stanley raised his eyebrows at his wife. Patience is a virtue, he thought to himself, one which his wife certainly wasn't blessed with.

Striding into the room, seemingly unapologetic about the fact that he was once again late for dinner, Jonathan sat in his usual place, between his dad and his brother.

"There's no point in me standing out in that kitchen cooking for you if by the time you get in here your dinner's cold," Bernie said pointedly.

Jonathan smirked and poked at his food.

"Mm, salmon again; what a nice change," he said, picking at the fish with his fork. Salmon was his mum's favourite; they ate it at least twice a week. "Pass the salt, Tommy."

Jonathan kept his head down, knowing that just the sight of his parents, sitting there looking stilted and false at opposite ends of the 'formal' dining table, as his mother liked to refer to it as if they were royalty would set him off giggling at how ridiculous they looked. He knew that this pretentiousness wasn't his dad's fault: he was a wet blanket and mostly just did as he was told so that he could have an easy life. It was his mum who wanted to be seen as 'proper'.

Bernie watched, irritated, as Tommy passed Jonathan the salt pot. Jonathan snatched it out of his hand and covered the piece of fish in a thick layer of it.

"Salmon costs a lot of money, you know," she said. "You don't realise how lucky you are to have such nice dinners made for you; some children eat microwaved junk every night."

Stanley scoffed, louder than he had meant; his wife moaned so much that even now when she had a valid point no-one bothered to listen. She never knew when to stop.

Glaring at her husband, Bernie slammed her cutlery onto her plate. Dinner was ruined. "Why I bother to make lovely home-cooked meals for the three of you,

I really don't know. I have a husband who sits there mocking me, making me out to be just some old nagging housewife, and an ungrateful son who can't even have the decency to come inside when he's called to eat the darn thing."

"What about me? I love your dinners, Mum." Tommy tried to soften his mum's mood as he ate another mouthful.

"Arse-licker," Jonathan whispered. Tommy was such a suck-up. Jonathan wished that his brother was more like him, so that they could team up and cause their mum some real grief. But Tommy was far too good to behave like that. Their mum had done nothing but suffocate them since the day they were born and her hen-pecking had paid off when it came to Tommy. He was a total mummy's boy. But her clinginess had had the opposite effect on Jonathan, resulting in her irritating the life out of him. He went out of his way to be dismissive of everything that she said or did. He loved that the more he pushed her away the more she tried even harder to keep him firmly in her radar and each time failed miserably. He relished the hurt that he caused her. Even as a toddler, he had been a master at playing games with her. His father had told him not long ago, in another of his feeble attempts at having some kind of a conversation, about how he had driven his mother mad as a small child. Whenever Bernie had tried to make Jonathan go to the toilet, he would deliberately save himself until they were all in the car or even better he would wait until they were at one of her snooty friends' houses. The sight of her looking mortified as she cleaned his poo off people's sofas and carpets had delighted him, and Jonathan had turned his incontinence into a regular occurrence. After a few of these incidents, his mother's friends had started not to invite her to coffee mornings and that was when Bernie reached the end of her tether and finally took Jonathan to see the doctor. A behavioural specialist made five-year-old Jonathan sit on a potty, on which he obediently went to the toilet with no trouble at all. He had taken great pleasure in making his mother out to be a liar in front of the middle-aged male doctor. He had even said pardon when a fart had escaped his bottom. His mother had watched, shocked that all of a sudden the little boy was capable of going to the toilet properly. Bernie could almost see the thoughts whirling around the specialist's head, such as whether her concerns about her child were fabricated and the questioning of her parenting skills had been the ultimate insult. After that toilet training was never an issue again; Jonathan had succeeded in his mission of making his mum suffer. Ten years on and still nothing pleased Jonathan more than scoring points against her.

"So, what have you been doing today?" Bernie asked, as she watched Jonathan continue to push his food around the plate. She hoped that her son would, for once, engage in a normal conversation with her. Looking him up and down, she wished that he wouldn't wear such dark, dreary clothing. She also didn't like the way his long, greasy hair hung on one side of his face. Her eyes went from him to Tommy, who was always dressed immaculately and had his hair cut without so much of a word of complaint. She couldn't understand how identical twins could be so different.

"Oh, you know, nothing much," Jonathan said, as he put a potato into his mouth. Eating it with his mouth open, he noted the annoyance in his mum's eyes: she was reacting as he knew she would to his bad manners. He chewed loudly, seeing her trying her hardest not to scold him.

Stanley winced as Jonathan let out a belch and Bernie, unable to ignore her son's behaviour any longer, tutted. Jonathan laughed; he had won yet another game: his mother was too predictable.

"Jonathan, what's got into you? Where are your manners? Say pardon me." Bernie used to believe that it was her son's awkward transition from child to teenager that was causing him to act so rudely, even though this was not the case for Tommy. She could understand hormones. But he seemed to be getting worse, and she feared it had nothing to do with puberty: Jonathan was just plain rude.

"Pardon you, mother," Jonathan said.

Sensing another battle of wills coming on, Stanley didn't want to get involved. "Right, that was rather splendid, Bernie. I'm just off to finish potting up those hydrangeas. Leave the plates on the side; I'll do them when I'm finished."

Having an electrical point installed in his shed had been one of the best things that Stanley had ever done. He had insisted that he would need it for his lighting and electric tools, but generally the only appliance that required any power was his portable TV. Escaping to his sanctuary to watch it had become a welcome release from his nagging wife's constant gripes and his spoilt son's demands, and Stanley once again couldn't wait to escape the pair of them. Jonathan may be rude to Bernie but he was completely dismissive to Stanley. The boy never had the time of day for his father, unlike his Tommy. It was almost time for the match to start: Arsenal was playing, and Stanley was looking forward to watching his team in peace.

"No, you go off and sort out your plants, Stanley. We'll clear up the dishes," Bernie insisted. It was the least Jonathan could do after ruining her dinner.

"Okay then. Do you fancy giving your old dad a hand... with the potting up?" Stanley asked Tommy. He knew that his son would jump at a chance to escape the other two as well. Tommy loved hiding out in the shed with his dad and watching the matches.

Jonathan watched as his brother and his dad made a quick exit from the room before turning back to his mother who had started on again with her nagging.

"Right then, you can make up for being so late, Jonathan. I'll wash, you dry," she said, shooting her son a firm look.

"I can't, Mum, I'm going out." His mum asking him to do chores with her was just a ploy to get them to spend time together.

"No, you're not. Not until you've helped me do the washing up," Bernie said, losing patience with her son. Jonathan hardly spent any time at home; when he wasn't at school he was always going off somewhere, usually with that silly camera in tow. He was so secretive. She tried hard with him, but he constantly spoke to and treated her like she was an inconvenience.

"And what are you going to do to stop me, huh?" Jonathan leaned back in his chair; he was intrigued to see how she would react to his challenge. He could see the tears in her eyes: she looked like she was fighting hard to hold them back. "Are you going to lock me in my bedroom or spank my bum?"

He laughed.

Bernie knew that once again, her son was challenging her. She never won an argument with him; the more that she insisted on something, the more he refused to do it. It was as if he was trying to break her down, and lately she had felt that it wouldn't be long until she would have to give up trying with him. After fifteen years, he had nearly worn her out.

Jonathan pulled his chair out, stood up and threw his mum a triumphant look. Whistling as he went, he strolled out of the room.

Staring at her selfish child's back, Bernie gathered the plates and cutlery. The thought of another lonely evening in the house on her own made her feel sorry for herself; family life was not how she had envisaged it. She and Stanley had never been madly in love, not even in the beginning. Stanley had employed Bernie to do his books for him. He ran his father's garage, but had no time to do any of the accounts or paperwork. Bernie had been a natural. She had answered the ad that he had placed in the local newspaper and in no time at all, she had whipped the place into shape. Stanley had very quickly come to depend on her. After his father's death, Stanley took the garage on as his own and by then Bernie had become irreplaceable to him. They worked so well as a team, and Stanley could see that

Bernie was fond of him. He reasoned that it would be in both of their interests if they married. As the business rapidly went from strength to strength Stanley was ecstatic when a few months after they had tied the knot, Bernie announced that she was pregnant.

Ever since the twins had been born, their relationship had been strained. Bernie gave up her role at the garage to concentrate on bringing the boys up, and now all these years later they no longer agreed on much anymore. It was rare that they were in the same room for more than half an hour these days, and even when they were the only thing they shared was an uncomfortable silence. Stanley favoured Tommy so blatantly, struggling to bond with Jonathan. Bernie constantly pulled her husband up on it, but she knew deep down that it was so hard not to be biased. Tommy was so considerate and caring and he couldn't do enough for anyone he met. Jonathan, with his dark moods and his constant sneers, seemed like the devil in disguise. Bernie had often guiltily wondered if Tommy had got all the good genes and Jonathan the bad ones. No matter what she or her husband did to try and get through to the boy, nothing worked. It was as if Jonathan had no emotions. Suddenly feeling extremely sorry for herself, Bernie dropped the plate she was holding onto the floor and flung herself onto a chair. Placing her head in her hands, she started to sob.

She had never felt so lonely.

Chapter Three

"Good morning, my beautiful little dumpling-bum." Nessa O'Hagan pulled back the curtains and let in a stream of bright sunshine. Now that there was light in the room she could get a proper look at her gorgeous granddaughter who was sprawled out on the sofa.

"Rascal, get down from there you blinking eejit," Nessa said, as she pushed the little Jack Russell off the chair that he was desperately trying to claw his way up onto, so that he could greet their sleepy-looking guest.

Sophia couldn't help but laugh at the sight of her nan wearing her usual morning attire of a fluffy leopard-print dressing gown and a head full of purple rollers, as she swatted the yappy little dog off the furniture. Rascal was in his element now, leaping around the room, thoroughly enjoying the fact that he was now the centre of attention. He began to move faster and Sophia giggled even more as she watched the nutty little dog pick up speed and wag his tail as he went.

Nessa managed to catch up with her demented pooch and pulled him up into her arms. "Should have called him blinking Loopy, not Rascal, always acting the maggot so he is. So, how do you fancy some brekkie, my lovey?" Nessa was delighted that she would have her granddaughter's company for breakfast, although she was also aware that the privilege had come at a price. It was the second night in a row that she had woken to find her sleeping on the couch, and Nessa didn't need the brains of Einstein to work out that her shithead of a son Jamesie was up to his old tricks again. Nessa wished to God that the man would cop on to himself and stop being the no-good bully that he was. What poor Sophia and her mother had to put up with on a daily basis from her son was totally unacceptable, and Nessa was losing her patience. Silently thanking God that her house was just across the road, and Sophia didn't have to go very far to get here Nessa decided not to start questioning the poor girl just yet as she made her way through the open archway into the kitchen. Sophia would tell her in her own time.

"Yes, please, Nan, I'm starving. What are we having?" Her nan always bought Sophia the chocolate cereals and other sugary treats that she loved, unlike at home where she was lucky if she could find a slice of toast most mornings.

Sophia rubbed her eyes and stretched her arms out, giving a dramatic yawn. She had been awake much of the night with a hard metal spring from the sofa poking into her back. What with that and a head full of worry, she had probably only had about three hours sleep in total and she knew if she milked the fact that she was exhausted, her nan would feel sorry for her and let her off school again.

Nessa shook the cereal boxes and realised that they were all empty. How that girl stayed so slim, Nessa couldn't fathom.

"Oh, I tell you what, I've got some tasty stew left over from last night's dinner. It was bloody delicious, you know. Albert brought it over; he makes the fluffiest dumplings I've ever seen: the size of footballs they are. Think he was trying to win me over, as he was worried that it probably didn't taste as good as how us Irish make it," Nessa said. "I told him the secret is in the spuds."

Nessa was proud of her friend's culinary skills. She had known Albert for years and since he had retired from working long hours as a busy GP, he mainly filled his days cooking the most amazing dishes. His specialties included delicious curries and tasty posh French cuisine, the names of which Nessa couldn't even pronounce, and as for his cakes: well, they were something else completely and she was surprised that she wasn't the size of a house with the amount of food he brought over for her. Albert seemed to be in the habit of making so much food that there were always leftovers. Nessa knew that the old boy had a soft spot for her, but he had never made a move or said anything. He had just insisted that he feed her well in return for her great company and Nessa was only too happy with the arrangement. Albert was a real gentleman, but although Nessa was very fond of the man she would never want anything more than his friendship. It went without saying that the only man that Nessa O'Hagan would take to her bed these days was the hairy mutt variety: aka, little Rascal.

"Stew... ew!" Sophia cried. Only her nan would eat stew at seven-thirty in the morning.

Seeing her granddaughter scrunch up her nose in distaste and stick out her tongue at her suggestion, Nessa added: "Well, there's not a lot in, I'm afraid. I haven't had a chance to do me shopping this week yet."

She placed Rascal onto the floor so that she could see what food she could dig out from the back of the cupboards.

"You know, if you weren't here, I'd think nothing of eating that stew. Don't matter to me what time of the day it is, food is food, makes no odds to me; goes in one hole and out of another," Nessa shouted into the direction of the lounge as she giggled to herself whilst she continued to root around for something her granddaughter might find acceptable.

Sophia rolled her eyes at her nan's bluntness then stood up and shook out the blanket that was always left out for her 'just in case'. Folding it and placing it on the arm of the sofa, she made her way to the kitchen.

Deciding that soda bread and honey was the safest option, Sophia settled down on the pine kitchen bench as her nan fussed around her, clanging the cups before pouring tea into them.

"So, darling; what happened last night? Has that son of mine been causing you girl's grief again?" Nessa asked, trying to keep her tone light.

Jamesie was the bane of Nessa's life: of his whole family's life, in fact. He was a violent bully and he caused poor Sophia and her mother Kaitlin nothing but misery and aggravation. He was a wretched git at the best of times, and Nessa could only imagine the tense atmosphere over at that house now he had lost his job. Nessa didn't envy poor Kaitlin and Sophia having to live with him while he moped about the place drinking all the time, wallowing in self-pity. She couldn't even bear to visit him, so God only knew what living with the man must be like.

"Yeah, you could say that, Nan." Sophia looked down at her hands. She took a deep breath before she continued: "He came in late, drunk again, so I snuck out the front door while he was shouting."

Sophia looked up and met her nan's worried eyes.

"He didn't lay a hand on you, did he?" Nessa felt her body tense in apprehension as she asked the question. Her suspicions that he was hitting Kaitlin were bad enough, but if he had hurt Sophia Nessa would kill him.

"No, Nan. No, he wouldn't. Besides, I didn't give him the chance; he didn't even know I snuck out. He only hurts Mum; she just lets him. I don't know why she puts up with it," Sophia said miserably, unable to understand why her mum tolerated her dad's behaviour.

Nessa could tell that Sophia was relieved that she could confide in her, and Nessa was glad that she was able to. If it wasn't for her granddaughter filling her in, she wouldn't have known the half of what went on. Kaitlin was a lovely woman but she and Nessa weren't close, not like how she and Sophia had always been. Nessa also knew that Kaitlin had her own problems. The woman popped so many pills that she almost rattled when she walked. 'Happy pills' she had called them

26

when Nessa had caught her in the kitchen a while back eating the things like sweets. Nessa had told her to ask for a refund, because 'happy' certainly hadn't made any sort of appearance in her life in a long while.

"I don't know what's bloody wrong with that man," Nessa said, feeling the familiar anger bubbling inside her at the thought of her son's controlling temper and what this poor girl had to witness on a regular basis. "Had I known that he was going to turn out the way that he has done, I would have held his stubborn little head down in the bath water when he was a boy and drowned the bugger. I should have thrown him away and kept the bleeding stork."

Nessa hated to see worry etched on her young granddaughter's otherwise perfect face. Her skin was flawless, a pale milky white, and Nessa adored Sophia's vibrant red curls. She felt so protective of Sophia: she was the light of her life. She reminded her so much of herself, although looks-wise they were total opposites. Her granddaughter had real beauty, a trait which Nessa had never had the good fortune to be blessed with even in her younger days. Now in her early seventies Nessa was convinced that she had shrunk with age, whereas Sophia was very tall and skinny: 'all limbs', as Nessa liked to say. But it was the young girl's personality that reminded Nessa so much of her own. Sophia had the same inner strength that Nessa possessed, and they both knew their own minds as well as sharing a sense of humour. It deeply saddened Nessa that one day, if Jamesie carried on the way he was going, he would break the poor girl's spirit with his outbursts and acts of intimidation.

"Your father was always a stubborn eejit, even as a lad, it was always 'his way or no way'." Nessa sat down at the table, and spread honey onto the soda bread. She had no idea why Jamesie had turned out like he had, but she often wondered whether things would have been different if her late husband, Patrick, had been around while her son was growing up. Nessa had been widowed when

Jamesie had been just eight months old, and it still felt like yesterday. Patrick had been killed in a car accident, his death brutal and sudden, and Nessa had never really got over his loss, he had been one of the kindest men she had ever known. After his death, she had been forced to leave Dublin. Being a single mother in Ireland during the recession of the sixties was nigh on impossible. There was no money to bring up a child so after a lot of wavering she finally decided that it was time to leave. Hackney had been her home ever since. It had been hard for her at first, but she had managed to find herself a cleaning job and a little place to rent. Working almost every hour that God sent and raising a son alone had been an uphill struggle. Nessa had had no time, nor desire for a man in her life, and maybe, she thought to herself now as she looked into her granddaughter's sad eyes, that had been her downfall. Maybe that had been what Jamesie had needed all along: a strong male role model? Nessa had dedicated herself a hundred percent to her son and had tried to be the best mother that she had known how to be. She wasn't sure where it had all gone wrong for Jamesie, but one thing she did know for sure was that she hadn't raised him as someone who would think that it was okay to treat women in such a vulgar, despicable way. Hitting women was disgraceful, and Nessa was deeply ashamed of her son's behaviour. She had very little to do with him these days because of it. In fact, if it wasn't for her beautiful granddaughter, she would have cut all ties with him long ago. Nessa was baffled at how some mothers condoned their son's abusive behaviour, making up excuses for them like 'he was driven to it' or 'she probably deserved it'. They were too blinded by denial to admit that their own sons were a disgrace: well, not Nessa. With her a spade was a spade, she would rather disown Jamesie than join that delusional crowd.

"Mm, this is really lovely," Sophia joked, as she popped the buttery piece of bread that her nan had smothered in honey into her mouth. Her nan looked deep in thought; the last thing Sophia wanted to do was cause her more worry. "You keep giving me food like this, Nan, and I might have to move in."

"Well, pet, if I had the room you'd be more than welcome. You know you can have the sofa whenever you need it. It ain't much, I know, but it's the best that I can offer, what with this place being so blooming pokey. Either that or you could 'top and tail' with me, but... I would strongly advise against that option. I've enough wind inside of me to launch a few kites some nights." Nessa giggled and once more Sophia rolled her eyes, although she couldn't help but smile: her nan cracked her up.

"So, I guess I'd better get home and get my uniform on. I'm so tired I really don't know how I'm going to concentrate..." She left her words hanging in the air; her Nan would take the hint, she was sure.

"You can't keep taking time off, Sophia," Nessa said sharply. Her granddaughter's education would be affected if Jamesie's antics kept on driving the poor mite out of her own bed every night. Nessa had already given Sophia a key so that the poor girl could escape here for some respite if things were bad at home, and she always left a blanket out on the sofa. Nessa was glad that she could offer Sophia somewhere to run to, and she knew that Kaitlin was glad of it too. It was an unspoken arrangement that was supposed to be a means to an end: Nessa had truly hoped that Jamesie would stop his appalling conduct, especially if he managed to find himself another job, but it was becoming a habit. Jamesie seemed to be getting worse.

"Ah, okay... I'll write you a note just this one last time, Sophia," Nessa said, unable to say no to the large puppy-dog eyes that Sophia was now turning in her direction. "But this really is the final time. Your father and I will be having words about this, if this carries on, mind! I don't know what he thinks he's playing at."

Sophia hugged her nan. She really did feel exhausted today, and a day chilling out with her nan would be just what she needed.

"Actually, it'll help me out if you're here. You'll do a few chores for me, won't you my lovey? Rascal could do with a walk, and if I give you some money you could just pop in to the Co-op and grab me a few bits." Nessa was already planning the shopping list. Albert would probably pop in again later with his next meal that would give Gordon Ramsey a run for his money, but she did need a few bits and pieces too, such as lunch for her and Sophia.

"Of course, Nan. Come on, Rascal, shall we go for a little walk?" Sophia pulled her trainers on as Nessa went and fetched the dog's lead from a drawer. "I'll take him down to the Lea, Nan; wear him out a bit for you."

Nessa smiled as Rascal once again started jumping about the place as soon as he saw the lead. A walk down to the river would be just what the little mite needed to burn off all that energy and knowing how fond Sophia was of Rascal, it would do her the world of good too.

"Pick me up a pint of milk, a loaf of bread and some cheese, make sure it's a mild one, my stomach doesn't agree with those strong whiffy ones, and get yourself some lemonade and some chocolate too." Nessa rummaged around in the bottom of her handbag for some change before handing the coins to Sophia. She watched her walk down the front path with little Rascal at her side, waggling his tail as he went.

Glancing over the road at her son's house, Nessa saw the curtain in the larger bedroom window twitch; she guessed it was Kaitlin. She thought about waving, but in case it was Jamesie looming behind the curtain decided not to. She was fuming with her son: it was high time that she went over there and gave him a piece of her mind. Not today, though. Closing her front door after watching Sophia disappear from view, Nessa looked forward to a lovely day with her granddaughter. Time was precious, and she was going to make the most of it.

Jamesie could wait.

Chapter Four

"Go on, then, what are you waiting for?" The camera balanced on his shoulder, Jonathan felt like a director on a Hollywood film set. He loved the fact that he could zoom in on every detail and watch back the footage he captured over and over again. Aiming the camera at the little red motorboat that he had named *The Hackney Warrior*, Jonathan looked around the lens.

"Press it then, Tommy!" he said, impatiently.

Tommy ignored his brother's commanding tone. Moving the boat with his foot along the muddy track, he positioned it so that it was facing the river's edge. Tommy felt nervous: what if, after all their hard work and effort, the boat didn't work? They had spent so long on this project, and they would both be gutted if there were any last-minute mistakes.

The project had been Tommy's idea initially: he had wanted to impress Jonathan with it. Jonathan dominated situations, and it had made a change for Tommy to be in control; he had taken great pleasure in being the one to tell Jonathan what to do for once. When Tommy had explained how the motor would work and what they needed to do to build the boat, Jonathan had actually listened. Now it was the day of the filming; this was the final part of their assessment and all the kids in Mrs Winter's physics class would show their videos tomorrow morning: Jonathan, now in film-director mode, was back to his normal bossy self, acting as if the motor boat was all his idea.

Tommy pressed the red button and steered the boat forwards using the remote control they had made out of scraps of metal and plastic. He felt a flutter of excitement in the pit of his stomach. They had spent almost three weeks working on the project, and Mrs Winters had said that if they managed to film the boat moving on land and then floating on water they should both get an A in their reports. He wasn't going to let his brother's domineering behaviour spoil it for him.

"Okay, here goes," Tommy said excitedly.

The engine whirred loudly, and the boat moved towards the river, slowly at first as its little black wheels gathered speed. Tommy was careful with the steering: he didn't want it to go too fast at first in case it tipped over before it reached the water. Slowly, it rolled forward. Leaving the path, it flattened the grass as it crossed the muddy verge. Then, gracefully, it tilted its nose into the water.

Tommy held his breath.

"Oh my God, it's going in... it's actually going in," Jonathan said. He stared at the boat, impressed with their design. It plopped off the bank and slid into the dark-green water, and Tommy used the controller to make it speed along.

"We did it." Tommy laughed, as impressed as Jonathan with what they had achieved. They were bound to get top grades; their mum would be so proud. "Did you get all that?"

The loud whirring that the engine had been making abruptly stopped and the boat came to a halt. They looked over to where she now bobbed aimlessly in the middle of the river.

"What's happened?" Jonathan asked. He placed the bulky camcorder onto the grass, annoyed that he had to end the recording.

"I don't know. I guess the engine must have just stopped." Tommy pressed all the buttons, but nothing happened. "Maybe the remote's batteries have run out."

"Here, give it to me." Jonathan snatched the controller out from Tommy's grasp. "Didn't you get any spares? I told you those ones I gave you weren't up to much. I pinched them out of the remote; they were probably on their last legs. I thought you were going to get some more." Jonathan was fuming: how dumb was Tommy?

Tommy felt his cheeks flush as he watched his brother smack the bottom of the controller with the palm of his hand in a desperate attempt to bring it back to life. He felt so stupid; the batteries had been his responsibility, and looking over to the boat in the water, he knew that he had ruined their project now.

"I'm sorry, Jonathan, I must have forgotten," Tommy said.

"Well, you're just going to have to go and get some from somewhere, then."

"I can't."

Jonathan looked at him angrily. "Why not?"

"I haven't got any money," Tommy said, checking his pockets, although he knew that it was pointless: they had no money in them.

"Go home and either get some batteries, or get some money so we can buy some new ones." Jonathan was defiant. Tommy had messed up their project; he could sort it out.

"But I can't go home; what if Mum sees me? She'll kill us if she finds out that we're bunking off." Tommy knew he shouldn't have listened to Jonathan this morning when he had persuaded him to skip school. They should have both come down here at the weekend as they had organised, instead of leaving it to the last minute. It had been Jonathan who had suggested that they skip their first lesson to test their boat out, and Tommy had gone along with it. Jonathan had said that they wouldn't even be skiving off, as technically they were doing their school work. Tommy hadn't been too sure at first, as he didn't want to get into any trouble, but Jonathan had been so insistent and so Tommy eventually, instead of saying no, had done what he always did and just gone along with him.

Now Jonathan was looking furious, and the project had turned into a disaster. Tommy knew that Jonathan wouldn't let it go; he was so obstinate when he got an idea into his head.

Jonathan was thinking about what Tommy had said. He didn't fancy getting caught bunking off school either. Tommy was right, their mum would go nuts and probably ground them. She might even take his camera away, and he couldn't risk that. Tommy was right; neither of them could go home just yet.

"Okay, then, there's only one thing for it. You're going to have to get in there and fetch our boat." Jonathan nodded towards the water.

"Why me, Jonathan?" Tommy whined. Just when he had thought the morning couldn't get worse Jonathan was going to force him get into the water, which had a film of slime covering the surface in places. It was also freezing, and the thought of having to take his clothes off and get into the river was the last thing he wanted to do.

"I'm not getting in there because I can't swim! Besides, this is your fault. You were supposed to bring the batteries and you forgot them. It's only fair that you get in there and bring our boat back."

Tommy gulped. He may have got away with not having to go home but there was no way Jonathan was just going to leave the boat out there.

"What if we wait till three o'clock? I can go home then... pretend I've been at school," Tommy suggested, beginning to panic.

"Three o'clock is hours away. And what if someone comes, huh? Then we'll have to leave the boat in the water. I'm not going to risk it. Besides, look at it, it's going to sink if we leave it. Either you go home and face Mum, or you have to get in there." He wanted the boat back, and Tommy had to be the one to get it. Jonathan sat on the path, next to the camcorder, and waited.

Knowing that it was pointless arguing, and remembering that at least he had a towel packed in his PE bag, Tommy reluctantly started to undress. He laid his purple school blazer down on top of his sports bag and shivered; he dreaded to think about the temperature of the river if it was this cold just standing on the bank.

The marshes were silent this morning, and as Tommy looked around he was grateful that there no-one could see him taking off his clothes. This side of the River Lea was lined with trees and even though their leaves had started to fall, there was just enough coverage for him to remain reasonably undetected by any people who might be inside the houses on the opposite bank. Jonathan had said earlier that if any nosey parkers asked them what they were doing there, he would just say that the school had given them permission to test out their boat. They were both wearing their uniforms under their big black puffer jackets and had their science books with them.

Jonathan took out a packet of Marlboro Menthol cigarettes, which he had stolen from the newsagents that morning whilst the shopkeeper was distracted, from his trousers pocket. He lit it up as a pasty-looking Tommy stood beside him, now wearing just a pair of white boxer shorts, a matching vest and a look of dread.

"Go on then." Jonathan nodded towards the river as he inhaled the minty smoke. He screwed his nose up: he didn't enjoy smoking, he just did it for effect. He loved the thrill of knowing that he might get caught, another thing that would piss his mum off; that alone had been a good enough reason as any to start as far as he was concerned.

Tommy watched his brother blow out a thin grey stream of smoke. He had hoped Jonathan would relent, that any minute now he would laugh at Tommy standing there like a twat, shivering in his underwear, and say that he could leave the boat where it was. It was, after all, November, and looking at the water made him feel the cold right down to his bones.

But Jonathan just sat there, staring back at him as he smoked, waiting.

Tommy dipped his toe into the water. He swiftly took it back out again as a chill blasted up his spine.

"I don't think I..." Tommy protested, before he was pushed in. His body slapped the dirty water.

"What did you do that for?" he shouted at Jonathan, as he fought to tread water.

The sight of Tommy's quivering lips and chattering teeth was too much for Jonathan. He laughed so hard he thought he would wet himself.

"I was doing you a favour: you looked like you needed a nudge in the right direction. Go on then, get our boat."

Coughing and spluttering as he spat out a mouthful of water, Tommy was annoyed. Jonathan knew it was freezing cold in the river. However, he was here now, he may as well get the bloody thing. Swimming towards the boat, Tommy dreaded to think what was on the riverbed. Trying to block out the images that he had seen on the News a while back, about chopped-up torsos in suitcases in the Thames, Tommy swam quickly, the iciness of the water stinging his limbs.

Jonathan watched from the bank, impressed at how slick Tommy looked as he glided through the water. Jonathan had refused to take swimming lessons as a younger child: the more their mum had insisted, the more he had dug his heels in and said no. Tommy excelled at it and had won numerous badges, coming first in most of the competitions he entered.

Tommy held the boat above the water with one hand, like a trophy; all that fuss he had made about getting it and it had taken him only seconds to reach it.

When he saw Tommy's head dip beneath the water's surface, Jonathan thought his brother was winding him up. "What are you doing? Stop messing about!"

Tommy emerged, waving his hands in the air, signalling that he was in trouble. Jonathan didn't believe it: his brother was such a good swimmer; he couldn't need help.

But watching as his brother's head dipped back under the water, Jonathan began to feel unsure. Tommy hadn't surfaced for about thirty seconds.

"Tommy, what's happening?" Jonathan shouted, as his brother's head broke through the water's surface.

"Help, Jonathan! I've got cramp," Tommy screamed, expelling the little air that he had left in his lungs in his panic, before he went under for the third time.

Jonathan still wasn't convinced that this wasn't Tommy's way of getting him back for pushing him in the water, but he still hadn't come back up after a few seconds and it wasn't like him to be a practical joker.

Seeing only bubbles on the surface of the river, Jonathan realised that Tommy might be in danger. Maybe he hadn't been winding him up.

"Tommy?" Jonathan yelled, feeling helpless. He wouldn't be able to reach Tommy even if he tried. He would only put himself in danger too. Desperate, Jonathan looked around to see if there was anyone nearby. "Help me, someone; help me, please."

No-one came. Jonathan looked into the middle of the river again. There was no sign of his brother.

Tommy had gone.

Chapter Five

There was a sharp pain in Tommy's leg. Then, he felt like he was being weighted down. His calf throbbed, making his whole leg seize up and stop working. Panic set in.

Thrashing about under the water's surface, Tommy desperately tried to swim back up. The water was dark and murky, just as he'd imagined it would be, and he had never been so scared in his life. In amongst his panicked thoughts was a feeling of disbelief that this was happening to him. He was a good swimmer. He remembered the coach informing the class about muscle spasms but Tommy had only vaguely paid attention, not really believing that the advice would ever apply to him. He remembered the two main instructions that she had taught them: keep calm; try not to panic. But that was easier said than done, he thought now, as he frantically clawed his hands through the water. He was running out of air. His natural instinct was to try and breathe but every time he attempted to he gulped down big mouthfuls of water that choked him.

He began to feel weak and disorientated. Tommy fought to remain conscious, knowing he was starting to lose the battle: sinking in the water, his body gave in.

Hands seized his waist.

Feeling immense relief sweep over him, he realised that someone was rescuing him. Was it Jonathan?

Tommy tried to turn in the water so that he could cling to the figure, the thought of being saved and the panic of wanting to breathe fuelling his newfound strength. He didn't mean to, but in his desperation his hands grabbed at the arms that gripped him, causing him to drag his saviour down deeper into the water with him; clawing with every touch he fought with every last ounce of his strength to push himself up.

The hands around his waist spun him around in the water; bringing them face to face.

Tommy thought that he was hallucinating. Through the darkness of the water he could see the face of a pretty girl with long red hair; she looked how he imagined an angel to be. As he stared into her green eyes and saw the look of determination on her face, he knew that he could trust her. She was helping him. He was going to be okay.

That split second was all she needed. Quickly taking her opportunity she grabbed the boy under his armpit, sliding her arm around the back of his head to support his neck and hauling him up to the water's surface with all the strength she could muster. She grasped him firmly as she kicked her legs as hard as she could so that she could make it back to the bank. She had no time to check how the boy was, nor even if he was still breathing. The CPR training she had done with St John Ambulance a few years before, a compulsory Girl Guides course, had bored her silly at the time but now those few hours of mind-numbing boredom were paying off; she just prayed that she could remember what to do. First things first, she knew that she needed to get him out of the icy water and quickly.

Pushing herself up against the grass verge, she shouted at the boy who stood on the bank looking at her with the weird expression on his face whilst she panted for breath.

"Are you going to help or what?"

Holding the other boy afloat, she watched as the boy on the grass stepped forward. He grabbed the boy who had been in the water by the arm, dragging him up onto the verge. The girl hoisted herself out of the river, her clothes stuck to her body.

The boy was sprawled out on the grass, his lips blue. The girl ignored the waves of exhaustion that washed over her as she tilted his head back, before pinching his nose between her thumb and forefinger and gently placing her lips over his. She slowly breathed into his mouth as she watched for movement in his chest just as she had been taught. She wished that she had paid more attention to the course leader now. The boy she had dragged out of the water seemed to be in a bad way, and the responsibility that she now felt to save him was overwhelming. Suddenly, he coughed and inhaled long gulps of air into his lungs and then, turning onto his side, he threw up all over the grass.

Worn out and shivering, the girl flopped onto the grass, relief sweeping over her and making her feel suddenly very tearful.

She had saved him. She had actually saved him.

Then she remembered. Turning to the other boy who was standing next to her in silence, clutching his camcorder, she shot him a look of contempt.

"What sort of a sicko just stands there and films someone who's drowning?"

Chapter Six

Bernie was in her element fussing over her son. Ever since they had brought him home from the hospital she had made sure that he had stayed tucked up in bed, while she fetched him bowls of soup and big mugs of his favourite hot chocolate. The dreadful phone call two days ago from the hospital had left her shaking with fright and even though she knew that she should be furious that Tommy and Jonathan had bunked off school in the first place, she couldn't help but feel anything other than relief that her boy was now okay.

"Lean forward, darling," Bernie instructed as she fluffed up Tommy's pillows for the fifth time that afternoon.

Tommy did as he was told, knowing that where his mother was concerned it was just easier that way.

Jonathan, sprawled out on his bed opposite, watched as their mum showered Tommy with attention. He wondered if she knew how desperate she looked. It was like she was grateful to finally have something to focus her attention on.

"Jesus Christ, Mum, he's not an invalid," Jonathan said. "Anyone would think that he lost his arms and legs in the river the way that you're carrying on. If you're that desperate for something to fuss over, maybe you should get a cat."

Just as Bernie was about to give Jonathan a mouthful for his backchat, he stomped out of the room. Hearing the doorbell chime and her husband's voice as he answered, Bernie made sure her son was comfortable before leaving him to relax and going to see who was at the door.

"Hello, Sophia," Stanley said as he gave the pretty girl a warm welcome. He and Bernie had met Sophia at the hospital. The ambulance crew had said that if it wasn't for her, Tommy would have drowned. Stanley had hugged the girl and thanked her repeatedly, before he had realised that he was probably embarrassing the poor thing.

"Hi Mr Jenkins, I just wondered how Tommy was doing. Thought I'd pop by and say hello to him if that's okay? I bought him these," Sophia said, holding out a small box of chocolates.

"Of course you can see him, love." Bernie glided down the stairs. "Can I get you a drink; something to eat?"

Sophia shook her head.

"He's just up here, come on up, love. Knock knock," Bernie sung, as she tapped on the door. "There's someone here to see you, Tommy."

Sitting up in his bed, Tommy looked both surprised and abashed as his mum showed Sophia in. Bernie said that she'd leave them to chat and quickly left the room, closing the door behind her.

"So..." Sophia stood at the end of the bed. "You look a lot better than when I last saw you, Tommy."

Sophia remembered how blue Tommy's lips had looked and how transparent his skin had been. "You gave me a scare."

Tommy sat back against the pillows and moved his legs to make space at the end of his bed so Sophia could sit down.

"I got you these." She smiled as she passed the box of chocolates to Tommy.

Tommy didn't know what to say. He was the one who should be buying the chocolates: he owed his life to this girl. And here she was sitting on his bed, offering him presents.

Noting the empty bed across the room, Sophia asked: "Is your brother not around?"

She hoped that he wasn't. The very short time that she had spent in Jonathan's company had made her dislike him. Even at the hospital he had been acting strangely, clutching his stupid camcorder to his chest as if it had more value than his own brother's life.

"Oh, he's around somewhere. He's probably outside having a sneaky fag. Mum has been fussing over me like a demented woman; I think she was doing his head in."

There was a silence. Sophia, knowing that Tommy was shy, started chatting about school. "It's weird, isn't it, that up until now we've never even spoken to each other at school," she began.

Tommy and Jonathan were joined at the hip at school, and while Sophia could tell that Tommy was a really nice boy it was clear why everyone gave him a wide berth; if they were friends with Tommy then they'd have to be friends with Jonathan too and he was just plain creepy. "You'll never guess what. Everyone at school has been talking about you. There must be ten different stories going around about what actually happened, and some prat in Year Ten has started a rumour. He told everyone that you'd been starved of oxygen for so long that you have severe brain damage, he said that you can only communicate by blinking and that when you come back to school there are going to be compulsory blinking classes for everyone so that we can show you our support. One blink for yes, two for no, three blinks if you need a wee, four if you need a... well, you know."

Sophia had thought that Tommy would find this funny, but catching the look of alarm on his face she quickly added: "Don't worry; I put him straight for you."

Tommy couldn't help smiling at the thought of Sophia putting the boy in his place, he could tell by how confidently she spoke that she didn't take any crap from anyone. As he was the opposite, it was a quality that he admired. He had never even properly spoken to a girl before, let alone been friends with one, and the fact that she had stood up for him made him feel really special.

"Everyone's talking about me?" Tommy hadn't thought about the kids at school starting rumours about him. Most of the time he felt invisible there: Jonathan didn't fit in and Tommy took it as his responsibility to stick with his brother, at the cost of Tommy's own popularity.

The door opened.

"Oh, I didn't realise that your guardian angel was visiting," Jonathan said, as he saw Sophia sitting on his brother's bed. He stared at her coldly, giving her the feeling that she was intruding. "Float down from your cloud in the sky, did you? Here, what's that chat up line I heard on the TV the other day? Oh yeah that's it, you say to the girl, 'Did it hurt when you fell from heaven?' The girl thinks it's a compliment, they love mushy shit like that but then you say 'cause your face looks fucked.' Ha, classic." Jonathan laughed.

"You really are a dickhead," Sophia said. Jonathan could bugger right off if he thought for a second that he would make her feel uncomfortable for being here.

"Ooh, give us one," Jonathan said. Without waiting for a response, he took the box of chocolates and started to unwrap the cellophane.

Sophia snatched them back. "They're Tommy's," she said, as she placed them on Tommy's bedside table.

"Alright, Red, don't get your knickers in a knot. They're only bloody chocolates."

"My name is Sophia, not Red," Sophia corrected him, as she returned his glare.

Tommy shuffled uncomfortably in his bed. He barely knew Sophia, but she clearly had a fiery temperament. Unfortunately, so did Jonathan.

Popping her head around the door and seeing the steely looks that Jonathan and Sophia were giving each other, Bernie sensed instantly that something was up. "Are you alright in here? You're not causing any trouble are you, Jonathan?"

"We're fine, Mum," Tommy answered.

"Good," Bernie said, only half-believing him. "Are you sure I can't get you a drink, Sophia?"

"I'm fine, thank you, Mrs Jenkins." Sophia smiled.

"I bet your parents are ever so proud of you," Bernie said. What she had done had been so courageous; who knew what would have happened had she not been walking down by the river that morning?

"I guess they are." Sophia shrugged. She hadn't put much thought into how her parents must feel about her rescuing Tommy: they certainly hadn't said much about it. Her dad had been more concerned by the fact that Sophia had taken yet another day off school and his 'interfering' mother had encouraged her to. At no point had he figured out during his rant that he had been the reason behind her recent absences. His main worry was that the school may send someone to his house because of it. Sophia's mum had just been fearful that Sophia would get hypothermia from swimming in the cold river. Neither of them had hailed her as a hero, the only person who had done was her nan: for the past two days it was all she had gone on about, singing Sophia's praises to anyone who would listen.

"Do you think they'd like to come to dinner? It'd be lovely to meet them," Bernie said. Sophia seemed such a lovely girl and, if Bernie pushed relations between the two families, who knew what would happen between her and Tommy.

"Oh, I'm not sure." Sophia tried to think of an excuse that would be acceptable to Mrs Jenkins without offending her or making her suspicious. "My dad isn't very well at the moment. I think it's quite serious; he hasn't been at work for a few weeks now. Maybe my nan could come: I'm spending a lot of time with her at the moment, what with my dad being so ill."

"Oh, you poor thing. That must be so worrying for you and your mum. What's wrong with him?" Bernie enquired.

"We don't know exactly. But he's really ill," Sophia said, realising that she wasn't actually lying. Alcoholism was a disease. Feeling everyone's eyes on her as she spoke about her dad was starting to make her feel extremely uncomfortable.

Bernie could see by the girl's pained expression that the subject was clearly a tough one so changing the subject she said, "Oh, well, maybe we can arrange something when he's a bit better then. Anyway, I'll leave you kids to it. Tommy, if you need anything just give me a shout."

"So, when do you think you'll be back at school?" Sophia asked as she turned her back on Jonathan, excluding him from the conversation.

"Well, Mum wants me to stay at home a little bit longer but I feel so much better now. So my dad has persuaded her that I'll be fine for tomorrow." Tommy could feel himself regaining his energy and boredom was creeping in. He didn't think he could manage another day at home being fussed over by his mother. Two days was more than enough.

"Thanks for what you did." Tommy said quietly, embarrassed as he realised that he hadn't thought to thank her sooner. "Thank you doesn't really cut it, I know, but honestly..." he trailed off unable to find the right words. Almost drowning had been the scariest experience of his life, and whatever he managed to say, he would never be able to thank Sophia enough.

Jonathan's loud scoff stopped Tommy from saying any more.

"Jesus, Tommy, if you could hear yourself mate." Jonathan snorted. "You sound like the Queen at Christmas when she makes one of her boring speeches."

Instantly feeling furious, Sophia bit her tongue and pretended to ignore Jonathan as she shrugged to Tommy as if to say don't worry about it. She knew that Tommy was grateful, but he didn't need to be. She had just acted on instinct when she had heard Jonathan's call for help and without a moment's thought she had leaped straight in, the same as anyone else would have done. Anyone else except that creepy Jonathan.

"I'd like to thank Sophia for being my hero, my guardian angel, my saviour..." Jonathan mimicked. "We get it, Tommy, you fancy her."

Sophia had had enough. Jonathan was a jumped-up little shit, and it wasn't as if he had been any help.

"Well, I'm glad I was there. Otherwise, who knows what would have happened."

"I can't swim," Jonathan said frostily, wishing Sophia would bugger off home. She was a stuck-up bitch.

"I'd find it pretty hard to swim too if I was holding a camcorder in my hand the whole time. Oh well, hopefully you got some good footage." Just looking at Jonathan made her skin crawl. She had been so angry with him: fair enough, he couldn't swim, but standing there and filming it all with a look of enjoyment on his face was just plain weird.

"Anyway, Tommy," Sophia said, not waiting to give Jonathan any more opportunities to butt in. "I guess I'll see you at school tomorrow then?"

"That would be nice; I mean cool." Tommy felt himself blush. He couldn't believe that she might want to be his friend.

"Cool," Sophia replied, before planting a kiss on Tommy's rosy-red cheek. "See you tomorrow."

Shooting Jonathan a filthy look, Sophia left. Tommy stared at the door after it had closed, dumbfounded.

"Do you want a tissue? You're drooling," Jonathan said, trying to hide the fact that he was equally dumbstruck. "You don't seriously like her, do you?"

Tommy shrugged, not wanting to give away how he felt: he knew his brother would only try and ruin the moment. But sitting back against his pillows, he couldn't hide his smile. Sophia was like a whirlwind: she had so much energy and, unlike him, she oozed confidence.

Tommy closed his eyes. The way things were going, he was beginning to think that nearly drowning had been the best thing that could have happened to him.

Chapter Seven

"Why can't you just give her the praise she deserves? You should be bloody proud of that girl, she's a heroine. The *Hackney Gazette* wants to run a piece on her saving that boy's life," Nessa said to her son, who was leaning back in his chair looking right through her as she spoke.

"A heroine?" Jamesie smirked. "Bloody nonsense, Mum. Bunking off school and knocking about with the local scallywags aren't the acts of a heroine."

Jamesie took a big swig from his can of lager. Spilling some down his jumper, he wiped the trickle of liquid with his hand before leaning forward and glaring at his mother, and then at Kaitlin who was sitting in the chair opposite doing her usual silent routine and not backing him up. "And the only reason the local rag got wind of it all is cos you bloody called them. Right old busybody, you are. Well, you might be happy for everyone to know all your business, but I'm bloody well not. I've said that she is not doing an interview and that's the end of it. So just drop it."

Nessa hadn't come over to the house to ask Jamesie's permission; it was nothing to do with him, as far as she was concerned. This was Sophia's moment of glory, and Jamesie was doing his utmost to stop the poor young girl from gaining the recognition that she ought to have. Nessa wasn't having it.

"No, I bet you don't want people prying into your business, Jamesie. You have a lot you don't want people finding out about you." Nessa felt rage build up inside her as she spoke. Her son was a smug bastard. She wouldn't let him intimidate her. He may be in his late thirties but it was all she could do to stop herself from leaping on him and giving him a bloody good hiding. Especially after the stories she had been hearing about him lately. The sight of him sitting there slurring as he laid down the law, like he was better than everyone else, made her blood boil.

"What's that supposed to mean? People finding out about what?" Jamesie shifted in his chair. "What have you been spouting your mouth off about now, Kaitlin?"

Nessa watched as her daughter-in-law fought to control her trembling hands as she placed her cup of tea onto the table, next to Jamesie and Nessa's untouched ones.

Seeing the look that her son had just shot her daughter-in-law, Nessa knew that she had said too much. Kaitlin was sure to get a hiding if Jamesie thought that his wife had been telling tales. Either that or, once he had worked it out it would be her poor Sophia who would bear the brunt of his fury.

"Shall I leave you both to talk?" Kaitlin asked nervously, getting up from the chair. She could feel the tension building between mother and son and thought she was better off leaving them to it. She herself had a fair idea where Nessa had been getting her information.

"Sit your arse back down," Jamesie commanded, his suspicions fuelled by her action.

Nessa was dumbfounded as she watched Kaitlin immediately do as she was told as if her husband's word was gospel. She shook her head at her son; she was so ashamed of him.

"I haven't got shit in my eyes, Jamesie; I see you for exactly what you are. No-one needs to tell me anything. Going out and getting langers every night and causing all your ructions. There is nothing that anyone can tell me about you that I can't work out for myself." The words tumbled from Nessa's mouth. She had been holding in her thoughts about her only child for a long time. If it hadn't been for her son acting like such an ignorant pig she would have picked a better time to let him have it, preferably when Kaitlin hadn't been in the room. The woman was petrified of Jamesie. Looking over at the woman, silent and hanging her head, Nessa felt heart-sorry that she had said anything at all. She regretted being so hasty in coming here, she had probably increased the likelihood of Jamesie being violent towards Kaitlin, but she had been so swept away in the excitement of speaking to the reporter from the newspaper, who wanted to do a feature on Sophia saving Tommy Jenkins' life, that Nessa had come straight over to tell the girl without considering that she would end up arguing with her son.

"Hello, I'm back," Sophia announced as she walked into the lounge, feeling the tension. She had been listening at the door and had thought it was as good a time as any to interrupt before things blew up between her dad and her nan. "Hiya, Nan."

"Well, girl," Nessa said to her granddaughter, "I was just speaking to your father about the *Hackney Gazette*. They rang me today, asking if they could interview you about rescuing the boy from the Lea."

"Rang you? Why would they? She lives here," Jamesie said.

"My friend Heather's daughter works as an assistant to one of the reporters, and Heather passed on my number." Nessa gritted her teeth.

Sophia could see from her dad's expression that if she agreed to the newspaper piece, it would only antagonise him more.

"Oh, Nan, no... I'm too shy," Sophia said weakly.

"Shy?" Nessa laughed. "Sophia O'Hagan, one thing you ain't is shy. You should do it. You should be very proud of yourself."

"She said she doesn't want to do it, so flaming drop it will you," Jamesie said. His mother could try and interfere as much as she wanted, but he ruled the roost around here.

"Where have you been, anyway, Sophia?" he asked, noting the time on the clock, suspicious of why she had strolled in so late from school.

"Oh, I just popped in to Tommy's to see how he's doing. Looks like he'll be back at school tomorrow," Sophia said, uncomfortable as her dad's eyes bore into hers.

"See," Jamesie shot to Nessa. "She's knocking about with the local dregs."

"He's not a dreg," Sophia said, more forcefully than she had intended. "He's really nice."

"Of course she wanted to see how he was doing," said Nessa. "The poor mite almost drowned. It's a big shock, something like that: for the pair of them."

"I don't want you hanging around with him, Sophia," her dad said, "or any other boy for that matter. You're fifteen: too young to be knocking about with boys."

Sophia wanted to say that she was nearer to sixteen than fifteen: her birthday was next week. But she knew better than to argue with her father, keeping the fact that most of her friends had had boyfriends for years to herself. She had never really been interested in boys: or not until now; Tommy was lovely and Sophia was so looking forward to seeing him the next day. But she had learned a long time ago that it was easier to agree with everything her father said, and what he didn't know couldn't hurt him.

Nessa shook her head in dismay: Jamesie was a control freak. She couldn't bear to be in the same room as her vile son any longer. She had nothing left to say to him.

"I'm off home; Albert will be over shortly with some dinner. I'll leave you all to it." Nessa stood up. "Pop over sometime for a cuppa, Kaitlin," Nessa added, knowing that her son would forbid his wife from doing so now that he thought she was telling tales, but she wanted Kaitlin to know that the subtle offer of support was there.

"See you soon, lovey," Nessa said as she hugged her granddaughter tightly.

Nessa didn't bid Jamesie goodbye, and she slammed the front door behind her on her way out.

"Fucking woman!" Jamesie erupted. He flicked through the TV channels. "Who the fuck does she think she is coming around here and butting her nose in? I don't know why she thinks she can have a say in your life, Sophia. I'm your parent, not her."

Recognising the signs of her husband starting one of his rants, Kaitlin gathered up the untouched cups of tea from the table.

"And if I find out either of you are going over there and telling tales to that interfering old bitch, there'll be trouble. Do you hear me?" Jamesie looked from Kaitlin to Sophia.

"We won't, Jamesie," Kaitlin stuttered. "I mean, we don't. We don't do that, do we, Sophia? Our business is private; we know that."

Jamesie looked from his wife to his daughter, as he took in their nods of agreement. He noted their striking similarities. Sophia had her mum's natural understated beauty although their daughter was slightly taller and Kaitlin skinnier, her posture stooped, as if she was apologising for existing.

Temperamentally, Sophia was more like her nan than her mum. Jamesie had never been able to really understand the girl. She certainly wasn't intimidated by him; in fact he seemed to repulse her. He often caught her looking down her nose at him and lately her dismissive attitude towards him was starting to bother him.

"Yeah, well, you had better bloody not. The last thing I need is her poking her nose in our lives every five minutes," Jamesie said, staring hard at his daughter. "And as for you, no more hanging around with boys, do you understand? More trouble than they're worth at your age. Only after one thing."

"Yes, Dad," Sophia said, as she opened the door for her mum who was taking the cups out to the kitchen. "I understand."

"Good, now get me another lager."

Sophia grabbed a can of lager from the top shelf in the fridge and then turned to see her mother standing at the sink, holding a bottle. She watched her as she opened it and swallowed a couple of her pills and then stood with both her arms tensed as she clutched the basin and stared out of the window, as if she was in a trance.

"Mum? Are you okay?" Sophia saw how worn out and defeated her mum looked.

"I'm fine," Kaitlin replied, sounding weary. "Just be careful what you're going off and telling your nan, okay? It's all well and good you needing to talk to someone, Soph, but her coming around here and interfering like this is only going to cause us more grief. You know what he gets like. The more he drinks of this," she pointed to the can on the side, "the more he winds himself up, and it's me he takes it out on."

Kaitlin turned on a tap, emptying the tea into the sink and staring at the brown liquid as it swirled around the plughole before being washed away.

"Mum, it's not right what he does to you." Tears stung Sophia's eyes.

"Your father is going through a difficult time at the moment, Sophia," Kaitlin replied. "You have got to stop going over to your nan's and telling her what goes on in this house, do you hear me? It's more trouble than it's worth."

Kaitlin knew that Nessa had infuriated Jamesie. He would work himself up into a state as he stewed on her words.

Sophia was angry that her mum would put up with being smacked around whenever her dad was in a bad mood. He was a bully. And standing here listening to her mum justifying his actions was hard to bear. Sophia didn't know if her mum was weak or stupid, but either way her dad's temper was becoming more erratic and her mum was just accepting it.

Vowing that she would never end up being controlled by a man, Sophia slammed the lager down on the worktop. "You can take this to him. I'm going to my room." There was no point in discussing the situation anymore. Sophia knew that her mum would never do anything about her abuse. Well, if she wanted to stand there and make excuses, it was up to her; Sophia had had enough.

Chapter Eight

Sophia sat in an armchair watching Nessa. Her grandmother fiddled with the buttons on her blouse, before looking into the mirror to check that she had no lipstick on her teeth.

"How do I look?" Nessa asked, as she twirled around to face her granddaughter, pleased with her effort. "I'm wearing my best Ester London lippy, you know, not some cheapie from the Pound Shop."

"It's Estee Lauder," Sophia laughed, "and you look really lovely, Nan."

Her nan looked very elegant in her light-grey tailored trousers, which she was wearing with a crisp white blouse and a long string of pearls. "I can't believe that you're in your seventies, Nan; you'd give women ten years younger a run for their money."

"Ten? I do hope you mean twenty years younger, my lovey... And you're sure that Tommy's parents said it was okay to bring Rascal along? You know what he's like; he doesn't like being left alone, especially in the evening."

"Tommy's dad loves animals, and he said that Rascal's more than welcome."

"In that case, what do you think of this?" Nessa bent down and scooped Rascal off the floor and tied on the black bowtie that she had bought for tonight around his neck. "Can't have him letting the side down, can we? There you go my gorgeous little babby. He looks the bee's knees doesn't he?"

Nessa put Rascal on the floor by her feet. He wagged his tail happily at her praise. His fur was sticking up, and the contrast of this with the posh bowtie he was wearing really did make him look very cute.

"Tommy sounds like a lovely lad, and so do his parents. It's just this Jonathan that we have to keep our eye on, is it?" Nessa gathered her purse and Rascal's lead.

"Honestly, Nan, he makes my skin crawl. He's so nasty and sarcastic and it's almost as if he goes out of his way to be horrible to me. Wait till you meet him and then you'll see what I mean." Sophia shook her head. If it wasn't for the fact that Jonathan was going to be there tonight, she would have been very excited about the evening. But she could imagine him sitting opposite her and rolling his eyes, mocking her every time she spoke.

Hearing the taxi beep its horn, Nessa switched off the lights. "Well, don't you be worrying about him tonight. One nasty word out of his gob about you and I'll wipe the floor with him and smile with glee while I do it. In fact, I can't wait to meet him."

***

Bernie had been cooking all day. She had made one of her mum's famous family recipes, homemade ham-hock and creamy leek pie. Her mum hadn't left her much when she passed away, but the small handwritten recipe book had been one of the gems of her possessions that Bernie cherished.

Chopping the last of the vegetables, she glanced at the clock and realised that they would be here any minute and she hadn't even got changed yet. Pleased that she had made the prawn and crab cakes and a seafood bisque for starters early that morning, along with a lemon tart for dessert, and thus had no more preparation to do, Bernie put the last of the carrots into a pan of water before wiping her hands on a tea towel and rushing off upstairs to make herself look half-decent.

Passing her husband on the stairs, Bernie said, "You're not wearing that, are you, Stanley?"

Glancing down at his blue V-neck jumper and brown cords, Stanley shrugged. He had thought he looked smart. "Well, it's clean and we're only eating in..."

Seeing his wife frowning, he added: "But you're right, I'm not wearing it. I'll change, shall I?"

It was quicker and easier to go along with Bernie's wishes. Changing his jumper would take just minutes whereas her giving him earache could go on all bloody night.

"Good," Bernie said, satisfied with her husband's reply as she followed him back up the stairs. As she passed the boys' bedroom, Bernie was surprised to see that her sons were washed and dressed. "They are going to be here any minute. Tommy, can you listen out for the door and Jonathan, can you go down and turn the oven off?"

Bernie was looking forward to meeting Sophia's gran. It was a shame that her parents couldn't make it but from what Tommy had told her Nessa O'Hagan was a real character, and Bernie also loved an excuse to throw a dinner party.

If Tommy did have his sights on Sophia, then it was right that they invite the girl over. Bernie was sure that she was a lovely girl, especially after what she had done for Tommy, but these days you never knew. Some children were dragged up, not brought up, and Bernie wanted to make sure that her son was mixing with the right kind of people.

Putting on a black shimmery dress, she saw Stanley standing behind her in the mirror.

"You've not finished dressing. You're not wearing a bowtie." Bernie scowled as Stanley walked out of the en-suite wearing smart black trousers and a shirt.

Stanley sighed. He had had no intention of wearing one. "I didn't realise that we were going to be so formal tonight, Bernie. I hope that they don't think we're snobs."

"Snobs: us? Don't be silly, Stanley. We're making an effort, that's all. There's nothing wrong with that, is there?"

"Mum," Tommy called up the stairs. "They're here."

Smoothing down her dress then giving herself one last admiring glance in the mirror, Bernie made her way downstairs.

"It's lovely to meet you at last." Bernie beamed at her guests, before ushering them into the dining room and indicating chairs for them to sit on. She had been looking forward to tonight ever since the other day when Sophia had popped over to see Tommy.

"Ah, and you must be our honorary guest, Rascal?" Bernie noted the little dog's bowtie approvingly. She was glad that she had made Stanley wear his now: she couldn't have him upstaged by a dog. "Wait until Stanley sees this little fellow. He loves dogs."

"I can feel my ears burning," Stanley said, as he entered the room. He kissed both Sophia and Nessa on the cheek.

Rascal, instantly taking a liking to the man, started wagging his tail excitedly as he tried to jump out of Nessa's arms.

"Oh look at us," Stanley laughed as he took the eager dog from Nessa. "We're matching." Sitting down next to Tommy at the table, Sophia smiled as Tommy stood up and awkwardly shook Nessa's hand.

"Lovely to meet you, Mrs O'Hagan," Tommy said.

"Ah you must be Tommy." Nessa beamed at the polite boy, noting that his brother didn't acknowledge her.

"Alright, Red?" Jonathan leered from across the table to where his brother and Sophia sat. "This is all very cosy, isn't it? Shame your mum and dad couldn't make it. What did you say was wrong with your dad again?"

Tommy had filled him in on why Sophia had lied about her dad being ill: apparently it was because she was ashamed of him being such an old drunk. Jonathan hoped he was making the girl squirm as she'd now have to re-tell her lie to everyone, and in front of her gran.

"It is a shame, isn't it?" Nessa quickly chipped in. "But hopefully in time he'll be well again. We can only hope."

Nessa put on a BAFTA-worthy act of sadness. Sophia had been right about Jonathan being a jumped up little shit; the second he walked into the room she had felt the air go cold. What the boy hadn't banked on was the fact that Sophia had told her about the lie. Jamesie was a complete disgrace, and there was no way the girl would have wanted to introduce him to Tommy's family, so Nessa could see exactly why she had lied. Looking at Jonathan, she could see what Sophia meant when she said the boy made her skin crawl; Nessa felt the same.

Smiling smugly at Jonathan, Sophia felt Tommy squeeze her hand under the table. She could tell that Jonathan was in one of his irritating moods but, with both her nan and Tommy here tonight, she should just about be able to tolerate him.

"Stanley, my love," Bernie said, "I'm going to check on the food, can you get our guests some drinks?"

Stanley tried to hide his smirk as his wife put on her usual public show of perfection.

"What can I get you, Nessa?" Stanley asked as he put Rascal onto the floor, leaving him to have a sniff of his new surroundings. "Gin; vodka; wine?"

"Oh, go on then, I'll have a glass of wine, but you better only make it a small one, goes right to my head that stuff does." The family seemed lovely, Nessa thought. Bernie was a bit stuffy, but she seemed like a very nice lady all the same. And Tommy was a credit to them both. Sophia certainly seemed smitten.

"Oh, I don't bloody believe it," Bernie shouted in the kitchen as she opened the oven door only to have black smoke pour out, filling the room. The pie was cremated, dried out with a black crust.

"Excuse me for just a moment, Nessa, then I'll be back with your drinks," Stanley said awkwardly, as the smoke alarm started beeping.

"I'm going to bloody kill Jonathan," Bernie cried, as Stanley rushed into the kitchen. "Look, Stanley, it's burnt to a bloody crisp. I bet he did it on purpose."

Bernie flapped the tea towel around exaggeratedly as she panicked, wafting the smoke around the kitchen.

"No, not Saint Jonathan; he wouldn't do such a thing, surely?" Stanley opened the kitchen window to let some fresh air in. "You must have turned the oven up too high yourself, Bernie, when you were in here earlier flapping around like a crazed woman."

Bernie searched the fridge and cupboards for something she could cook instead of the charcoaled monstrosity on the worktop. "I had it on a hundred and sixty. That's what the recipe says, and that's what I had the oven set to. I told Jonathan to turn it off earlier and now look: it's on the highest setting."

"Is everything alright, Mum? Do you want a hand with the drinks, Dad?" Jonathan wandered into the kitchen. He was sick of watching his brother and Sophia making eyes at each other, like they were auditioning for the parts of Romeo and Juliet. And as for Sophia's nan, what a weirdo: she kept staring at him. "Mum, what the hell have you done to the dinner? We can't eat that. We'll break our teeth."

Stanley opened the larder door. Pretending to look for a dinner substitute, he stifled a laugh. It was obvious Jonathan had ruined the dinner on purpose. And for the first time ever, Stanley was revelling in it. Bernie was so obsessed with being the perfect host: the fact that tonight was quickly turning into a complete disaster was quite amusing.

Bernie gritted her teeth. "Jonathan, I told you to turn the oven off."

Jonathan shrugged. "Oh, I thought you said turn it up. Sorry."

Bernie could see Jonathan was anything but. "Oh, just go and sit down, will you."

For once, Jonathan did as he was told. He could tell that his mother was furious with him.

"What am I going to do, Stanley? We haven't got anything in. I used everything up to make the pie," she said as her husband closed the larder door and stared at her blankly.

"We've got the starters and the pudding, all we need's a main. I'm sure there's something we can rustle up," Stanley said; realising that his wife was close to tears, he felt guilty that he had found the fact that Jonathan had deliberately burned the dinner so funny. "I'll tell you what: get Nessa a glass of wine: make it a large one, then she won't notice the food. You have one too. Go on, sit down and leave this to me."

***

"Well, I have to say, I've never had a fancy seafood starter followed by beans on toast before, but that was lovely," Nessa said, as she placed her cutlery on her empty plate and took another mouthful of her second glass of wine. She didn't normally drink, and was starting to feel tipsy.

"Cheesy beans on toast is the best," Stanley said. "It's not gourmet unless you delicately sprinkle cheese over the top and follow with a dash of salt and a dusting of pepper, don't you know."

Stanley remembered the look of horror on Bernie's face when he had bought out the plates of baked beans on toast.

"Shall me and Tommy take Rascal out, Nan? I think he may need a wee," Sophia interrupted as she watched Rascal jump up and down at the kitchen door, hoping that she and Tommy could then be alone for a few minutes.

"Oh, Tommy, can't you use the toilet like everyone else?" Stanley winked at Tommy.

"You're drunk." Tommy laughed at his dad's feeble attempt of a joke.

"Of course you can, my lovey," Nessa said, "as long as that's okay with Bernie and Stanley. He might leave one of his little presents out there, I'm afraid. Rascal by name, Rascal by nature..."

"Oh, Stanley won't mind if he does, will you, Stan?" Bernie slurred her words; she was on her third glass of wine due to the evening being such a disaster.

Her annoyance was compounded by the fact that Jonathan had sat there all evening grinning like the Cheshire cat.

And Stanley's contribution to the chaos... bloody beans on toast. A dull and common meal to match the company, Bernie thought, wishing she hadn't bothered to get out her finest china. Nessa seemed nice enough, but she was hardly worth rolling the red carpet out for. Bernie had needed to drink to get through the painful evening.

"You can be on poop-scoop patrol tomorrow morning, can't you Stanley? He doesn't mind getting his hands dirty," Bernie said, then hiccupped loudly.

"I'll come outside too," Jonathan said quickly. His parents bored the arse off him at the best of times, and after a few drinks they were worse than normal. "I've got a tennis ball upstairs; bet Rascal would love a game of catch."

Sophia couldn't hide her disappointment.

***

"Okay, I've got another one for you," Nessa said, as Stanley poured her another glass of wine. "What's the difference between an Irish wedding and an Irish wake?"

"I don't know," said Stanley.

"One less drunk." Nessa roared with laughter.

Seeing Bernie's shocked expression only made Nessa and Stanley laugh even more.

"Well, apparently it's okay for the rest of the world to take the piss out of us Irish, so we may as well join in. One thing they can never say is us Irish haven't got a humour," Nessa said.

"You certainly have," Bernie said; the sound of Nessa's laugh grated on her nerves.

Seeing the disapproving look on Bernie's face, Nessa added: "Bernie, as my dear old mammy used to say, it doesn't matter how high up you sit on your throne, at the end of the day you're still just sitting on your arse. There were no airs and graces in our house. A spade was a spade, and we could laugh at ourselves along with the best of them."

She could tell that she was rubbing the woman up the wrong way but she didn't care. Stanley was hilarious and Nessa hadn't had this much fun in ages but, realising that she was slurring now too, she said to herself that she wouldn't have any more wine after this last glass.

Stanley's chest ached from laughing. Nessa had got funnier as the night went on, not mincing her words at all, while his wife had been the complete opposite. Her tightly pursed mouth resembled a cat's arse, he thought, as he gathered up the plates.

"Who's for pudding?" he asked.

The women shook their heads. Nessa couldn't eat another thing, and Bernie just wanted to keep drinking.

"So, looks like Sophia and Tommy are getting on really well," Nessa said to Bernie as the women sat in silence looking out the window to where the two children were huddled up close to each other on the garden bench. She could see Rascal yapping away and playing happily with Jonathan, and she was pleased that the boy must have taken the hint and given Sophia and Tommy some space. Her little Rascal would keep the boy busy.

"Tommy is smitten with her, I have to say," Bernie agreed, observing her son as he sat next to his very first girlfriend with a big smile on his face. Bernie had never seen him look so happy. Even Jonathan seemed to be behaving, she thought, as she watched him run up and down the garden bouncing the tennis ball on the ground, Rascal jumping around his feet. It must be hard for him to see his brother with Sophia, though; before Tommy met her, he and Jonathan had been joined at the hip. Bernie made a mental note to spend a bit more time with Jonathan: maybe tomorrow she would buy him those new trainers he had mentioned.

"Right now, how about some of this," Stanley said, as he held out the bottle of Limoncello that had been tucked away in the back of the freezer since their holiday to Italy the previous year.

"Oh, go on then," Nessa replied cheerily, as she held out the shot glass that Stanley had placed in front of her: one for the road wouldn't hurt.

***

"I think my parents are a bit tipsy." Tommy hoped Sophia hadn't found them too embarrassing. Typically, that night was one of the few times that he had seen his mum let her hair down, and she had chosen to do it in front of Sophia and her nan.

"That's alright, my nan's in the same boat. She normally only has a sherry at Christmas or birthdays. She'll be wasted on all that wine." Sophia was glad that everyone seemed to be getting on. Even Jonathan seemed happier now that he was running up and down the garden like a lunatic, with Rascal chasing him for the ball.

"Are you cold?" Seeing Sophia's teeth chatter, Tommy shuffled nearer to her on the bench, hoping he could keep her warm. Sophia smiled. She felt so comfortable with him, like they had known each other forever; although it had only been a week since Tommy had returned to school, in that time they had become inseparable. Tommy had changed her life. The tension at home was becoming unbearable, but spending time with Tommy helped her to forget it while she was with him.

Sophia had confided in Tommy about her dad's abusive nature. He was the only person other than her nan that she had spoken to about it. Tommy had listened intently and he hadn't judged her mother for putting up with her father's behaviour when she told him of the times she had caught her dad hitting her mum, or grabbing her by her hair. Her mother tried so hard to hide her bruises, but Sophia had seen them.

Tommy had told Sophia that he would be there for her no matter what, and she was so grateful for that. He was the opposite of her dad. Sophia could tell that Tommy was a genuinely good person. Sophia's nan had always said that you can tell how a man will treat you by the way that he treats his mother. And Tommy was very kind to his mum.

Tommy tapped his fingers on the bench. He felt stupid and awkward. He didn't have the guts to wrap his arms around Sophia and pull her close. He wished he had the courage to tell her how he felt. But he was too scared in case she didn't feel the same way. They hadn't known each other long, what if he was reading the signals wrongly: what if she just felt sorry for him after what happened at the Lea?

"What's up, Tommy? You've gone all quiet. What are you thinking about?" Sophia asked. They had sat in silence for a couple of minutes, and she could tell there was something on his mind. She wondered if he liked her as much as she liked him, but Tommy had yet to make any kind of a move, and Sophia didn't want to seem pushy by being the one to initiate things unless he did first.

"Oh, I don't know, it's silly really, but I was just thinking..." Tommy started, unsure if he should tell her how he felt. But maybe now was as good a time as any.

"How are you two lovebirds getting on?" Jonathan smiled at Tommy knowingly before plonking himself down on the edge of a wall opposite his brother and Sophia.

Feeling his cheeks burn, Tommy shuffled further away from Sophia.

Sophia sighed loudly: Jonathan was a pain in the arse. He followed Tommy around like

a bad smell. Sophia wished he would get some friends of his own.

Jonathan took a crumpled pack of cigarettes and a lighter from his jacket pocket and lit up a bent cigarette.

"You'll get caught if you do that out here," Tommy said, worried that their mum and dad would then think that he was smoking too. Or even worse, that Sophia had been smoking. Knowing his mum, she would probably ban her from the house if she thought that Sophia was a bad influence.

Jonathan shrugged.

"Where's Rascal?" Tommy asked, hoping that Jonathan would go off and look for him.

"At the back of the garden; he was sniffing out a rabbit hole or something when I left him." Jonathan breathed in smoke. "Want a puff, Red?"

He had caught Sophia glaring at him, enjoying the fact that his presence was winding her up and knowing she hated it when he referred to her by the colour of her hair.

Sophia shook her head. She had tried to tell Tommy a couple of times about the expression on his twin's face on the day that Tommy had nearly drowned; it had almost been as if he had enjoyed seeing Tommy's seemingly lifeless body lying there. Sophia couldn't understand how someone as kind and lovely as Tommy could be related to someone as weird and cold as Jonathan.

"Have you asked her about the party yet?" Jonathan asked, betting that his brother wouldn't have plucked up the courage.

"What party?" Sophia asked Tommy.

Tommy gave his brother an annoyed look. He had wanted to tell Sophia how he felt about her first, and then he was going to mention the party. Jonathan had ruined his plan.

"Well, it's up to you, Sophia," Tommy said shyly, "but my mum said we can have a party for our sixteenth. And when she found out that your birthday is in a few days' time she said we should move it forward to make it a party for all three of us. She's got this crazy idea in her head that it would be a great way of thanking you for what you did for me, she said what with your dad being ill and all that..."

Tommy went red as he spoke: Sophia would probably think that it was a stupid idea.

"A party?" she asked.

"We could get some of the kids from school over: you can invite whoever you want... Mum said that she and Dad would go out for the evening. She must really want to thank you, because from the way she was talking she sounds like she wants to pull out all the stops."

A big smile spread across Sophia's pretty face.

"That would be amazing," Sophia said as she placed her hand on top of Tommy's and squeezed it tightly.

"She's been acting like you're royalty or something, Sophia. But whatever, it sounds like the perfect opportunity to get off our tits on cider," Jonathan added.

As he watched the lovey-dovey exchange, he felt a twang as he recognised the bond they had.

Light spilt out on to the grass, and they looked in that direction to see Stanley standing in the kitchen doorway.

"Sophia, I've just called a taxi. Your nan is a bit drunk, love," Stanley said, as he held Nessa upright while she giggled like a young girl. He regretted insisting she knock back three large shots of Limoncello now that she could barely walk.

"Oh, Nan." Sophia laughed, before standing up and calling for Rascal. As he was normally so well-behaved, she was surprised when he didn't come at her first call.

"Rascal?" Sophia called again, with Tommy following suit. "Rascal, here boy," he called.

"He's probably gone down that rabbit hole, knowing him," Sophia said, as she made her way to the back of the garden, thinking that it was typical that her nan was drunk and Rascal playing truant on the one night she had wanted to make a good impression.

"Rascal, darling," Nessa called, as she staggered onto the patio, almost tripping. "Rascal, come on my little babby, we have to go home. Ooh, dear. I feel a bit queasy."

Stanley helped Nessa walk to the end of the garden, thinking that a bit of fresh air might help, and failing that at least they could help to find Rascal: then he could put Nessa in a cab so that she could go home and sleep it off. That Italian stuff he poured them must have been stronger than he realised because even he felt quite tipsy and Bernie was already in bed.

Stepping through a pile of leaves, Sophia leaned in towards a big spray of climbing roses that Stanley grew up against the back fence.

She thought she could hear a whimper.

Searching on the ground, she couldn't find any rabbit hole but she was sure she could hear the dog, and then she heard the whimper again.

"Rascal's here, Tommy," she called, as he came running over, hearing the panic in her voice. "I think he must be stuck somewhere. I can't see him, but I can just about hear him."

Pushing through the bushes, Tommy didn't care that his arms were bleeding from the scratches as the thorns tore at his skin.

"Oh my God: Rascal," Tommy cried, as he reached the wire fence that was hidden behind the dense rose bushes, and spotted Rascal's little furry body tied to it. His feet were dangling above ground level, while he hung limply by his neck, his bowtie wrapped tightly around the metal like a noose.

Sophia peered over Tommy's shoulder and screamed as she caught a glimpse of Rascal's body hanging there limply. Tommy pushed her out of the way to protect her from seeing any more than she already had.

Rascal's mouth had gone grey and his eyes were vacant, but as soon as Tommy touched him, he could feel that he was warm and that he had a faint heartbeat.

"Don't let your nan come back here, Sophia," he commanded. He ripped at the bowtie fixing the dog to the fence, and released him from his suffering.

"What's going on?" Stanley and Nessa had found Sophia crying and shaking, and Tommy crouched over on the ground.

"Don't let my nan see," Sophia implored. "Rascal has had an accident. Please, Stanley, don't let her see."

"Dad, we're going to have to call a vet," Tommy called, as he cradled Rascal in his arms, relieved to see that the dog was breathing, his chest rising slowly up and down. Sophia was crying hysterically, the sight of Rascal just hanging there had been too much to bear.

"Rascal must have jumped up to get his ball and got the bowtie caught up on the fence, Nan, he was just hanging there..." she whimpered.

Nessa clasped her hand over her mouth in shock; the sight of Rascal's body lying limply in Tommy's arms was instantly sobering. "Oh Rascal, my poor boy; it's all my fault. That stupid bloody bowtie could have killed him."

Tommy placed Rascal in Nessa's arms. Lying there weakly, he wagged his tail and Nessa started to cry. Rascal was a child and a best friend rolled into one; she would be lost without him.

Tommy and his dad exchanged glances. Tommy nodded over to where his brother was sitting on the bench with an expression on his face that looked like he was thoroughly enjoying the drama that was unfolding in front of him.

Tommy whispered: "He didn't get caught up, Dad; his collar-tie had been tied into a double knot." Tommy felt sick; a few more minutes and Rascal would have been dead.

Stanley couldn't speak. Jonathan had tried to hang Nessa's dog.

Chapter Nine

"It's not exactly the party of the century, is it? I thought you said that there was going to be booze," Megan Farrow muttered to Sophia as she half-heartedly swayed her body in time with the awful music that was blasting out, hoping that she would at least look like she was having a good time even though she really wasn't. Tugging down her mini-dress, Megan wished that she hadn't gone to so much effort; she couldn't help but notice the stares that she was getting from most of the boys in the room. The other girls were just wearing casual tops and jeans.

As for the venue, the house itself was okay but it wasn't exactly a happening and cool place unless you were into floral prints and dingy looking furniture: she should have brought her gran. Megan was willing to give the party a chance though, Tommy's parents may not have had much taste when it came to décor but she could see that they certainly had money and she thought that her friend Sophia had landed on her feet with this new boyfriend. Apparently he had a twin, too.

Scanning the room, however, she felt let down. The boys at the party were just that: boys. Megan liked men and, because she looked older than her age with her hair done and her make-up on, they liked her too. As Megan glanced around the room she turned her nose up at the lack of talent. The room was full of immature boys throwing themselves about to the music and they all had more chance of pulling a muscle than they did at pulling her tonight.

Even the food was disappointing: cheese-and-pineapple sticks and overflowing bowls of sausage rolls sat cluttered on a bright pink tablecloth strategically placed around the grand centrepiece: a home-made Victoria Sponge birthday cake. The whole thing reminded Megan of a child's party.

"They do know you're sixteen and not six? It's a bit shit, don't you think?" Megan said sulkily, as she searched the table for anything alcoholic. The Spice Girls' squeaky voices were now blaring out of the stereo at full volume and she figured that she would need a few drinks to help her through the evening.

"I'm having a good time," Sophia said.

"I can't believe that I let you drag me here." Megan scowled. "When you said party, this," she indicated the kids that were dancing dementedly around her, "wasn't what I had in mind. This Jonathan had better be worth it."

Sophia sighed. Megan was hard work sometimes, and why she was clutching on to the idea of Jonathan she had no idea: Sophia had warned her that he was nothing like Tommy. In fact he was the complete opposite. As for the party, her own thoughts couldn't have been more different. Tommy had clearly gone to a lot of effort for her, and she thought that the party was amazing. Okay, so the buffet and the music were cheesy, but that's what birthday parties were supposed to be and unlike her friend, Sophia thought that the trouble Tommy had taken to make tonight special was sweet.

"Oh my God, please tell me that we're not drinking fucking Ribena all night." Megan had spotted the cartons of soft drinks all lined up in a neat row on the sideboard. Realising that she was about to launch into another of her long-winded rants, Sophia nudged her hard in the ribs.

"Shush, here come the boys."

Tommy and Jonathan made their way to where the two girls were standing. Sophia gave Tommy a beaming smile, ignoring Jonathan.

Staring from one twin to the other, Megan sniggered. They were dressed in matching red checked shirts and black jeans. "Oh my God, don't you think you're taking the whole identical thing a bit too far? Are you wearing the same pants too?"

Megan vaguely recognised the boys as being in her year, but up until now she had never actually spoke to either of them. Looking from one boy to the other she tried to see if she could spot any differences. Sophia was smitten with Tommy, and Megan could see that out of the two he did seem to be the nicer one. He seemed softer around the edges, and came across as shy. The other boy, Jonathan, had beady eyes and the way he was standing there leering at her didn't help. Either way neither of the boys were the heartthrobs that Sophia had made them out to be and wealthy or not, Jonathan didn't stand a chance with Megan.

"God, don't ask." Tommy pretended to laugh, feeling stupid. He had meant to change after his mum had gone, but she had been so busy fussing that by the time everyone they had invited from school had started to arrive Tommy had forgotten. Tommy didn't realise how many people would actually turn up. They had to be here for Sophia, he and Jonathan had barely been given the time of day by most of these kids normally. Hopefully, things were going to change for the better after tonight. Glancing down at his shirt, Tommy shrugged. He and Jonathan both looked ridiculous but their mum had insisted on them wearing the new shirts that she had bought especially for tonight, in her element as she tried to dress them up as she had when they were small on special occasions. To keep the peace, Tommy had gone along with it, especially after the effort his mum had gone to helping him to get the party ready for Sophia. He had been surprised when Jonathan had gone along with it too, normally he would kick up a fuss. He'd even, for the first time ever, agreed to get his hair cut in the same neat style as Tommy, which their mum had been over the moon about. She had taken at least twenty photos of the boys before she had left.

"Tommy, I can't believe how great it all looks," Sophia said, seeing Tommy's cheeks colour at Megan's words. She thought the matching outfits were cute. "This must have taken you ages."

"So you like it then, yeah?" Tommy asked. His main aim tonight had been to impress Sophia and by the smile on her face he had a feeling that he had succeeded.

"Took us ages to get rid of Mum and Dad, didn't it, Jonathan?" Tommy wanted to include his brother in the conversation. Jonathan hadn't been able to do enough to help Tommy with the preparations, and he hoped that Jonathan would be prepared to put his differences with Sophia aside too. Jonathan was prone to having tantrums even at almost sixteen but Tommy hoped that today was the start of his brother finally growing up. Ever since the other night, when Rascal had had his accident, Jonathan had been behaving impeccably. When questioned, he swore blind that he hadn't done anything to Rascal, as much as his dad had shouted at him. Tommy and Stanley both knew that he was lying, but Bernie believed Jonathan. Rascal was a little terror with boundless energy: he had dashed about the house sniffing everything out. Getting caught up on that fence would have been easily done.

"Yeah, Mum was a bloody nightmare," Jonathan concurred. "I don't think she wanted to leave in the end. She said something about staying to wish you a happy birthday, Sophia; you know, after all you did for Tommy. I think she just wanted to check up on us. She's convinced that we're all going to start getting off our heads on drink. I thought Dad was going to throw her over his shoulder at one point and carry her out."

Their mother had been her usual annoying self today and Jonathan and Tommy had practically had to push her out of the door to make sure she left. She had been so concerned about the state of her house and garden that Jonathan had wondered why she had suggested they had the party in the first place.

"Not much chance of getting off our heads on blackcurrant juice, is there?" Megan spoke glumly. She grimaced as she watched one of the boys from school stuff two large sausage rolls in his mouth at once and spit pastry as he chewed them. "Looks like we're going to be playing pass-the-parcel and musical chairs like good little children then."

"Well, actually..." Jonathan grinned at Megan as he pulled out a bottle a big bottle of Coca-Cola from behind a chair and held it up like a prize trophy.

"Just when I thought that it couldn't get any worse," Megan cried. "Shoot me now! Please tell me that you're not actually excited about drinking poxy coke."

"Ah, see, that's where you're wrong." Jonathan grinned. "It isn't coke." Unscrewing the lid, Jonathan passed the bottle up to Megan's nose.

The aroma of alcohol wafted up her nose. "What's in it?" Megan asked, suddenly feeling hopeful.

Tommy, however, was feeling stressed. They had promised their mum that no-one would be drinking.

"But Mum will know that we've drunk it," Tommy said. Their mother would have made it her business to know exactly how much alcohol they had in the drinks cabinet, she was sure to notice it was missing.

"For fuck's sake, Tommy; I'm not a complete moron. I poured a bit of everything in here. Gin, vodka, rum, whiskey. It's a bit of a concoction really. And don't worry, Tommy, I topped all the bottles up after. Trust me, they won't have a clue."

"So it's a cocktail then?" Megan said, smiling for the first time since she had arrived.

"It is. It's called... Sweet Sixteen."

Megan took a glass from Jonathan and held it out eagerly. Sophia did the same, and Jonathan poured out generous measures for the girls and Tommy. Jonathan, Tommy and the girls clinked glasses and said 'Cheers', before tipping their heads back and drinking the large shots down in one.

Jonathan spluttered from the strength of the alcohol, and then laughed. "Wow, a few more shots and this will be the best party you girls have ever been to. Let's do another."

Jonathan poured more drinks. Tommy shook his head. The alcohol had burned his throat and the fumes had shot up his nostrils, making him wince.

"Oh, come on, Tommy, don't be such a pussy. She's sixteen, let's celebrate in style." Jonathan smiled, happy that the girls were keen for more alcohol. Tommy was just making himself look like a coward, and Jonathan thought it was hilarious that he would act so pathetically in front of the girls. Sophia would soon realise what a wet blanket he could be.

"Nah, but you go for it. That stuff tastes rank," Tommy added, surprised when Sophia downed a second glass. Because of what Sophia had told him about her father's addiction to alcohol, Tommy had expected her to abstain. It was her sixteenth birthday too, though, and although Tommy didn't want to get drunk, he wasn't going to try and stop Sophia.

As the evening went on and the drinks kept flowing, Megan thought that Jonathan had been right: now they had all had a few drinks the party was fun. Feeling tipsy, Megan threw her head back and sung along with the music at the top of her voice.

Feeling herself swaying even though she had been sitting down for at least fifteen minutes, Sophia slumped back onto the sofa as she tried desperately not to throw up.

"Here you go, Sophia, have this. You don't look so great, and if you're feeling a bit sick, my mum swears that lemonade settles your stomach. She gives it to me and Tommy every time either of us have a dodgy stomach." Jonathan handed Sophia the glass and watched as she threw her head back and drank it down in one. The 'lemonade' was more vodka than anything else. That and the six large shots of his cocktail she had just done should be enough to do the trick he thought to himself nastily. His mum had deviously drawn a line in pencil along the label of the vodka bottle so that she would know if it had been touched, but always one step ahead Jonathan had even more deviously topped up bottle with water, replacing the alcohol so that his mum wouldn't notice it had been taken. "You're welcome."

He smiled before walking off.

***

"You alright, Soph?" Tommy asked, a few minutes later as he sat on the sofa next to her. He had been so busy making sure that everyone had drinks and topping up the crisp bowls as his mother had instructed him that by the time he had thought to check on Sophia she was slumped over on a chair.

"I feel a bit sick, Tommy," Sophia said quietly, wishing that she hadn't done so many shots this evening. She had managed to dance for a couple of songs with Megan, but then she had started to feel dizzy and had needed to sit down. She had only drunk the shots because she knew that Megan wanted her to. Now Megan was grinding away on the dance floor, enjoying herself, leaving Sophia alone to fight the puke that kept threatening to come up at the back of her throat. The lemonade that Jonathan had given her hadn't helped at all, in fact she felt worse than ever.

"You don't look very well," Tommy said, seeing Sophia's skin looking even more transparent than normal and beads of sweat on her forehead. "Do you want to go upstairs and lie down for a bit? On your own, I mean... not with me. Not that I don't want to come with you. But if you're feeling sick..."

"Yeah, I need to lie down." The room was spinning, and Sophia felt like she might throw up. She had no idea how her dad managed to knock back as much as he did on a daily basis. This was the first time that she had been drunk and the way she felt right now it would be the last. With blurry vision, Sophia unsteadily let Tommy guide her out of the room and up the stairs. Walking past Megan who also looked like she had had too much to drink, Tommy shook his head at her snogging the face off some lad who was at least a foot shorter than her, while the boy groped at Megan's chest. Tommy would have to check on her once he had made sure Sophia was okay.

"And where are the two little lovebirds off to?" Jonathan watched his brother escort Sophia upstairs. "Mum said upstairs was out of bounds, remember? Mind you, if you're going to do what I think you're going to do, then mum's the word."

Jonathan winked at Tommy, thinking that finally his brother was going to lose his virginity. He couldn't help feel impressed that Tommy was willing to have sex with Sophia when she was paralytic. Maybe Tommy wasn't such an innocent after all. It was probably the only way he'd get into Miss Snooty-pants' knickers.

"Sophia doesn't feel very well, so she's going to lic down for a bit. 'Someone' gave her too much booze, and now she's wasted," Tommy replied. He held on to Sophia, who was wobbling on a stair. Tommy was furious with Jonathan. He had been pouring drinks down Sophia and Megan's necks all night, and now Sophia's night was ruined and Megan didn't look too far behind her. She was in such a state that she was probably going to miss the rest of the evening while she slept off the alcohol's ill effects, if she didn't puke her guts up beforehand.

Shaking his head at how upset Tommy sounded over his pathetic lightweight girlfriend, Jonathan walked off, smiling, pleased with himself that his plan had worked. He had guessed that stuck-up little bitch wouldn't be able to handle her drink.

***

Sophia opened her eyes and took a few seconds to remember where she was. She looked around the room, taking in the unfamiliar blue walls covered in Arsenal posters. Music thudded beneath her, the loud bass causing the floor to vibrate. She was at Tommy's house, at their sixteenth birthday party.

She didn't know how she had ended up in Tommy's room. She vaguely remembered feeling ill earlier and seeing a bucket on the floor next to her, and a glass of water on the bedside cabinet, and she guessed it had been Tommy who had looked after her.

As she sat up, the room started to spin and Sophia felt like she was going to be sick; her stomach was churning and she felt hot and clammy. Unable to do anything else she turned back on to her side and shut her eyes tightly, willing the nauseous feeling to go away as she fell back to sleep.

***

"Looks like we weren't the only ones drinking," Jonathan slurred, as he pointed to the corner of the room where a boy was leaning and throwing up into the large pot that contained Bernie's favourite plant.

"Mum is going to go mental," Tommy moaned, as the boy moved away from the plant only to spew the contents of his stomach halfway up the wall as well. "I guess I'm going to have to clean it up, aren't I?"

Tommy glared at his drunken brother, who looked in no fit state to help him.

Tommy had been getting more and more frantic as the night went on. The party had quickly got out of hand. The drinks cabinet had been ransacked and the house was getting trashed. Tommy had spent half the night cleaning up puke.

His parents had told him that they would be home at eleven-thirty, and it was almost eleven now.

Fetching another bucket, Tommy was thoroughly pissed off. The whole point of tonight had been to impress Sophia but she had been upstairs, passed out, for most of the evening.

"Here, bro; let me help," Jonathan offered, as he tried to grab the cloth from Tommy's hand and almost fell over.

"No, don't worry, Jonathan. I'll do it all," Tommy said sarcastically, as he snatched the cloth back before stomping over to a puddle of vomit on the carpet.

Tommy tried not to retch himself as he cleaned. Even if he managed to get most of it up, he was still going to be in big trouble when his parents got home. Hearing his brother over the other side of the room shouting and jeering as he encouraged some of the younger kids to down their beers, Tommy stood up and watched as a boy choked on the frothy head of lager as it bubbled up his nose.

Coughing, the boy spat out a mouthful onto the floor as Jonathan roared with laughter.

Tommy shook his head, feeling defeated. Jonathan looked like he didn't have a care in the world: it was clear he was enjoying wrecking the place. He was doing everything that their mother had made them promise not to do, and encouraging everyone else to join in. The worse thing, in Tommy's view, was that he had managed to get Sophia so drunk that she missed her own party. Tommy suspected that had been his plan. He should have known that Jonathan being helpful earlier was just an act.

And who was left to pick up the pieces? Tommy: the sensible twin. Tonight had been a disaster and Tommy just wanted it to be over.

Just as he thought things couldn't get any worse, there was a scream and Tommy looked up to see what was happening. One of the boys in the group dancing around Megan, who had been doing an impersonation of Michael Jackson, had swung an arm out wildly and managed to knock down the large green urn that had been sitting in the middle of the mantelpiece.

"Tell me that this is not what I think it is," Megan said, looking like she was about to break down in tears as she stood deadly still in the middle of the floor, holding her hands out accusingly, praying that she was wrong as everyone around stared at her. But she could already tell from Tommy's horrified expression that her worst fears were true.

The large ceramic urn had flown through the air and hit Megan, covering her completely with Tommy's grandmother's ashes. Tommy placed his head in his hands. His mother would crucify him for this.

"Oh my God, Tommy, this is so disgusting. Get that stuff off me," Megan cried frantically as she spotted small bone fragments amongst the pile of dust at her feet. Then, tasting the dry powder on her lips, Megan freaked out. She jumped up and down like a lunatic, flapping her arms as she tried to brush off the ash that clung to her dress, which had been purple and was now grey. She couldn't get it off her. Unzipping her dress, Megan stepped out of it and threw it on the floor sending another cloud of dust rising up.

Tommy stood rooted to the spot. The group of boys who had been dancing were laughing their heads off at the sight of Megan jumping about and shouting in her underwear. Then something snapped inside Tommy.

"Right, that's it, people." Tommy went over to where the stereo was placed on the Welsh dresser, and yanked the plug out of the wall. "The party's over."

***

Waking from a very peculiar dream, Sophia opened her eyes. The room was dark, and as her vision adjusted she smiled as she saw Tommy standing above her.

"How are you feeling?" he asked softly.

"I don't know. Not too good," Sophia muttered. The room was spinning and it was difficult to focus on him. "How long have I been up here?"

"About an hour, I guess. You were in a bad way earlier," he said, as he sat on the bed.

"I feel in a bad way now," Sophia said, feeling ashamed. "I'm so sorry about this, Tommy. I've ruined the party, haven't I?" Sophia knew that Tommy must be pissed off after all the effort he had gone to, even though he wasn't showing it. She wished more than anything that she hadn't drunk so much now.

Tommy shrugged.

Hoping to make it up to him, Sophia reached out and took Tommy's hand.

85

She felt Tommy tense up, seemingly surprised, before he responded by leaning down and kissing her. Feeling him move his hand up her chest, her heart thudded.

"So, have I ruined your night?" she asked teasingly. She could tell from the bulge in his trousers that he was enjoying the kissing as much as she was. Sophia moved Tommy's hand down and guided it underneath her top.

Tommy pulled his hand away. He looked at her questioningly.

"It's okay, Tommy. I want to." Sophia moved her legs apart.

"Are you sure?" he asked, and she nodded.

"You feel the same about me as I do about you?" Tommy kissed her gently on her forehead.

Catching a strong whiff of alcohol from his breath as he spoke, Sophia nodded before turning her head to avoid it; even just the smell of alcohol made her feel rough.

She did love him: of that there was no doubt. In the short time that she had known him she had thought of nothing but him. Tommy was the most decent, caring boy that she had ever met. He made her feel safe.

However, she stiffened as his warm palm caressed her stomach. Suddenly, she felt apprehensive. She wasn't sure that she was really ready to do this. But she wanted to make it up to him for ruining the party, and the stroking sensation was quickly soothing her worries away. Gradually, she began to relax as Tommy moved his hand down further.

"Are you sure you want me?" he asked, as he pushed her skirt up around her hips, grazing her thighs with his hands.

He moved his hand away, which made her crave his touch once again.

"I'm sorry," she said. "I do want to; it's just that I wanted my first time to be..."

She was too drunk to finish explaining and the warmth of Tommy's body, and the way he had gently touched her skin, made her doubt everything that she had believed. Putting his hand back on her body, she nodded at him to carry on.

"What do you mean?" he asked.

"I don't know. I wanted it to be special, I guess," she whispered. She wondered why she was vacillating. She was sixteen now: old enough. And she was curious. Megan had told her all about the night she had lost her virginity; she had boasted enough times about how amazing it was, and how she had had her first orgasm. She said there was no feeling in the world like it.

"It will be special. I'm going to make it so special for you," Tommy whispered back as he pulled her knickers down and moved awkwardly on top of her.

"We need a condom, Tommy," Sophia said suddenly feeling very nervous that they were going to actually do this.

"Hang on," he reassured her as he fiddled about with himself before straddled her body once more.

At first she liked it, but then the weight of him pinning her down made her feel claustrophobic and nausea washed over her in waves. As Tommy moved on top of her, she tried to focus on her breathing as a way of distraction. Her heart was beating loudly. Tommy's breath rasped against her cheek as he kissed her hard on her mouth. She screwed up her face at the sudden sharp pain that she felt as he pushed himself inside her without warning.

"Tommy," Sophia managed to say quietly, still lightheaded from all the cocktails.

She felt like she was suffocating underneath him. The room was still spinning.

Tommy grunted in her ear as he moved his body up and down on top of her, gathering momentum as he pushed her back and forth on the bed. Pounding on top of her, he thrust himself harder into her. Sophia gritted her teeth and tried to hold back her tears. She hadn't imagined that her first time would feel like this. She had imagined it as gentler; more intimate.

She could feel the bile at the back of her throat, but she forced herself to gulp it down. The acidity burned her throat.

Sophia felt Tommy's body tremble and convulse and was glad it was over.

Her feeling of relief was quickly replaced by one of increased nausea. Tommy had barely rolled off her, when Sophia realised she could no longer hold back the urge to be sick. Flinging her head over the side of the bed she puked up the contents of her stomach into the bucket.

"I'll get you some more water," Tommy said, dressing quickly.

As she watched him, she saw the crumpled cigarette packet sticking out of his back pocket. She felt her blood run cold.

"Jonathan," she said, her voice so quiet she could barely hear it.

Jonathan turned and smiled. "Yes?"

"No... I don't understand. I thought you were Tommy."

"Don't play games, Red. It was me you wanted. You don't think my brother would have been able to fuck you like that, do you?"

"But I... I thought... You tricked me," Sophia cried.

She had known that it hadn't felt right, but she had thought it had been because she was still drunk, and unsure about the act itself. It was her first time; she didn't have anything to compare it to. She couldn't stop shivering. She felt as if Jonathan's coldness was contagious and had crept out from deep within his bones, infecting her.

She should have known that Tommy would never have been so rough with her. If she hadn't been so drunk maybe she would have realised in time. She could have stopped it.

"You pulled me on top of you, Red, remember? You were gagging for it. You can't beg me to fuck you and then start playing these little games." Fucking Sophia had been the perfect opportunity for him to finish her and Tommy. Tommy wouldn't believe that Sophia hadn't realised who she was having sex with, nor would he forgive her. By the look on her face, she knew that too.

"See, Red, I told you that I'd make your first time special." He looked her up and down.

Sophia grabbed the duvet and pulled it around her. She leaned back over the bed and started retching violently until her stomach ached and her throat burned. Through her tears, she saw that Jonathan had gone.

Dragging herself off the bed, Sophia straightened her skirt and put on the rest of her clothes. Struggling to balance, she staggered and leaned on the bedside table for support.

She hated herself, but she couldn't begin to imagine how much more Tommy would when he found out what she had done. Jonathan was right, she had instigated it. Tommy would never believe that Jonathan had tricked her. And even if he did, he wouldn't want her now. Not after that.

Weaving out of the bedroom and down the stairs, she prayed that she wouldn't bump into Jonathan on her way out of the house, or worse still Tommy.

The only place in the world that Sophia wanted to be was at home.

Chapter Ten

The pain in Kaitlin's head was excruciating. Rubbing it gently, she then checked her hand for blood and was surprised there wasn't any. Jamesie had bashed her head so hard on the laminate floor that she felt like her skull had been dented.

"Go on then, you miserable cunt, what are you going to do now? I know... why don't you go and tell my interfering old bitch of a mother what I've done?" Dribble seeped from his lips as Jamesie slurred the words; he was barely capable of speech. Kaitlin looked Jamesie in the eye, searching for a hint of compassion. There was none; all she could see was a sneer on lips surrounded by red and blotchy skin, another side effect of the constant alcohol abuse.

This was the worst state she had ever seen her drunken husband in, however. He had been goading her for a row all day, and even though she had tried her best to pacify him she had known that this would be the outcome. Every day since Nessa's visit, a week ago, she had sensed his anger brewing. Now he had finally started to punish her, the only option left was to let him get it finally out of his system. Looking at the clock she was grateful Sophia was at her party and would be for some time, she desperately wanted to shield her daughter from Jamesie when he was like this, hating the thought of the poor girl seeing her own mum dragged around and beaten. She had already witnessed enough as it was.

"Jamesie, I told you I didn't say anything to your mother. I swear," Kaitlin pleaded half-heartedly, knowing that it was pointless trying to reason with him. Her husband had spent the past few days tormented with paranoid thoughts. He believed what happened behind closed doors should stay there and his mother knowing what he had done, and thus looking down her nose at him, enraged him. He would not have her interfering in his business.

Kaitlin knew that she should take the blame so that Sophia wouldn't be in the firing line. She had known that from the second that she had opened the door to Nessa last week. Nessa hadn't needed to say a word; the pitying way that she had looked at Kaitlin had spoken volumes. Kaitlin also knew that when Jamesie was very drunk, there was no talking sense to the man. Tonight, he had drunk eight cans of cider and half a bottle of Scotch before letting out his pent-up anger. And he didn't seem to have finished.

Catching Kaitlin by her hair, Jamesie wound his fist down to the roots and dragged her screaming onto her feet.

"Look at the state of you, crying like a fucking baby." His wife standing in front of him, whimpering like a wounded animal after all the grief she had caused him, made him want to beat ten shades of shit out of her. He hated her weakness; he wouldn't do this to her if she didn't let him.

Kaitlin would let him say whatever he liked. She knew that whatever she said would be the cause of his next punch or kick. If she stood in silence for long enough, he would rant and rave and swear but, going by his past outbursts, it wouldn't take him too long until he burned himself out. Gearing herself up for it, she knew that she could handle the odd punch and kick until then.

Then there came the sound Kaitlin had dreaded the most: a key in the front door.

"Mum?" Sophia wiped away tears as she hung up her coat then walked into the lounge. How she had managed to find the strength to get out of Tommy's house and make her way home without breaking down she wasn't sure; she had run all the way.

Sophia stared in horror at the scene before her, her face paling. "What's going on?"

But Sophia knew exactly what was going on. Her father stood in the middle of the room like he was king of the castle, holding a fistful of her mother's hair in his hand. Her mum couldn't even look at her. Blood trickled down from the cut on her lip, and she clutched her head in pain.

"Mind your own business, Sophia; this is between me and your mother. Go to your room," Jamesie said coldly as he tried to control his swaying.

Tears ran down Sophia's cheeks as she stared at her unflinching mother, unsure of what she should do. Her legs felt heavy and her body was rooted to the spot.

"Go upstairs, Sophia; its okay, I promise. I'm okay." Kaitlin spoke quietly, pleading with her daughter. The only saving grace in Kaitlin's depressing existence was that Jamesie had never laid a finger on Sophia, and Kaitlin didn't want to put her in a position where that would ever even become a possibility. She had to get her out of the way. "Please, Sophia, go upstairs."

Sophia stared at her dad, watching him wobble from side to side; he was clearly drunk out of his mind once again. She hated what he had become, and she hated what he was doing to her mother. Her mum had told her that he only drank so much because he was depressed. Her mum had said it to make Sophia understand why her dad acted the way he did. Her mum always justified it. Even if it was the combination of the two diseases that made him like this, the mixture was lethal and as far as Sophia was concerned her dad was ruined as a man. Looking at him now was like seeing him for the first time. He was pathetic; a wreck of a man, who had destroyed himself. And now he was destroying his family.

The reality of how drunk she had been tonight made Sophia feel ashamed, remembering how she had stumbled about, she had probably looked just like her father did.

Everything about the evening disgusted her, and it was all down to alcohol. She had lowered herself to the level of a pathetic drunk whom she despised. And look where it had got her. Sophia had never felt so angry.

"Get your arse upstairs. This is your mother's fault, Sophia, not mine," Jamesie said, in a pitiable attempt to justify his actions.

Sophia's mother said that when she had first met Jamesie, he had been different. He had been kind. Sophia had found her mother's words hard to believe, and lately she was convinced they were untrue, because her only memories of her father were as a violent drunk who took out his anger and his shortcomings onto her mother. She had seen the tears and the bruises and had spent countless nights lying in bed with a pillow covering her ears so she could block out the endless name-calling. Lately her father's outbursts had become more frequent, ever since he had lost his job at the factory. At least when he was at work he would stay away from the bottle during the day. Now he was at home, he just drank himself into a stupor from almost the minute that he got out of bed until the minute he passed out back in it.

"Go on, Sophia, get the fuck out of here," Jamesie bellowed, losing his patience.

Sophia heard her father's command, but she couldn't move her legs. She wanted to run to the sanctuary of her bedroom, where she could bury her head under her pillow and forget everything, pretend tonight hadn't happened. But she had been pretending for too long: she couldn't do it anymore. If Sophia did as she was told again tonight and left her mum alone with her dad in the state that he was in, he would kill her.

There would be no more pretending.   Looking into her dad's eyes, Sophia shook her head.

"Get your hands off her, Dad." The words tumbled out of Sophia's mouth and after they had, she couldn't believe she had said them. She had never so much as openly disagreed with her father, let alone had the courage to speak to him so boldly. Feeling her body shake as she spoke, she wasn't sure if it was with anger or fear and she no longer cared.

"What did you just say?" Jamesie said, shocked at his daughter's tone and the insolent look on her face. For a split second, he could see his mother's expression staring back. Sophia's hatred and disgust was clear. She was just like all the rest: everyone he knew despised him. Did they think that they could treat him like he was nothing? He was sick of it.

Clenching his fists, Jamesie stepped towards his daughter.

"Who do you think you're talking to?" Jamesie wouldn't accept his daughter's dismissive attitude. He knew that he had never possessed the same power over Sophia that he had over her mother, but it had only started to bother him recently. Sophia was growing up and he could tell in her eyes that she had not one ounce of respect for him.

"Have you been drinking?" Jamesie demanded, as he neared his daughter and smelt a strong odour of drink. Then he noticed the make-up that was smudged under her eyes, and that she was wearing a miniskirt. "What the fuck do you think you are playing at, going out of this house looking like that? You look like a cheap tart. You better not have been with that little fucking scroat Tommy again."

Jamesie felt rage surge through his veins. He knew how young boys' minds worked. Those dirty little bastards would be all over his daughter like a rash in her current state.

Ignoring her father's words, Sophia repeated herself. "I said, leave Mum alone. You can't use her as a punch bag."

Sophia sniffed back tears, although they were now of pure anger. Tonight had been horrendous, and she didn't know how much more she could take.

"Don't poke your nose in where it's not wanted." Then the realisation hit Jamesie like a brick. He had known all along really, his wife was too feeble to be going around telling tales. Of course it had been Sophia. She was over at her nan's every five minutes. "It was you, weren't it? You sneaky little bitch. How fucking stupid. You were the one telling your nosy cunt of a nan our business, weren't you?"

"Jamesie, just leave her: please," Kaitlin implored. "Sophia, do as you're told and go to your room; it's me that your dad's angry with: you don't need to get involved. Jamesie, you've got it wrong, it was me. I spoke to your mum and I'm sorry, but please don't take it out on Sophia. It was me."

Jamesie clenched his fists tighter. Staring hard at his daughter, as she glared back at him, he knew he was right. He was having none of his wife's nonsense. Of course it was Sophia who had been running her mouth off, telling that old bint tales. He felt stupid for not realising it earlier. It had obviously been Sophia: the girl was always at her nan's house. And now he knew why. The pair of them must spend their time badmouthing and disrespecting him.

"You've been running your mouth off to your nan, telling her stories about me, haven't you? You ungrateful little bitch, after all I've done for you. Where's your respect for me? I'm your father," Jamesie snarled.

Before Sophia knew what was happening, Jamesie had launched himself at her, knocking over the bookshelf that she was standing beside. They both crashed down, his body pinning hers on the floor amongst a heap of books. He grabbed her throat, squeezing it. She tried to scream but could only make a choking noise.

"Get off her," Kaitlin cried, trying to push him off Sophia. Jamesie was completely out of control, but Kaitlin's maternal instinct was far stronger than her fear of her husband.

Jamesie was too strong for her though, and as he held Sophia's throat as she spluttered in panic, trying to breathe, he used his other hand to hit his wife.

The force of the blow sent Kaitlin flying across the room, and her body landed in a heap. Unbalanced by his drinking, Jamesie went flying across the floor too.

Sophia's instincts were to run, but she couldn't. Holding her throbbing neck, she was petrified. She stared at her father, who lay sprawled out on the floor as he panted loudly like a wild animal. Staring ahead of him as if in a trance, the shock on his face at what he'd done was clear. She followed his gaze to Kaitlin's seemingly lifeless body. Her mother lay motionless and Sophia could see the trickle of blood running from her head, down one cheek.

"What have you done, Dad? What have you done?" Sophia's screams filled the room.

Chapter Eleven

"Which room do you think is hers?" Jonathan whispered, as they crouched down behind the low brick wall that framed the tiny front garden.

It was almost two am and, apart from a glow of light coming from the hallway, the house stood in darkness. Squatting down near to his brother, Tommy was shaking and thought he might throw up; he deeply regretted the second helping of dinner that he had gorged on earlier this evening.

"I don't know about this, Jonathan. Shit... what if her dad comes out and sees us?" Tommy was starting to sweat. His desire to make sure that Sophia was okay was gone, replaced by fear.

It had been two days since the party, and he hadn't seen or spoke to her in that time. He had gone upstairs to check on her after everyone had finally left only to find an empty bed and the bucket next to it full of vomit. He hoped that she wasn't avoiding him now because she was embarrassed about getting so ill. Tommy was glad that Sophia had gone when she had, though; he would have hated the thought of his mum seeing her in such a state. Things were already bad enough as it was. His mum had come home as he had gone upstairs, and on finding her house trashed had started bellowing at Tommy and Jonathan like she was the anti-Christ. Tommy had never seen her so angry. And once she saw that her mother's urn had been knocked over, the tears started. Their dad, who rarely lost his cool with them, had shouted at them as she sobbed. Tommy had tried to reassure his mum that he had managed to pick up almost all of the ash and put it back, but Jonathan had brazenly dropped him in it by telling her that he had vacuumed up much of it. After hearing that and seeing the large grey patch of ash that was engrained in the carpet Bernie had grounded Tommy and Jonathan indefinitely. They had spent the following three hours on their hands and knees scrubbing away sick and picking up broken pieces of glass. And Bernie had vowed to never so much as let them have a friend over again, let alone a party. Since then, the only chance Tommy had to see Sophia was at school, but she hadn't been there. More worryingly, no-one had heard from her.

Tommy knew that something wasn't right. He racked his brains to think of what he could have done to upset Sophia, and came up with nothing. Worried out of his mind that she was still sick from the alcohol that she had drunk, or worse still that she had got in serious trouble with her dad when she got home Tommy just had to see that she was okay.

Now, he and Jonathan were standing outside Sophia's house in the moonlight. Tommy wasn't convinced they were doing the right thing but Jonathan had insisted that if Tommy was going to see her, he would come too. Just to make sure that she was okay.

Tommy was glad that his brother had come; he knew if he wasn't there he would have gone home, though why Jonathan had thought it necessary for them to dress up as though they were something from the Special Forces branch he couldn't fathom. Tommy's balaclava not only made his skin itch, but the musty odour that it gave off was not helping the feeling of nausea that was rapidly sweeping over him as his nerves set in.

Jonathan rolled his eyes up at his brother, as he watched him fiddle with his hands nervously. Jonathan knew Tommy better than anyone, and he could tell that he was losing his bottle: he should have guessed that Tommy would try and chicken out now that they were here. Jonathan was hoping that Sophia was avoiding his brother because she was so ashamed and embarrassed about having sex with him at the party. The only reason that he had suggested coming along was just in case the stupid bitch decided to tell Tommy what had happened. He thought that when Sophia saw him here pretending to be all concerned about her it would just add insult to injury, which Jonathan couldn't resist.

"I don't know about this, Jonathan, what if we break the glass? Her dad will catch us, and he might really hurt us." Tommy's eyes were wide with panic. He couldn't see how this was going to have a good outcome: he shouldn't have listened to Jonathan earlier. This was a stupid idea. Sophia would probably be back at school tomorrow.

"What if, what if? Will you just chill out, Tommy? Nothing's going to happen to us, you Muppet. Trust me!" Jonathan looked up to the window and tried to suss out which bedroom belonged to Sophia. Jonathan guessed that the one directly above them was the master bedroom, as it was the largest, so that probably belonged to her parents. "I bet Sophia's is around the back. Come on."

Jonathan kept his body low as he led the way around the path to a large wooden side gate. "Stay close behind me, Tommy."

Jonathan knew that Tommy would have skulked off home if he could have, but Jonathon wouldn't give him that option. They were here now, and the sooner that Tommy saw that Sophia was okay the better. Then they could go home, and hopefully Tommy would stop harping on about her the whole time.

Carefully pushing opening the gate, the boys traipsed through the overgrown grass as they crept around to the back of the house.

"Sophia's dad's not exactly Alan Titchmarsh," Jonathan observed, as he searched around by the back door for any small stones. "Guess it wouldn't be wise of him to 'drink and mow' though eh? Didn't you say that he's an old pisshead?"

Jonathan found several stones that were a suitable size to throw. He bent down, scooped them up and indicated to Tommy that he should take them. Tommy did, then stood there looking at his hand. He didn't know for sure it was Sophia's room that they were standing below, let alone whether the stones would wake her up without breaking the glass.

"Go on then, Romeo. You're her boyfriend, aren't you? You're the one that wants to make sure that she's okay. The last thing that Sophia would want to see when she opens her window is my ugly mug staring back up at her," Jonathan said.

Tommy reluctantly threw a stone at the window. There was a small tap and then it bounced straight back off it. The boys crouched down in the long dewy grass, shivering from the cold. Tommy looked up to see if they had been heard.

There was no response.

"You got to throw it with a bit more force, Tommy: like this." Standing up, Jonathan lobbed the stone with more power than his brother had. This time the noise of it hitting the window was much louder. Jonathan ducked down into the grass where his brother was crouching down. "She's got to have heard that, surely?"

They both stared up at the window.

After throwing a few more stones, the boys realised that their plan wasn't going to work. Tommy started to feel frustrated. "What are we going to do, Jonathan? She's either in there asleep and can't hear us, or she isn't in there at all... and either way, we're back to square one because I still don't know if she's okay or not."

Tommy looked up at the house, confused, wondering if they had been throwing the stones at an empty bathroom. But the curtains indicated that it was a bedroom window.

"We may as well just go home. This was a stupid idea anyway," Tommy declared, feeling completely useless. He couldn't understand why no-one had come to the window. Unless, he thought, something really bad had happened to her.

"Well, if you really want to see if she's okay, there is one more thing that we could do." Jonathan lifted up his balaclava and reached into his backpack, pulling out their dad's torch that he had taken from the shed earlier when no-one was looking. He switched on the button and shone the light under his chin as he said menacingly: "Let's break in."

Tommy watched the creepy shadow that the beamed out from the torch, as it lit up the big grin on Jonathan's face before he realised that his brother was actually being serious. Seeing Jonathan pull out a screwdriver, Tommy gulped.

"I knew this would come in handy," Jonathan said smugly. As he noted the look of alarm on his brother's face he added: "Don't worry, Tommy. If anyone was awake in there, they would have heard the noise at the window by now; they didn't, did they? They're probably all sparko. We can sneak in, make sure Sleeping Beauty is okay and be back out of there within ten minutes. You do want to see she's alright, don't you?"

Standing underneath Sophia's window would have been enough to freak her out once she saw that he was there too, but the idea of her waking up to find him at the end of her bed excited Jonathan even more. The stuck-up little cow would be distraught.

Tommy wasn't sure about this new plan. Chucking stones at a window was one thing, but breaking into someone's house in the middle of the night: well, that was a whole other.

Before Tommy had a chance to protest, Jonathan had made his way to the back door and stuck the screwdriver in the gap between the door's edge and the PVC frame. Levering it back and forth as he tried to force the door open, he placed all his body weight behind the screwdriver as he twisted the metal tool hard. Tommy watched Jonathan struggle, praying that he wouldn't be able to force the door open. He had a bad feeling about this and the sooner they got out of here the better. But to Tommy's disappointment, after a few more twists of the screwdriver, the door popped open.

"Fucking hell, Tommy, I think I've found my true calling," Jonathan smirked, pleased as punch with himself for getting the door open so quickly. "Come on."

From what Tommy had heard about Sophia's dad, Mr O'Hagan, he was a nasty bloke and Tommy was so terrified at the thought of him catching them in his house that he couldn't even talk. His heart was beating loudly inside his chest, thumping so hard that he was convinced that even though Jonathan was a few steps ahead of him he could hear every beat.

The boys stepped inside the house then tiptoed through the dark lounge. Jonathan shone the torch around the room, checking the floor was clear. The beams of light cast shadows around the room as it reflecting off surfaces and lit the way. The place was a mess. The stagnant smell of stale cigarette butts sitting in an overflowing ashtray on the coffee table hung in the air, and Jonathan stepped over a pile of empty beer cans that had been crumpled up and left scattered about on the floor. He turned his nose up in disgust, surprised that Sophia lived in a house like this.

No wonder she had told Tommy that he wasn't allowed to come here.

"Be careful," Jonathan whispered, as he shone the torch onto the floor. The light revealed a bookcase turned on its side, and books strewn everywhere.

"Looks like Sophia wasn't exaggerating when she told you her old man had a temper. Do you reckon that this was him kicking off?"

Jonathan didn't wait for an answer, as he peered into the narrow kitchen. Spotting a large knife block just inside the doorway, he grabbed a bread knife and concealed it up his sleeve, hiding it from Tommy as he knew that he would freak out if he saw it. From what Tommy had said about Mr O'Hagan and going on the state of the place, Jonathan thought it was wise to have a Plan B in case they did run into the old nutcase. Jonathan looked into the lounge to see Tommy standing in there, unmoving.

"Come on, we're here now, Tommy, stop being such a pussy," Jonathan whispered. They had come this far, Jonathan didn't want to go home without finding Sophia.

"But Jonathan..."

Jonathan shone the torch up to his face and placed his index finger up to his lips, signalling to Tommy to be quiet.

"Your bloody whining is what will get us caught, Tommy, now come on."

Wishing that he had the guts to stand up to his brother, Tommy followed him up the stairs.

***

Having spent the last few hours tossing and turning, her mind reliving the past days' events, Nessa decided that she may as well get up and make herself a cup of milky tea, maybe then she would be able to get herself the forty winks that she needed.

Tucking the duvet around a snoring Rascal, Nessa smiled down at him. He was a little twicher tonight. Daft mutt, she thought, as she watched his tiny legs moving rapidly in circular motions; she imagined that was mimicking running around in some field chasing rabbits. Quietly getting up, Nessa left him to his dream.

Treading quietly on the stairs, Nessa went into the kitchen. She put the kettle on and got a mug from the cupboard before tiptoeing over to take a peek into the lounge.

"Are you alright, sweetie?" Nessa whispered, surprised to see she wasn't the only one awake. Sophia was sitting on the floor, her back against the sofa that her mother was lying on. Nessa saw that Kaitlin had her eyes open, and Sophia was stroking her mum's hair.

"Kaitlin lovey, how are you feeling?" Nessa beamed, relieved that her daughter-in-law looked a bit better than when she had first arrived here.

Since she had got here all Kaitlin had wanted to do was sleep. The poor woman was more hurt emotionally about what Jamesie had done to her than she was physically. Heartbroken, she was.

It had been two days since Sophia had turned up on her doorstep propping up her very battered and dazed-looking mother. Nessa had been amazed when she had seen them both standing there. The pair of them had looked like they were in a right old state. Sophia had been crying hysterically; Kaitlin had been silent.

"Oh, sweet Jesus, girls... what in the name of God has happened to you both?" Nessa had asked, horrified at the sight of them. Sophia looked battered and bruised and Kaitlin was covered in blood, Nessa felt her stomach turn at what her son had done.

"I swear to God, Nan, I'm going to kill my dad for this. Look what he's done," Sophia wept, her voice trembling as she fought to hold up her mother.

"I'm going to kill him," Sophia said loudly, over and over again. She was convinced that her father had almost murdered her mother and had started to go into shock at the trauma. Glancing over the road, she was terrified that her dad would come over and continue with what he had started.

"Everything okay Nessa dearie?" Mary Simpson leaned out of the neighbouring window to see what all the commotion was about. She was one of the many who knew that Jamesie O'Hagan was a wife beater: once he started with his ranting, the whole street could hear. Mary would be telling the ladies at the Gala Bingo hall about this.

Nessa ignored her neighbour's question, Mary's ears were probably honing in on the conversation like bloody satellite dishes, dismissing Mary with a mere shake of her hand. Her granddaughter was deeply distressed and Nessa needed to get her safely inside: she didn't have the time or the energy for anything else.

"Oh well pardon me for caring," Mary said as she continued to rudely gawp at the two women who were clearly anything but alright. Taking in the cuts on the woman's face, Mary knew that her friends would all have a field day with this information; they loved a bit of drama.

"Albert," Nessa shouted as she rolled her eyes at her neighbour's blatant rudeness as she continued to lean out of the window and have a good old gawp, "come and help me get Kaitlin in, will you? Perhaps you'd like to borrow my camera, Mary? Then maybe you could take a bloody photo? Or better still perhaps you would like me to get some crayons out and draw you a fecking picture."

Nessa shot down her neighbour with a glare before Mary finally took the hint, and looking indignant scarpered back inside her own house slamming the window behind her.

Nessa was glad that Albert, who had stayed later tonight so they could watch a film, had been on hand to help. He had rushed to the doorway on hearing the panic in Nessa's voice, gasping as he saw Sophia holding her barely conscious mother upright. He wrapped his arms around Kaitlin's waist to help take some of the pressure off a now distraught Sophia. Carefully he assisted them both to the sofa, where Kaitlin had collapsed.

When Sophia had managed to stop crying, she begged her nan not to call an ambulance; the only thing that her mum had been able to say as they had made it across the street had been not to let Nessa call the authorities. It was the only thing that she had asked, and she had made Sophia promise her on her life that she wouldn't, knowing that it would only make things worse for them in the long run.

If it hadn't been for Albert being there to give Kaitlin a once-over and make sure that she wasn't badly injured, Nessa would have been left with no choice but to go against the girl's wishes. Albert had seen many an injury in his career as a doctor at Homerton Hospital, and he assured Nessa that Kaitlin's injuries looked worse than they actually were. She had been beaten black and blue, and was by no means a pretty sight, but this time she had been extremely lucky and nothing had been broken.

"I think she'll be okay after some rest. She's taken a thorough beating, that's for sure. She's in shock and exhausted. So make sure that you keep an eye on her at all times," Albert warned, "if she deteriorates in any way, then you must call an ambulance. Don't take any chances in case she has concussion."

The past two days had felt like the longest ever to Nessa, as Kaitlin fell in and out of sleep without eating any food. The only thing she would do was sip water. Sophia hadn't left her mother's side.

Nessa had been worried sick as she prayed to God that Kaitlin would be alright. She was convinced that they should have taken her into A&E, and constantly tried to shake off the horrible thoughts of severe concussion or even worse bleeding on the brain. Who knew what damage that reckless son of hers had caused? It was only Sophia being so adamant that Nessa mustn't call anyone and of course Albert's reassurance that had caused her to finally let it go. She couldn't describe how relieved she felt now that Kaitlin had woken up.

"You must be famished, my lovey, shall I warm up some soup or make a nice sandwich?" Nessa asked Kaitlin.

Slowly shaking her head, Kaitlin tried to sit up. A pain spread through her chest, causing her to lie back down. She felt like she had done ten rounds with Lennox Lewis.

"Stay as you are, Mum, you need to rest," Sophia ordered as she looked at her worriedly. "It's alright, Nan, she only wants some water at the moment; she only woke up about half an hour ago. Maybe we can do her something to eat a bit later on."

"Well, I'll make us a hot drink then, Soph. I could do with something a bit stronger than a cup of PG now, but that's all I have in so it'll have to do."

As Nessa busied herself in the kitchen, Kaitlin tried to prop herself up against the arm of the sofa wincing as she moved. Thinking of her husband and what he had done to her, she clenched her fists. This was the worst beating he had given her. She knew that over time his temper had been getting worse. Up until now she had made excuses for him: he was depressed, he had lost his job, they had no money and too much debt... even when he caused an argument about nothing, she had blamed herself. Maybe she had wound him up; maybe she really was a terrible wife, she would think. She must be, because she couldn't make him happy. But after what he had done to her in front of Sophia, there was no going back: if she did then the next time she got away from him would be by being carried out of that house in a body bag. There would be no more excuses. Jamesie was a violent bully, and Kaitlin had walked around with blinkers on for too long in the hope that his behaviour would change.

"You alright, Mum?" Sophia asked. "Do you need painkillers?"

"No, darling; I'll be fine." Kaitlin looked at her daughter, and the sadness in her heart deepened. She recognised the look of hurt and confusion behind Sophia's pretty green eyes that were now shadowed by ugly dark purple bruises. Her face looked sore and swollen. Jamesie had hurt her Sophia, and Kaitlin had never felt angrier.

"I was dreaming about when I had you, Sophia," Kaitlin said quietly, as she closed her eyes, willing her dream to return. "You were a tiny baby. Beautiful, you were. I lay in my bed at the hospital, and the midwife wrapped you in a blanket and placed you in my arms. You were the most delicate, precious little thing I had ever seen: let alone held. I couldn't believe that you were mine. I promised you that I would love and protect you for the rest of my days... Oh God, Sophia: I am so, so sorry!"

A single tear slipped out from the corner of Kaitlin's eye.

"Don't be silly, Mum," Sophia said, feeling a lump form in the back of her throat and her own tears escaping as she spoke. "You have nothing to be sorry for; this isn't your fault."

"Where is he?" Unable to speak his name, Kaitlin wondered if Jamesie had bothered to check that he hadn't killed her.

"I think he's still over at the house, Mum," Sophia said. She hadn't seen him leave, and she had been watching out of the window constantly since they had arrived. She wanted to know what he would do next, reckoning that her dad had probably been expecting a visit from the police, and half-expecting him to do a runner as he was such a coward. But as far as she could tell, he hadn't left the house. He normally went to the pub around five pm, but she hadn't seen him leave, and the lights had been on each evening and switched off around midnight. She hoped that he was festering inside, driving himself mad as he waited for a visit from the Old Bill. He must have been going out of his mind not knowing what was going to happen. Sophia had wanted to call the police, maybe getting him locked up would be the wake-up call he needed. But she would never go against her mother's wishes. Even after all he had done, she knew her mum was too scared to involve anyone, especially the authorities. Sophia had even had to snatch the phone from her nan's hand at one point, begging her not to call them. Nessa had been shocked at how forceful the girl had been, and had agreed that she would leave it for now, but only on the condition that once Kaitlin was feeling a bit stronger, they report Jamesie.

Sophia had never seen Nessa so angry. She had told Sophia that Jamesie might not have factored in her life for a long time anyway, but after what he had done this time he was dead to her. Nessa wondered if he realised that he could have killed his wife. Her intuition told her that it wasn't going to be just the physical scars that would need healing. And as for him touching Sophia: that was the final nail in his coffin. He was lower than low, as far as his mother was concerned; the scum of the earth. She no longer had a son.

"Here we go, my honeys." Nessa smiled as she returned, carrying a tray which held three mugs of tea and a plate of biscuits. "As my dear old mum used to say, pour yourself a cup of tea and count your blessings. She used to swear that there was not a situation in the world that a good cuppa couldn't sort out. We'll have you back to yourself again in no time, sweetheart."

Nessa spoke with more conviction than she really felt, however. She also knew she was kidding no-one. Jamesie had crossed the line by a mile this time. There would be no coming back from this one.

Chapter Twelve

"Wait," Tommy whispered, as he grabbed the back of Jonathan's jumper to stop him going any further along the landing. "I think I just heard something."

Tommy was terrified. He could have sworn he had heard a creaking noise coming from a room at the other end of the landing.

Jonathan stood still and listened. The only noise that he could hear was the sound of his brother's fast and heavy breaths, which were due to Tommy working himself up into a state.

"I can't hear anything; you must be imagining things, Tommy. Come on."

Tommy reluctantly obeyed Jonathan's orders again. He followed closely behind his brother as they made their way towards the back bedroom. Reaching the rear bedroom, Jonathan gently pressed down the handle and slowly pushed the door ajar. Shining the torch in, Jonathan reflected the light off the pink walls and saw the posters of Sophia's favourite band, The Backstreet Boys, plastered all over the walls.

Tommy peered in and nodded: it was definitely Sophia's room. Her purple Reebok rucksack was open on the floor. When Jonathan shone the torch over to the neatly made bed, Tommy felt disappointed when he saw that it was empty.

The bedroom door hit the wall and a man holding a baseball bat came into the room.

"What the fuck are you doing in my house?" he shouted as he lurched forward, swinging the bat about wildly. Straight away Tommy knew that this was Mr O'Hagan. He was gritting his teeth in anger as he spat his words out, his face red with rage as he shouted. He looked like a nutcase standing there wearing only his y-fronts and with a crazed look in his eyes, and Jonathan had a feeling that he could cause them some real damage with the bat if they didn't get out of there fast.

Tommy stood frozen to the spot with fear.

Mr O'Hagan swung the bat again, as he looked at the intruders. Jonathan tried to work out what to do. He wished that they hadn't taken off their balaclavas now. Mr O'Hagan knew what they looked like.

"Run," Jonathan shouted, failing to come up with a better idea. Adrenaline surged through his veins as he grabbed hold of Tommy's arm and tugged him out of his trance. "Fucking run, Tommy!"

Tommy didn't have time to think. Hearing his brother's words, he charged towards the door in a panic.

Seeing one of the boys running towards him, Mr O'Hagan brought the bat crashing down, just missing Tommy's head as it connected with the boy's shoulder and made a loud crack. The blow sent Tommy off balance. This caused him to charge straight into Mr O'Hagan as he made for the stairwell, sending the man flying into the wall behind him before Tommy made his escape down the stairs. Dropping the bat, Jamesie recovered and grabbed at Jonathan as he tried to get past him too. Jamesie gripped Jonathan by a clump of his hair. "Tommy? You better not be one of the fucking scroats that's been knocking about with my daughter." Jamesie was fuming now. If this Tommy thought that he could break in here in the middle of the night then Jamesie was going to enjoy teaching the little fucker a lesson.

He clenched his fist, ready to punch the boy in the face. "You boys must be fucking stupid coming in here."

The blow caught him off guard. He felt the hard sharp twist as the blade punctured his abdomen, sending a scorching pain all the way through him. Falling to the floor, Jamesie held his stomach as he writhed in agony. He clutched the handle of the knife that had stabbed him. The blade was deep inside him. Unable to gather his strength, he couldn't pull it out and even in his shocked state he didn't think that it would have been wise to do so even if he could have.

Jonathan stared at Sophia's dad, mesmerised by how powerless he looked as he squirmed about. He was at Jonathan's mercy, a lamb to the slaughter.

Jamesie spat out a mouthful of blood and held his hand up as if to plead with Jonathan. Jonathan smiled down at him: it was a sickly sweet grin that told the man he was enjoying watching his gruesome demise.

Jonathan stared at Mr O'Hagan for a few more seconds, fascinated as he listened to the strange gurgling noises that were coming from the man's throat before he reluctantly walked away. He and Tommy needed to get out of there as quickly as possible.

Reaching the back door, Jonathan could see no sign of Tommy and guessed that he had kept running in fear. Quickly, Jonathan contemplated what to do next. Mr O'Hagan had seen Jonathan's face and heard him shout Tommy's name. It wouldn't take long for the police to work out who had done the stabbing.

There was a shed in the O'Hagans' back garden. Jonathan expected it to be locked, but it wasn't: he pulled open the door and rummaged around inside, hoping to find something flammable. His luck was in; behind some deckchairs and a rusty old barbeque he spotted a Gerry can that was half-full of petrol.

Going into the lounge, Jonathan knew that he had to be quick. He checked that Mr O'Hagan hadn't managed to get down the stairs. Satisfied that the injured man was still upstairs, hopefully about to croak it, Jonathan poured the petrol generously all over the floor and sofa, dowsing them thoroughly in the liquid before running back to the safety of the back door. Lobbing the can in the room, he hoped that the evidence that he had used it would be destroyed along with the rest of the house.

Lighting a match Jonathan held it up for a second as it crackled, enjoying the last few seconds of calm. The smell of petrol filled his nose. Picturing Mr O'Hagan lying upstairs bleeding to death, Jonathan had never felt more powerful as he tossed the match into the room and watched as an inferno began to rage. The flames flickered up around him, licking the walls as the fury of the fire grew. His face warmed by the burst of heat that filled the room, Jonathan knew he had to get out, but stared mesmerised at the chaos and destruction. Wishing that he could stay to watch the damage as the house burned down around him, and disappointed that he wouldn't be able to hear the piercing screams of agony as the fire reached Mr O'Hagan, Jonathan turned and ran. He needed to get home quickly, before anyone saw him.

Chapter Thirteen

Sophia wriggled awkwardly on the rickety chair. She had thought her nan's sofa was lumpy until she had been forced to sleep in this old thing. After hours of trying her hardest to drift off, Sophia decided she was fighting a losing battle. She regretted not taking up her nan's earlier offer of swapping over the care duties and taking her bed for a few hours while her nan kept an eye on Sophia's mum. But Sophia had seen how tired her nan looked and after they had all had their tea had insisted that she would be okay on the chair; she would wait until the morning, when her nan was up, then have a lie-down in the bed. It had seemed like a good idea at the time, but she felt exhausted now.

Sophia looked over at her mum who was now sleeping peacefully, having finally given in to her and her nan's fussing; she had accepted a big mug of hot soup and some painkillers before she had fallen back to sleep.

Looking at the clock, Sophia thought how time was dragging by. She was bored out of her mind just sitting there staring at the four walls. She couldn't turn the TV on as she didn't want the noise of it to wake her mum and there weren't any books or magazines lying about that she could read. Feeling restless, she got up and went to sit at the window. She had been peering up and down the street constantly since they had arrived, her house being the main focus as she had hoped to catch a glimpse of her father. She needed to see if he was bothered by what he had done.

Looking out into the darkness once more, Sophia did a double-take. She was so tired that at first she thought her eyes must have been playing tricks on her.

Pressing her face against the glass so that she could get a better view she stared at her house, watching in horror as she realised that there really were tall flames inside the kitchen.

"Oh my God," she said to herself as she jumped down from the sill and made her way to the front porch. There was no time to waste; running out of the front door and across the road, Sophia knew that despite her dad's actions if he was trapped inside that inferno she wouldn't be able to live with herself unless she at least tried to help him get out.

Chapter Fourteen

"Are you sure that you're alright, Tommy?" Bernie wrapped her dressing gown tightly around her as she shouted through the bathroom door, concerned at the heaving sounds that her son was making. The poor boy had been in the bathroom for the past fifteen minutes, sounding awful. Pressing her ear against the door, Bernie was relieved to hear that his retching had stopped.

"I'm fine, Mum, honestly, go back to bed," Tommy called. Still bent over the toilet but no longer being sick, he wiped his mouth with the back of his hand.

"Okay, love; if you need anything, just let me know. I've left you a glass of water out here on the dresser." Bernie hoped that there wasn't a sickness bug going around; the last thing she needed at the moment was a houseful of people throwing up. She was still getting over having her carpet ruined. Deciding to check on Jonathan, Bernie peered around the bedroom door to find him sitting up in his bed completely wide awake.

"You're not feeling sick as well, are you?" Bernie asked, praying that she hadn't given everyone a dose of food poising. She would be mortified if it had been her lovely shepherd's pie that had made Tommy ill.

"No, Mum, I'm fine. I was fast asleep until I heard him puking up," Jonathan lied and then added: "Tommy probably ate too much that's all. His eyes are bigger than his belly; you know what he's like."

Hoping that her son was right, and that once Tommy had got it all out of his system and managed to get some sleep he would feel better, Bernie went back to her own bedroom to join her sleeping husband. Stanley was usually too busy snoring to notice anything that happened once he had gone to bed.

***

When Tommy came back into the boys' room a few minutes later with a face paler than a ghost's, Jonathan couldn't keep his temper.

"Tommy, you need to seriously get a grip. What are you trying to do, drop us both in the shit? You're supposed to be playing it cool, not drawing attention to us."

"I'm sorry, Jonathan," Tommy apologised, feeling embarrassed as he plonked himself down onto his bed and took another sip of water before laying back down against his pillow.

"My stomach always plays up when I'm worried, and my shoulder's killing me too."

Tommy added hoping that Jonathan would offer some sympathy for his ordeal tonight. His guts had been churning all evening but he did feel a bit better now that he had been sick. He knew that Jonathan thought he was acting like a wuss but he couldn't help it, he wasn't cut out for this kind of thing and his nerves had got the better of him.

"Yeah, you got a right whack. Bet you have a massive bruise tomorrow." Jonathan said sounding almost impressed with how hard his brother had been hit.

Earlier, when Jonathan had said to run, Tommy hadn't been able to stop once he had got started. He felt like he had a rocket launched up his backside, and running all the way home took just minutes as he was spurred on by the thought of being chased by a bat-wielding mad man. He had run so fast that he had thought his lungs would explode inside his chest. When Jonathan had finally appeared and tapped him on the shoulder, Tommy had been doubled over with his back against their back gate. He could barely get his breath to ask what had happened. Jonathan who, unlike him, hadn't even broken a sweat coolly informed Tommy that he had managed to outrun Sophia's dad, and that the bloke didn't have a clue who they were. Jonathan being so matter-of-fact about it all unnerved Tommy even more. Now, staring up at the ceiling as he continued to worry, Tommy knew that he wouldn't be able to sleep tonight.

"I'm just worried that Mr O'Hagan might have recognised us, Jonathan. You shouted my name out, remember? He knows who I am. What if he comes here? The police will know it was us that broke in." Tommy felt like crying, but he held it back; Jonathan really would think that he was pathetic. Tonight had been a disaster and he was none the wiser as to where Sophia was or if she was okay.

"Don't you worry about Mr O'Hagan, Tommy. He won't be saying a word to anyone," Jonathan assured Tommy.

"You don't know that, though," Tommy said in frustration: Jonathan didn't seem to be affected by anything.

"Look, just do as I say and you'll be fine. No-one knows jack shit, so keep your mouth shut because if it ever gets out that we broke into that house we will be in serious trouble. And I mean serious trouble: as in prison-serious," Jonathan warned, knowing that Tommy would be shitting himself at just the mention of prison. There was no way he would breathe a word of what happened to anyone.

"I won't say anything, I swear," Tommy said quietly.

"Good. Now try and get some sleep, yeah?" Jonathan yawned, as he reached over and switched off his bedside lamp. "Forget all about old O'Hagan, he's probably conked out himself by now."

Jonathan lay in the dark and smiled. As long as Tommy kept his mouth shut, they would be okay.

Mr O'Hagan wouldn't be saying a word to anyone.

Chapter Fifteen

Smoke billowed out of the small air vent at the top of the window. Sophia bashed her fists against the front door while she screamed at the top of her voice. No one came to help her. It was gone three am; no doubt the neighbours were all tucked up peacefully in their beds blissfully unaware of the inferno as it continued to grow. She wished she had woken her mum and nan up now before she had rushed out in such a panic, but there had been no time.

There was no sign of her dad, so he must still be in the house. Remembering the key that was in the jeans she was wearing, Sophia opened the door and forced her way inside. A blanket of black smoke escaped past her. Adrenaline was pumping wildly through her veins as the wall of immense heat hit her, but she was determined not to let it deter her as she continued to run through the hallway.

"Dad," she screamed, as looked out into the lounge that was now just a giant ball of flames roaring out towards her, spreading out into the kitchen and the hall. Trying to keep away from the heat, Sophia ran up the stairs.

"Dad," she shouted, growing more concerned with every step she took. The smoke was thick and she could barely see in front of her now. Coughing hard, she covered her mouth by tucking her chin inside her jumper.

Pushing her parents' bedroom door open, she struggled to see but after a few seconds realised that the room was empty. Holding the banister, she made her way back down the corridor through the dark smoke, feeling the heat rising from the floor beneath as she went. Reaching her bedroom, she screamed again. There was a body lying on the floor. It was her dad.

She bent down next to her father, thinking that maybe he had passed out from the smoke, but then she saw the blood surrounding him, which had seeped into the carpet, and the knife protruding from his stomach.

"Dad, what happened?" Sophia cried.

There had been many occasions on which she had wished death on her father, she could have murdered him for what he put her mother through on a daily basis, and this had been especially true over the last couple of days. But seeing him lying on the floor put everything into perspective. He didn't deserve to die like this: no-one did. Sophia had to try and help him.

Seeing his chest rise and fall, she sighed with relief. Then her father reached a hand out to her.

Jamesie knew that he didn't have much time; he could feel himself slipping away. He opened his mouth, desperate to tell Sophia who had done this to him and wondering if she already knew. But immense pain took over and he could only manage to let a hoarse moan escape his lips. He sprayed his daughter's face with splatters of blood as he died.

Wiping her face, Sophia saw how her dad clutched at his stomach and wanted to pull out the knife so she could take away his pain. Maybe if she did that, then she could stem the blood flow and he might be alright.

Trying to control her nausea, Sophia leaned over her father and tugged on the knife's handle as she struggled to pull it out of his stomach. She realised that she had done the wrong thing when she heard a sickening glugging sound as the blood bubbled up, filling the newly made space.

When she placed her hands over her father's wound the warm, sticky blood spread through her fingertips. Seeing the black smoke billowing up the stairs towards her, Sophia didn't know what to do.

She took deep breaths but the smoke was overpowering her; she was scared that she might pass out.

"Please," she cried quietly to herself. "Someone please help me."

She kneeled over her father, keeping the pressure on his stomach. She watched in horror as he took one long breath. Then his eyes went blank. The rasping noise that he made was one Sophia knew would stay in her memory forever.

Chapter Sixteen

Mary Simpson was in her element. She had her best bone-china cups out for the tea that she was serving with fancy biscuits and a Madeira cake on display on her coffee table. Had she known how today was going to unfold, she would have moved her cut-and-colour to the morning so that she looked her best: in case the paper wanted to take a photo of her.

"More tea?" Mary asked the young man sitting opposite her.

Mary had taken an instant shine to Terry James. He was nicer than the other reporters who had been hanging around outside in the street. A right bolshie lot they were, as they tried to ply information from the local residents about the past few days' events. They had all but bombarded her as she had tried to make her way to the shops. Mary had tried to push through the group who were standing at the end of her front path, blocking it. The rowdy reporters had been shouting at her and Mary had found them to be not only very rude but also quite intimidating. She could see why some of the other neighbours had nicknamed them all vultures.

Had they had not have been so aggressive, Mary would have otherwise been very happy to share her information: especially as she had heard one of the men mention that there would be a considerable sum of money paid out for any exclusive stories. After pondering on the reporter's words once she was back indoors, Mary had in the end decided to phone The *Hackney Gazette*. If she was going to sell her story, she would do it to the paper that she read and supported, and she couldn't have been more pleased when she had opened the door to this nice man.

Terry had more manners than the rest of the journalists she had seen that morning put together. He was a real dear. Not only was he dressed immaculately but he had started off by politely introducing himself and then had gone on to inform Mary that, going by the snippet of information that she had told him over the phone, he would very much like to run her interview on tomorrow's front page.

The front page, she couldn't believe it. Mary couldn't do enough to look after her guest after she had heard that: she started by forcing a biscuit and a slice of cake on him.

Terry hadn't expected Mrs Simpson to enjoy his company quite so much: because of this, she wasn't in much of a hurry to divulge the information that she had promised. He'd been at the woman's house for almost forty-five minutes and he still hadn't managed to get her to repeat to him what she had told him on the phone.

"So, back to the unfortunate events of two days ago, Mrs Simpson. You said on the phone that the murderer had confided in you? That Sophia O'Hagan told you that she was going to murder her father?" Speaking softly about the delicate subject, Terry tried to convey that he was sensitive that being the victim's neighbour, Mary Simpson may be grieving herself.

"Bloody scandalous, isn't it?" Mary took a bite out of her slab of cake, spitting out crumbs as she said: "Who would have thought that there would be a murder in this street? Nothing happens around here. And trust me, if it did, I'd know about it."

Terry nodded and smiled, trying not to let his eyes glaze over.

"I remember when I could leave my back door open and no-one would give a hoot. Can't do that anymore, can I? No, I'd end up being raped in my bed by some wild street gang if I did that now. The whole world's gone to pot."

Mary leaned forward, speaking in a hushed tone and staring into the reporter's eyes. "You can have this on the record, Terry. I heard that young girl say she was going to kill him just days before he was murdered. She said it out there on the door-step, bold as brass. Swore to her nan on the Good Lord's name that she was going to kill her father she did. I was up at my window, what with all the commotion they made, and I could not believe my ears at the venom in her voice."

Referring back to his notes on the incident that had taken place the day before, Terry was sure that this new information had yet to come to light in any of the other newspapers. He wondered if the police had been informed. He had heard from a friend who worked down at the local police station that they had found blood on the young suspect's clothing and that her fingerprints had been all over the weapon. His friend had also informed him that they had also managed to gather some information from other sources that the perpetrator seemed to have a solid motive for the crime. No one yet had mentioned the girl admitting to it, though.

"Have you told anyone else about this, Mrs Simpson?" Terry asked.

"Well, no, not really... I may have mentioned to a friend or two, but I haven't told any other reporters, if that's what you mean." Mary looked deep in thought before adding, "Do you think I should tell the police? Rita across the road told me that they were doing a door-to-door early this morning, gathering information, but I went over to my friend Edna's for a chat and a cuppa and must have missed them. Maybe I should give them a call. They should know, shouldn't they? Oh, the whole thing has shaken me right up. Just to think of what that girl did to her own father, her own flesh and blood. I mean don't get me wrong, that Jamesie was far from being a saint. The stories I could tell you about him... he was a nasty bugger. Sophia and her mum both looked like they had taken a battering, that's for sure. A few slaps here and there doesn't excuse stabbing someone though, does it? And how Nessa, that's her nan, will ever have the nerve to show her face down at the Gala Bingo hall after all this I really don't know."

Terry made notes on his pad as Mary continued to babble away. He couldn't believe his luck. She hadn't even reported her information to the police. If she had done, they would have advised her on no account to reveal it to the press.

Fifteen minutes later, once Terry had managed to get Mary's story transcribed, he held out his pen so that she could sign the consent sheet, certifying that everything she had discussed was accurate and that she was happy for it to be published. The *Hackney Gazette* would go flying off the shelves tomorrow with this story headlining and Terry was sure he would be in for a few brownie points with his editor. Shooting Mary a big smile as she handed back the document complete with her signature, Terry felt like kissing the woman.

"Do you know what, Mary, I think I will make room for another piece of that cake. Bloody scrumptious, it was. Just don't tell my wife, she's trying to get me to lose weight."

Chapter Seventeen

The rain lashed down, causing Nessa's knitted dress and long black coat to cling to her skin. She was drenched, but up until now had been completely oblivious to the pouring rain. The irony that 'the heavens had opened' on today of all days was not lost on her. She felt utterly numb after everything that had happened in the past week.

She held her breath, motionless as she watched her son's coffin as it was lowered into the muddy grave.

Glancing behind her, she saw Albert dutifully holding an umbrella up just above Kaitlin's head, shielding her from the rain as he huddled closely next to her beneath its cover. Albert had been a blessing to Nessa that week; she was so grateful to him for all he had done to help support her. She would have been lost without him keeping everything together like he had. Looking over to Kaitlin, Nessa saw that her daughter-in-law's eyes were vacant in her gaunt face. Kaitlin had been in this trance-like state ever since she had first been informed of her husband's murder and her daughter's arrest. Nessa wondered if Kaitlin was even aware that she was attending her husband's funeral.

"Earth to Earth, ashes to ashes..." Nessa heard the priest say as she turned back to the grave and shifted her concentration to the casket as it reached its final resting place deep down in the dark hole in the ground.

Jamesie hadn't been a popular man, and Nessa was glad that the service was being held privately. The only other people that would have attended other than herself, Kaitlin and Albert, if they had the chance, would have been the local busybodies and the press, and they would have only been there to add fuel to the gossip.

Nessa didn't have the time or the energy for any more questions. The press had hounded them like a pack of hungry wolves, greedy for any little titbit on offer regardless of whether it was true or false.

Since Jamesie's murder, Nessa's life had been turned completely upside down. She had tried her hardest to remain strong throughout all of it; God knows her daughter-in-law needed her more than ever right now, and having to be strong for someone certainly had helped her to stay focused. Poor Kaitlin was not coping. Jamesie's death had been such a shock for all of them, but it had knocked the wind out of Kaitlin more than anyone. The woman was already hooked on pills, and Nessa wasn't convinced that they weren't doing her more harm than good. Kaitlin was popping them like there was no tomorrow and still she seemed to be unable to function coherently. Nessa was worried about the woman but she was willing to take one step at a time, they could deal with that issue later.

Nessa knew that before all that they had worse to come. Having buried her husband she knew from experience that the funeral was purely a milestone in the grieving process, and once they managed to get through today, they would have to then face tomorrow and the next day, and the day after that. Those were going to be the hardest days. They were the days when the reality of the situation would sink in. Christ only knew how they were going to get through it, Nessa thought sadly as she looked down at the wooden coffin.

"Shall I take Kaitlin back to the car?" Albert asked, as he placed his hand gently on Nessa's shoulder when the service had finished.

Her eyes transfixed on the raindrops bouncing off the coffin's lid, Nessa answered: "Yes, if you don't mind, Albert. I'd just like a few more minutes."

Albert nodded understandingly, before he carefully guided an unresponsive Kaitlin back to the shelter of the awaiting funeral car.

As the rain continued to pour, and puddles started to form on the ground around the gravestones, the priest made his way over to where Nessa stood.

"I just want to say how sorry I am for your loss, Mrs O'Hagan. I'm sure that today has been very difficult for both you and your family," the priest said sadly as he touched her arm compassionately. He was acutely aware that a funeral was never an easy time, especially for grieving loved ones. But the funeral of someone who had been murdered, although thankfully rare, was even more difficult for people to cope with. "I hope that the strength that you possess deep within you will help you through your darker days."

Nessa started to laugh then, all of the emotions that she had been suppressing suddenly surfacing as she let a loud cackle emanate from her mouth: she was aware that it probably made her sound almost deranged, but she didn't care.

"Darker days? Oh, don't you worry about me, Father. I'm only here because I wanted to make sure that the bastard was properly dead and buried."

The shocked priest replaced his look of concern with one of disbelief.

"My son was evil right down to his bones. Today may be Jamesie's funeral, Father, but my son has been dead to me for many years. He was a woman-beater, the shameful coward. My mother used to say that God pays back his debts without money, and Jamesie got exactly what was owed to him: I hope he rots in hell."

Giving the grave one last look, she satisfied herself that Jamesie was where he belonged: six feet under. Nessa then turned on her heel and made her way to the car, leaving the priest standing alone and speechless.

Chapter Eighteen

"Undress and put your belongings in here. Officer Johnson will log down what's there and you'll get it all back when you leave," the female prison officer said in an bored tone as she passed Dolly a plastic grey box to put her possessions in, all the while looking Dolly up and down like she was something hot and steamy that she had stepped in.

Flashing the officer a bold grin, Dolly tugged down her miniskirt and thong, letting them drop to the floor, before lifting her tight black lace top over her head to reveal pert breasts. "Getting a good look, are you?" Dolly asked sarcastically, as she stood there confidently in all her naked glory, wearing nothing but her sweetest smile and her customary pair of thigh-high black leather boots. Dolly stared at Officer Johnson challengingly; nothing had changed since Dolly's last visit here, the woman was still a prize bitch. Finally the officer blushed and looked away, leaving Dolly feeling triumphant: no one intimidated her.

At twenty-three, Dolly had the tight little body that this frumpy old officer could only dream about. Look all you like, love, she thought to herself smugly as she slipped out of her boots and into a pair of grey cotton knickers that reminded her of something her grandma would wear. She pulled on the familiar prison attire of navy-blue jogging bottoms and a drab grey T-shirt; the outfit swamped her body but she instantly felt warm and cosy. Glad to be out of the uncomfortable six-inch heels she spread her bare feet out on the floor, the coldness from the tiles soothing.

"Right then, Dalton, I'm going to take you to your cell, where you'll wait until you're called by your personal officer. Follow me."

Following the plump officer through the wing, Dolly felt like she had come home. The officer jangled her keys, unlocking each gate as she went. Walking past one cell, the smell of excrement and bleach hit Dolly. Glancing in, she saw a team of cleaning specialists in protective clothing. Judging by the smell, and the streaks which had been smeared up the walls, one of the inmates had carried out a dirty protest. Scrunching her nose up in disgust, she tried not to heave. Dolly could never understand how the only way to get a point across was to wipe shit and piss all over yourself and your cell.

This place never changed, she thought, as she took in the doom and gloom on the prisoners' faces. She was in and out of here so often they may as well give her a key. Luckily, it was only short stints that she served and never for anything more serious than soliciting or getting caught with a bit of gear on her. However, her criminal record was rapidly growing into a list longer than her legs.

"Alright, Doll," shouted one of the women who were playing pool noisily in the main corridor. "Fancied a bit of Hotel Holloway again, did you?"

"Yeah, the all-inclusive option was just too tempting." Dolly smiled at the woman.

She knew loads of the ladies in here. She was popular because she treated them just as she did her punters. Smile and be polite and keep your private thoughts to yourself that was her motto. Dolly observed the group. The women were all laughing and joking as if they were best of friends; it looked cosy. But Dolly knew just how fickle people could be in here. They would be your best mate one minute and stab you in the back the next for just looking at them the wrong way: fake as fuck, the lot of them. Even the goody two-shoes housewives who found themselves banged up in here were full of surprises, and in fact they were the worst culprits. Dolly had seen it a hundred times over: while hubby and kids were both out of sight and mind, they were the ones who happily obliged in being 'gay for the stay'. There was more sex going on in this place than in most brothels. Generally, the women got into relationships with other inmates more for survival than anything, often latching onto the stronger and more intimidating inmates for reassurance, hoping that they would have the security of having someone to watch their backs for the duration of their stay.

Dolly may be a hooker, but she would never sleep with a woman. Not for any amount of cash or security. She guessed that a bit of muff-diving was a small price to pay for protection, but it certainly wasn't something that she was into. Besides, she didn't need to; she was more than capable of looking after herself. But she did understand why some of the girls did it: prison could send you out of your mind if you didn't have something to occupy your dark and lonely thoughts. Be it a relationship or a training course, anything to focus your attention was better than just staring at the grey grimy walls, enclosed with the sort of lowlife individuals that on the outside you'd cross the road to avoid, she thought.

"Here you are," the officer said as she showed Dolly the tiny cell that would be her new home for the next three weeks. "O'Hagan, you've got company."

Looking up from her book, Sophia eyed her new roommate.

"Lily Dalton, this is Sophia O'Hagan. That's where you'll be sleeping, Dalton." The officer indicated the bed opposite Sophia's. "Someone will be along shortly to take you to see your personal officer. I'll leave you girls to play nicely."

Sophia smiled at Dolly. Having spent the past eight years sharing a cell with just about every type of convict there was Sophia thought that this one didn't look too bad. And she certainly couldn't be any worse than the last one. Jackie bleeding Princeton had been a complete fruit loop. She had been convinced that she could hear voices that no one else was able to; this made her pull out chunks of her hair and bang her head against the wall. And the daytime had been even worse. She had regular psychotic episodes, often locking herself in the cell once she was alone and self-harming until someone took notice of her. Sophia had been relieved when the officers had worked out that girl wasn't just the average attention seeker that you got in here, and she was finally moved to the segregation unit. Sophia had enjoyed having the cell to herself. The solitude didn't bother her as much as it did other people.

"Lily, is it?" Sophia asked, wondering how old the girl was. If it wasn't for the fact that they were in an adult prison Sophia would have guessed that she was only fifteen.

"They call me Dolly. The kids at school started it; I guess it just stuck. They used to say that I looked like a little doll. Drove me nuts, it did, but I've got used to it now. It's better than Lily, anyway. Lily sounds like something posh birds would name their fanny, doesn't it?" Dolly said, smiling. She sat down on her bed heavily, forgetting how thin the foam mattresses were.

Sophia smiled back: Dolly may look dainty but her appearance was clearly deceiving.

"Only got three weeks this time," Dolly said. "I don't know why they bothered. Think the Old Bill was getting bored of seeing my face in the back of their cars each week so they slung me in here for a bit. Don't know why they think this is a punishment though. I'm glad of the bleeding break to be honest."

Dolly saw prison as a welcome release from her daily grind. She also got to lay her head down at night without anyone pawing at her. It wasn't the Hilton, but it was true what they said, a change was as good as a rest: especially in her line of work.

She had been pleasuring men for money since she was fourteen years old. And 'pleasuring' was putting it nicely. Some of the things she had been made to do had shocked her to the core when she had first started out. Even at just twenty-three years old, Dolly could safely say that she had probably just about seen and done it all.

"What's that you're reading?" Dolly motioned to the chunky book that her roommate held in her hand, guessing that she must be intelligent. "I flick through the glossies sometimes, if I get the chance. I can't get enough of celebrity gossip. Don't really read books, though."

"Oh, this is my course notes: I've been learning cookery. Dab hand at it now, I am," Sophia said, suddenly realising that she sounded like a swot. "You've got to do something while you're in here or you'll end up going mad."

Dolly nodded. She knew from her previous stays in jail that this was true. The smart inmates kept themselves occupied by signing up for training schemes and education courses, but Dolly had no desire to join them: there was no point. An NVQ food preparation course would be as useful to her when she got out as a chocolate teapot.

"Don't blame you, love. It's too late for me to think about a change of career, but if I had my chance again I would have done the same. Don't think I'd have been much of a chef, though, to be fair; my staple diet when I'm not in here is curry-flavoured pot noodles, and cheese and Piccalilli sandwiches. Hardly gourmet, is it? I wouldn't know where to start cooking a slap-up meal. But good on you, though," Dolly said with conviction.

Dolly wouldn't wish what she did for a living on anyone. Her line of work was dark: she had been in some really nasty situations. Luckily, she was so popular with her long list of regulars now that she didn't have to tout herself out to too many strangers anymore. But it was still hard graft. Some of her regulars were the type of blokes that only their mothers could love, and the only way they were ever going to get their leg over was to pay the premium for it. She had a few punters that wouldn't have known hygiene if it smacked them in the face with a wet flannel. Even some of her older clients were hard work. She had lost count of the amount of men that she had lain down with that had a fixation with her looking so young and childlike, which was the main reason why she was so popular in the first place. The men liked their girls younger and younger these days. Without her makeup, she looked like a school girl and wearing a tiny school uniform pleased many of the punters. Some of the old dirty gits even got her to call them daddy when she wore it for them, before they held her head down and made her suck them off or straddled her roughly from behind while spanking her and telling her what a naughty little girl she was. But though some of the blokes were weird, they could have been a lot worse. She had been lucky so far with her clients. She'd had the odd punter here and there over the years that had got a bit too rough with her, teaching her the hard way that some men liked to get their kicks by beating and forcing themselves onto women. It was all part of the job. If Dolly had seen one filthy old pervert she had seen them all and, as long as they didn't hurt her too much, she just got on with what she was paid to do. Being on the game was all she had ever known and, once she'd done her time in here, she'd be straight back out there flashing her clout to the highest bidder before the prison gates had even closed behind her.

Trevor would make sure of that.

"So, how long have you got left?" Dolly asked, as she kicked her legs against the side of the bed and looked around the room, brushing thoughts of Trevor quickly to the back of her mind. Scanning the cell for a glimpse at Sophia's belongings so she could gauge some clues about the girl's personality, Dolly noticed that other than a pile of books stacked up neatly on top of her locker Sophia's cell was bare. She didn't even have any posters on the wall.

"I'm getting out in two weeks," Sophia replied.

"Lucky you. Have you been in here long?"

"Eight years."

"Woo. Eight years is a bloody long time to be somewhere like here."

"I got ten originally, two of them I was in a young offenders' institute. And, you know, what with good behaviour and all that..." Sophia trailed off. She felt uncomfortable with the conversation. She hated people prying. She often had her head inside a book for that very reason. Seemingly too preoccupied to talk to anyone, people soon got the hint and generally just left her alone. That was how she liked it. She preferred the isolation that she had created, and wanted nothing more than just to blend in to the background and become invisible. Bitter about being in prison, she made sure that she distanced herself from the other inmates. They weren't the same as her. They were guilty.

Eight years may have been better than the initial ten, but no amount of time could soften the fact that she was in prison for something that she hadn't done. Eight years of her life had been stolen from her, and not one person, apart from her nan had listened nor cared when she had begged and pleaded that there had been a mistake. Every single person in prison claimed that they weren't guilty; they all sung the same song. It infuriated Sophia because, unlike all the real criminals, she really was innocent, but she had given up protesting about it long ago as her pleas fell on deaf ears.

"Ten years? Phew, girl, you must have done something really bad to get yourself that kind of a stretch," Dolly said, realising that she was probably over-stepping the line snooping into the girl's private business. She couldn't help it, though; Sophia looked as though butter wouldn't melt and it was unusual to find that type in here. Dolly knew that she was pretty but Sophia, with her long red bouncy curls tumbling over her shoulders and her piercing green eyes, was stunning. Just by looking at the girl Dolly couldn't imagine that she was capable of committing any kind of a crime; she seemed far too soft. It just goes to show, she thought to herself; it's true what they say, you can never judge a book by its cover.

"I'm in here for murder. They said I brutally stabbed my... somebody, to death." Sophia hoped the shock factor would cut the conversation dead.

Dolly heard the bitter tone in Sophia's voice. "They said? So you're innocent?"

"Yeah, I am; along with every other inmate in here." Sophia placed her book in front of her face to make it clear that their chat was over. She couldn't be bothered with the bullshit conversations in here anymore. She had given up insisting on her innocence a long time ago, so telling Dolly all about it now wouldn't make a blind bit of difference. Her new room-mate seemed okay but with just a couple of weeks left of her sentence Sophia wasn't interested in having a heart-to-heart with the girl.

Dolly lay back on her bed and stared up at the ceiling. She regretted giving Sophia the Spanish Inquisition. She couldn't blame the girl for not wanting to talk about her crime; she hadn't known her for more than five seconds. It was one of the unspoken rules in prison that you didn't poke your nose into other people's business.

Staring at a damp patch around the strip light, Dolly's thoughts turned back to Trevor. Big, bad Trevor Creevy would be doing his nut over his best little earner being holed up in prison again. She hoped he was stewing over this, it would serve him right. She worked her arse off for that man because she had no choice. He made sure of that, always there lurking in the background, 'keeping an eye on her'. He even let her have a room in his house as a reward while he counted the money that she had been forced to lie on her back and earn for him. He had eyes and ears everywhere, that bloke; he made it his business to know everything about each girl that he had working for him. Getting sent to prison was the only way that she could escape from him, that's why she wasn't so bothered about the pigs pulling her in all the time. This time she had played a blinder. Caught with her whole day's takings and a bag of gear from a generous punter for extras, Dolly had argued with and cursed at the officers until they had been left with no choice but to pull her in. What with the numerous offences she had stacked up against her, and her previous convictions, she had known she'd be sent down. It was only three weeks, but she didn't care. She had felt dog-tired lately and had been looking forward to her stretch. The system was a joke. Prison certainly wasn't the punishment it was made out to be; in contrast to her world outside, being inside was a saving grace, for a brief spell anyway.

Three weeks away from Trevor's controlling grasp with no slimy punters and a chance to get her head straight again was exactly what she needed.

Trevor would be doing his nut over it, and there was nothing that he could do about it. Her sentence would hit him harder than it did her, in the only place that hurt him: his pocket.

Smiling, Dolly closed her eyes. She was looking forward to some well-earned time off.

Chapter Nineteen

Except for the bed that she was lying on, the room was bare of furniture. The light above her flickered as she tried to stay focused.

Beads of sweat trickled down her torso as she writhed in agony. Her clammy hands slipped as she tried to grip the bed's metal handrail as she braced herself for another surge of pain.

The officer standing in the doorway had a detached expression; she remained silent as she watched. How could she stand there impassively, ignoring the suffering she was witnessing?

The pain was coming once more: stronger and more intense than before.

"Please," she begged. "Please don't make me do this." She shook her head and tried her hardest to control her tears.

She wouldn't give the officer the satisfaction of seeing her cry.

Feeling the pain build inside her again, she let out a shrill scream. After that she felt weak and faint, unsure how much strength she had left.

Her heart hammered inside her chest.

"Please help me," she pleaded, to no avail. The officer was seemingly void of all feeling.

Where was the compassion?

Retreating inside herself once more as the pain slowly started to grip her again, she took long controlled breaths, inhaling as though her life depended on it.

Her body was exhausted. She wanted to close her eyes and make it all go away. Make everything go away. She moaned, too tired to release the scream caught in the back of her throat.

She felt herself losing control.

Then she saw the blood.

Sobbing, she gave in to her tears. The scream that filled the small room was like that of a wounded animal as it howled in pain. Feeling her body convulse, she felt herself being ripped in two.

Then Sophia awoke. She was panting hard, her heart racing just as it had done in her nightmare. The delicate silvery light of the moon illuminated the room just enough that she could recognise the familiar outline of the window bars as they created a shadow in the middle of the floor. That and Dolly, sitting next to her on the bed, brought her back to reality.

"It's alright, Sophia; you're okay. It was just a bad dream. You're alright, mate. I'm here." Dolly's gentle voice was soothing as she leaned over Sophia and stroked her hair.

Dolly had been worried when she had woken up to the sound of Sophia tossing and turning in bed, crying out for help. Having thought at first that she was having a fit, it had taken her a moment to realise that Sophia was asleep. As Dolly tried to rouse her, Sophia had lashed out at her before waking up.

Realising that Dolly's arms were around her in a bid to comfort her Sophia took long, deep breaths to calm down. Then, she sat up and reached for her beaker of water from the top of her locker. Tonight's dream had been the same as usual. Even in her sleep, her demons caught up with her.

"Must have scared you good and proper, whatever it was you were dreaming about. Your hands are still shaking," Dolly said, as she placed her hands around the plastic cup, helping Sophia to drink the water.

Sophia took a long thirsty gulp. Gradually her heartbeat slowed.

"I used to have night terrors too. They'd be so bad sometimes I wouldn't be able to shake them off for ages," Dolly said.

Sophia flung her head back down on her pillow, exhausted.

"Thank you," she said, feeling emotional. It has been a long time since she had felt the warmth of someone's arms wrapped around her as they reassured her that everything was going to be alright. She was really grateful, but the dream had left her feeling so shaken up that she was scared that Dolly would make her talk about it. And she couldn't: not yet.

Dolly got back into her own bed and listened to Sophia's breathing quieten before turning into a soft cry.

"Sophia, are you sure that you're okay?" Dolly asked, concerned. She had barely known the girl for twenty-four hours, but it was crystal clear that Sophia had problems. Dolly had met girls like her before. They withdrew themselves from people and situations so that they couldn't get hurt, putting an invisible guard up, but it didn't fool Dolly, she could tell when a girl may appear strong on the outside but on the inside it was a completely different story.

"I'll be fine in a minute, and I'm sorry you woke up. Can't even remember what the dream was about now; just gave me a fright, that's all." Sophia wiped her tears away. She couldn't bear to talk about the recurring dream. There was barely a night that went by in here when she didn't have it. Every time that she gave in to sleep, it was like she was being haunted. She would close her eyes and, before she knew it, she was confronted by the ghosts of her past. Dolly would have to contend with this each night until Sophia left.

"You don't need to apologise, love; as long as you're alright. Just remember it was just a silly nightmare, it can't hurt you," Dolly said, feeling sorry for the poor girl.

Shivering, Sophia wrapped her blanket around her, feeling the warmth envelop her. She knew that she was in for a long night. Her night terrors often left her wide awake, her mind circling, unable to shake off the dreams that affected her so badly.

The nights were worse than the days in prison. Once the dark thoughts had crept in there was no escaping them. At least in the day it was possible to avoid thinking about things too much by keeping busy.

Soon, however, it would be over. In less than two weeks she would be out, catapulted back into a world that had almost forgotten her. A world that didn't know she existed anymore.

And once she was out, her bad dreams would be the least of her worries. Dolly was right, nightmares couldn't hurt her. But reality could.

Chapter Twenty

"Here, look at the state of her." Dolly nodded across the canteen as Ruth Parker marched past their table, her fists clenched, followed closely by her friends.

Ruth's angry face could have given a slapped arse a run for its money. Dolly watched as she stomped about, every part of the woman wobbling as she moved. She could tell by her body language that somebody had severely pissed her off and she didn't have to wait long to find out who it was.

Ruth strode over to the table where Imelda Grey was eating her breakfast alone, and sat down next to her, glaring. Imelda didn't react; instead she wisely kept her head and pretended that she hadn't noticed the woman that was now stationed next to her, with her cronies standing behind her as backup.

"It's all going to kick off," Dolly said, her cold and soggy toast halfway to her mouth.

"Ruth's a bloody head-case. She's in my cookery class: eats more pies than she bakes," Sophia said, as she glanced around to see what Dolly was looking at. "She did away with her husband because he was dipping his wick in places he shouldn't have been, Imelda being one of them. Ruth poisoned him, apparently, sent him to his grave after dishing him up his last supper, ended up getting life for it. Apparently when it all went to trial she laughed as she told the judge that if the cheating bastard didn't want her then he wouldn't be having anyone else. What are the chances that a year down the line Imelda would get banged up in the same prison? Silly cow only got a few months for benefit fraud or something stupid. Ruth is going to make her life hell for the duration."

"Jesus, what a fruit loop," Dolly said, as she looked Ruth up and down. "Even I wouldn't fancy my chances against that." Ruth looked more butch than most men: Dolly could see exactly how waif-like Imelda would have appealed to Ruth's late husband. Having sex with Ruth must have been like riding a fat-girl Rodeo in comparison to bedding skinny, sultry-looking Imelda; he probably thought he'd won the lottery.

"He told Ruth that he was going to leave her for Imelda. So Ruth blames Imelda for the whole thing. She's been gunning for her since the minute she heard she'd been sent here. The officers are all watching Ruth, but they can't keep an eye on her all the time can they? Imelda's probably crapping herself."

Ruth told her business to anyone who would listen, and Dolly was probably the only person in the prison who hadn't heard this sob story a hundred times.

"Oh, Soph, what am I going to do when you get out? Who's going to fill me in on all the gossip?" Dolly asked as she pushed her plate away.

Breakfast time in the canteen was becoming Dolly's most favourite time of day. She enjoyed sitting with Sophia while she kept her up to speed with all the ins and outs about the other inmates. It passed the time, and after being locked away in their eight-by-ten-foot cell all night, especially with Sophia having nightmares, the light-hearted banter they shared in the mornings was a tonic.

"Four days left, bet you're so excited to be going after all this time," Dolly said, wondering if this was true: Sophia hadn't said much about her family, nor about whom she had murdered and Dolly knew better than to pry. Sophia didn't seem the violent type at all; in fact she seemed like a really nice girl. And the more time that passed, the more she felt like Sophia was letting her in a bit. She was still secretive about stuff, but that was her prerogative.

Dolly felt that she had made a genuine friend inside: she would miss Sophia.

"I guess," Sophia said unconvincingly. "It's weird: eight years ago I would have skipped out the prison gates, but I feel a bit scared. I've kind of got used to this place. These walls are funny like that... You hate them with a passion at first for being the barrier between you and everything outside, and then get used to them."

Dolly couldn't imagine doing an eight-year run; short little stints were all she had experienced. She understood what Sophia meant, though. It was safer in here that it was outside for many of the girls. And they had a routine in here. Some of them managed to get clean and re-train. It was a different world.

"Have you got anyone on the outside waiting for you, to help you get back on your feet?" Dolly asked casually.

"My mum and my nan," Sophia said quietly. "My mum's in and out of hospital with her nerves, though. She had a breakdown just after my... just after I got sent down. She hasn't been to visit me for years. Seeing me in here made her a million times worse apparently."

Dolly listened; she was scared to comment in case Sophia clammed up again.

"My nan's all I have really, and she's getting on a bit: eighty last week. You'd love her: she's so funny. She's the only person who comes to see me. She's visited regularly since my very first day in here," Sophia said proudly before adding, "but she isn't too well at the moment, hasn't been in for over a month. When I get out of here it'll be my turn to make it up to her." Sophia longed to show her nan how grateful she was for her belief in her innocence. Her nan was the only one who felt like that. Her mum had said she did on the rare occasions that they had spoken since the start of Sophia's sentence. However, she had never said it with much conviction, and she was often barely coherent due to her heavy medication.

Having said more about herself during the breakfast than in the whole of the ten days that Dolly had shared a cell with her, Sophia went quiet again. Dolly knew that was all she would be getting for now, although she wanted to know more. The nightmares occurred every single night and even though Dolly had managed to catch the odd word that Sophia shouted out here and there, whenever she mentioned them to her cell-mate she quickly changed the subject. There was something that had happened that had greatly affected her, but Dolly was just going to have to wait until Sophia was ready to find out what it was.

"Can we stay in touch when you get out?" Dolly asked, surprising herself. She didn't really have any real friends as such, even on the outside, but Sophia was different.

"Of course," Sophia said, laughing at Dolly's coyness. "We're mates, aren't we? Oh, for fuck's sake, here comes Cockroach."

Dolly followed Sophia's eyes, seeing Officer Roache making his way to their table. She groaned. Although he was new, Roache had already earned himself a reputation amongst the ladies. If any of the women needed anything brought in, he was the man to talk to. Mobile phones; vodka; extra tobacco... you name it and he would get it, for a price of course. Sophia had warned Dolly about him and Dolly had assured her that she was more than capable of handling the little parasite's advances should she ever need to.

Roache smiled as he stopped at the girls' table, and then scanned the room as he checked none of the other officers was watching. "Dolly, isn't it? I need a word."

Roache nodded to her to get up, ignoring Sophia who he couldn't stand. She was a stunner, he would give her that much, but she was also a stuck-up little cow. He had tried it on with her, as he had done all the others in here, but Sophia had thought she was above him and had not only refused his advances but she'd also grassed him up to the governor, complaining that he was harassing her. Luckily for Roache, he and the governor were very good friends and the grievance had never gone any further than between the two of them. But knowing what a narky bitch Sophia could be, Roache had been careful to give the girl a wide birth ever since: the stupid little slag wasn't worth the agro.

Sophia looked at Dolly questioningly. Dolly nodded to indicate to her friend that she was fine, before she reluctantly pushed her chair back and gathered up her tray. Sophia watched as Roache followed Dolly out of the canteen all the while his greedy eyes staring at her arse as she walked. Shaking her head in disgust, Sophia looked to see if any of the other officers had noticed. It didn't look like it. The male officers were always supposed to have a female officer present when with an inmate on a one-to-one basis, but in reality that rarely happened. Roache was such a pervert Sophia couldn't fathom how he got away with all the stuff that he did. She guessed that the staff just turned a blind eye.

A voice boomed out behind Sophia, interrupting her thoughts. "You slag! My Harry's in the ground because of you. If you'd kept your dirty stink-hole to yourself none of this would have happened."

A tray of food landed face down on the floor next to Sophia's feet, along with a dishevelled-looking Imelda Grey.

Sophia jumped out of the way in the nick of time, as Ruth hurled a jug of boiling water into Imelda's face.

Standing back, Sophia watched in horror as Imelda screamed in pain as the water scalded her skin while Ruth's cronies circled around her, making it hard for any officers nearby to intervene. Sophia felt sick at the screeching sounds Imelda was making, but Ruth was laughing: she was obviously enjoying seeing Imelda suffer. Then, Ruth started raining blows down on the girl's face for good measure.

By the time that three officers had been able to pull Ruth off her, Imelda was seemingly unconscious.

***

"So, a little birdie told me that you're good at looking after men, Dolly, that you know what makes us happy," Roache said after he had followed Dolly into her cell, and locked the door behind him. Walking over to her bed, he indicated to Dolly to sit down. When she didn't move, he pushed her down and then moved in closer so that he was looming above her.

"What are you talking about; what 'little birdie?'" Dolly pretended to be puzzled. If this slimy pervert thought he was getting a freebie because he had heard she was on the game, he could get stuffed.

Roache ignored the girl's questions as he placed his finger inside Dolly's T-shirt and ran it slowly across her décolletage.

"I've got this mate, you see, and he owes me a few favours: big favours. He said that you would take care of me." Roache leaned in closer, standing in such close proximity that his crotch was almost touching her face as he spoke. He was enjoying his moment. Dolly wasn't being nice enough to him. But she soon would be.

"And who would that be?" Dolly scoffed, wondering what this bastard was playing at. She instinctively leaned backwards, trying to get away from the officer as he invaded her space, obviously trying to intimidate her.

Roache started to undo the fly on his uniform trousers, sucking in his paunch as he did so. Watched in shock as Officer Roache pulled his erect cock out of his pants and held it in front of her face, Dolly could see beads of sweat form on the officer's large forehead. His little piggy eyes greedily roamed her body and he licked his lips.

"See, just because you're in here doesn't mean that you're off duty." Roache brushed the tip of his penis along her cheek, before pressing it firmly against her lips. "And you better do as you're told, Dolly darling. Otherwise you're going to be in big trouble."

Roache leaned forward and gripped the back of Dolly's head, causing her to screech as he dragged her closer to him.

"Trevor Creevy ring any bells?" he added, enjoying the look on her face as she realised that even in here Trevor had managed to get to her. "He told me to make sure that you're paying your way while you're in here, and with the amount of debt that he owes me I reckon you're going to be a very busy girl." Roache smiled, enjoying the look of dread spreading across Dolly's pretty little face as she realised that he had her exactly where he wanted her.

Dolly wasn't bad looking for a bird that worked for Trevor Creevy, and Roache liked that she looked unusually vulnerable. She wasn't like the cold-hearted slags he was used to: the prostitutes who normally got banged up in here disgusted him; dregs of the earth, most of them. Dirty, cheap, immoral... they could have filled a Jeremy Kyle series. Most offered sexual favours in return for him smuggling them in cigarettes and vodka: always willing to get down on their knees as long as there was something in it for them.

This one was probably no different, deep down, although at least she had it going on in the looks department, being so young and pretty. She didn't have that cold, hard-done-by look that most whores got after being on the streets for a while.

And she did look very young, Roache thought, as he examined her body closely. But despite the innocent school-girl appearance, Roache would bet money on her being excellent in the sack.

Dolly closed her eyes, rigid with anger at what was coming. Disgusted that the officer had started playing with himself, she grimaced as he tugged himself off in her face, his cock bashing against the skin of her cheek.

"I reckon this is a good a place as any to start, don't you?" Roache flipped her over so she was face down on the bed, and then yanked down her tracksuit bottoms.

Positioning himself close behind her as he knelt on all fours, he rammed himself inside her, barely able to contain himself any longer.

Wincing, humiliated, Dolly had no choice but to do as she was told.

Outside she would have been ready for this; nothing fazed her when she was working, sex was what she did. But she hadn't expected it to happen in here and somehow she had let her guard down.

Even though she was locked away in prison, Trevor had managed to get to her. She had thought that she was getting a break from all that. She realised that she should have phoned him. He wouldn't have appreciated her playing games, and maybe because she had avoided calling him since she had been inside, enjoying the tiny bit of control that she had, he had thought he would teach her a lesson.

Dolly switched herself off from the grunting noise that Roache was making as he pounded against her buttocks: just like she did every time, with every man she had slept with.

It was just a job... just a job.

Roache gripped her shoulders, pushing himself harder and deeper inside her.

He wanted to keep fucking the girl. He wanted to make her sore, but he couldn't control the intense hot quiver as it spread through his body as he held on to her arse cheeks. Tipping his head back, he tried to stifle his groan as he ejaculated.

It hadn't lasted nearly as long as he wanted, but he would make sure that next time it did. As he zipped his fly up, he smiled.

Dolly Dalton was a prize fuck and after that little performance, Roache was going to enjoy every last minute that he spent with her before she was released.

***

Once the mayhem in the canteen had died down and the prisoners were able to go back to their cells Sophia strode through the busy corridor, eager to get back to her friend to check that she was alright and to fill her in on the horrific confrontation she had just witnessed. Even though the officers had finally intervened and dragged Ruth away, it was too little too late. Imelda's badly scalded skin and pulped face was a vision that wouldn't leave Sophia's mind anytime soon. The attack had reminded Sophia of how vulnerable they all were in here, and picking up her pace she just wanted to get back to her cell.

Seeing Roache coming out of the door as she approached, Sophia hoped that the dirty bastard hadn't tried his luck with Dolly: they had been gone long enough. Sophia was sure that Dolly would be able to handle herself, but she wouldn't put anything past Roache.

"Slow down, O' Hagan, I can't see any fire," Roache cautioned as he saw Sophia rushing towards him.

Sophia eyed the guard with suspicion as he grinned at her.

"There's no fire, but there was a crisis. The canteen has been on lock-down since you left. Ruth Parker just kicked off and napalmed poor Imelda Grey. Last I heard they were carting her off to the hospital and the governor was looking for you. She didn't look very happy that you were on the missing list," Sophia said coldly, hoping that he would get bollocked for his disappearing act. Just the look of Roache's fat smarmy face and his beady little eyes made Sophia feel sick. "And if you have done anything to Dolly, and I mean anything then, I'll be letting the gov know," Sophia spat.

Roache pushed her against the wall.

"The governor won't give a shit about you or any of the bullshit that you spout," he threatened. His face was puce and spittle escaped his lips as he spoke through gritted teeth. "Dolly and I have an agreement, and you better keep your fucking frigid nose out of it. Just you remember, O'Hagan, you're out in a few days. You won't be able to protect her then. One word of trouble from you and I'll make sure that Dolly gets passed around in here quicker than a cold. Do you understand?" He let her go, looking around to make sure that no-one of any relevance had witnessed his loss of temper.

Hearing another member of staff call out Officer Roache's name over the tannoy, Sophia pushed past his chubby frame and went to see how her friend was.

Chapter Twenty-One

Dolly was used to being devoid of sleep now. Two weeks in, and her body-clock had adjusted fully to her new routine. If it wasn't her cell mate's nightmares that kept her awake, it was the cries and shouts that carried up and down the wing, echoing in her ears. Some inmates weren't very good at coping anyway, and the long nights locked away in darkness made things seem even bleaker. Desperate cries, angry shouts and manic hysterical laughter were just some of the noises that filled the air each night.

Tonight Dolly was listening to a new inmate, a lifer apparently, as she frantically begged and pleaded to see her children. Dolly felt sorry for the poor cow. The first night in here was the hardest and with such a long sentence ahead of her, the officers probably had the woman on suicide watch.

The days in here weren't too good for Dolly either. Roache had kept his promise and every day that he had been working, he had made sure that they had sex. She hated it. He was the type that could only satisfy himself if he was causing someone pain.

Sophia had her suspicions but Dolly couldn't confide in her. Roache had already warned her that if Sophia got wind of their 'little arrangement' then she would tell the governor and Trevor would kill Dolly for jeopardising their arrangement and not paying back his debt. Dolly hated lying to her friend, but she didn't have a choice.

Hearing Sophia talking in her sleep once more, Dolly propped herself up onto one elbow and listened. Sophia was mumbling and kicking the covers around. Every night without fail was the same. It was as if she was struggling to get up, as if she was being held down. A couple of times Dolly had heard the odd word, but she hadn't been able to work out what it was that was upsetting Sophia so much. And Sophia always changed the subject as soon as it was broached. The nightmares had gradually got worse, though, and last night's outburst had worried Dolly sick: at one point she had thought she was going to have to call one of the officers to help her.

"Get off," Sophia shouted as she clawed the covers then kicked them off.

Dolly went over to Sophia's bed. It was their routine now. Sophia would kick and scream and cry, and Dolly would be there for her when she awoke, stroking her hair and reassuring her that she was going to be okay.

"Please," Sophia begged as she swatted her arms about, as if fighting off invisible attackers and almost hitting Dolly square in the face as she did. "Please take it away. I don't want it." Dolly saw fresh tears cascade down Sophia's cheeks as she continued to fight her night terrors. Her words were clearer tonight, and Dolly felt uncomfortable about hearing what she was sure Sophia wouldn't want her to. But what else could she do but try and help?

"Sophia," Dolly said gently, shaking her arm as she tried to rouse her.

"Take it away. Please. It's evil," Sophia shouted hysterically this time.

"Sophia, darling, it's me Dolly. Wake up, babe, you're dreaming." Dolly shook her harder. Sophia's fear was hard to bear; it was as if she was trapped in some parallel universe, like her nightmares were real.

As Sophia woke, she gasped for air as if she had just come up from being submerged under water. She panted, before bursting into tears and clinging to her friend as if for dear life.

"Shush," Dolly soothed. "It's okay."

It was Sophia's last night; if Dolly couldn't get to the bottom of what was causing Sophia so much pain and anguish tonight, she may never find out. Dolly felt so close to Sophia, she just wanted to help her. Maybe now Sophia would finally confide in her.

"Sophia, whatever it is that's upsetting you, I just want you to know that I'm here for you, babe. You can trust me. You don't have to tell me, but I think maybe it will help. Bottling whatever it is up clearly hasn't."

Sobbing, Sophia hugged Dolly tightly. Finally, after eight years of denial, Sophia gave in and spoke about the one thing that up until now she had tried so desperately to block out.

Dolly listened to her as she spoke of finding her father dying on her bedroom floor. Sophia wept as she spoke of her then-boyfriend Tommy, who when she was just fifteen she had fallen in love with. She spoke of how they had met that day at the river and of how horrible and mean Tommy's brother, Jonathan, was.

Once Sophia started to speak, it was as if a dam had been broken and she just couldn't stop, the words kept pouring from her mouth.

Then she went quiet. Dolly squeezed her hand to encourage her to continue.

Sophia felt ashamed as she went on to explain how Jonathan tricked her, how he had made her believe he was Tommy at her birthday party and how she had slept with him.

Dolly was silent as she listened. Sophia had held all this in for far too long; it would do the girl good to get it out of her system once and for all.

"There's something else, isn't there? You can tell me Sophia, whatever it is," Dolly said softly.

"I had his baby, Dolly; I had Jonathan's baby and then they took her away."

Chapter Twenty-Two

When he heard the doorbell chime, Stanley Jenkins was already in a foul mood. He had been pushed to his limits today. As he stepped over the bright yellow paint that had been smeared on the carpet and up the walls, he cursed as he realised that he had stepped in it. Wiping his shoe with a cloth, he dipped his hands into a bucket of warm soapy water; he swished them around then he dried them off and went to see who was at the door.

"I told you last time, Stanley, that if it happened again I would be ringing the police..." Geoffrey ranted as soon as the door opened, not bothering with the usual neighbourly niceties.

Stanley stood with his mouth open, unable to get a word in.

"That young'un of yours has only gone and bloody done it again. Look at poor Harry, I found him this morning. Lying dead on the floor of the aviary he was. And don't try and make up excuses. I've had enough." Geoffrey held out his hand to show Stanley one of his lovebirds, which was splayed out lifelessly in his palm. "This is murder, Stanley, murder. How's our Sally going to cope without him? Lovebirds depend on each other, Stanley. That girl of yours is out of control..." Geoffrey tried to remain in control of his emotions, but he loved his little birds so much, each and every one of them had a special place in his heart.

Stanley grimaced as he looked at the tiny bird's head hanging loosely from his crooked neck. He leaned back, the sight of the lifeless bird making him feel queasy.

"Look, Geoffrey, I'm sorry about your bird, really I am. But it's like I told you last time: you have absolutely no proof whatsoever. So by all means ring the police but unless you have concrete evidence, I'd really appreciate it if you didn't come around here throwing around unfounded accusations." Slamming the door in the disgruntled neighbour's face before he had a chance to respond, Stanley leaned up against the wooden frame and closed his eyes in despair. In the pit of his stomach, he knew that Geoffrey was right. She had done it. But he had had about as much as he could take for one day from the little madam, so he'd have to deal with this new crime another time.

"Who was that?" Bernie came bustling in from the garden to check the progress on the paint spillage that her husband had been clearing up. Stepping carefully over the bright splodges on the carpet, she could see by the look on her husband's face that something else had happened.

"That was Geoffrey from next door: again," Stanley said in a controlled tone. "'Somebody' has killed another one of his birds; snapped its neck."

Bernie instantly felt her heckles rise as she recognised her husband's accusing tone. Trust him to believe the neighbours over one of his own: typical. Bernie could just imagine Geoffrey's head turning the colour of a beetroot while he blamed one of his birds' unfortunate deaths on to a small defenceless child, whom he only disliked because of her natural high spirits; well, not this time, she wouldn't let him get away with it. And Stanley should know better than to believe it.

"That man is a bully. How does he know that the bird didn't die of natural causes? Maybe it broke its neck when it fell off its perch," Bernie reasoned angrily. "He's got nothing better to do with his time than make up lies. Nasty little man. "

Rubbing his temples, Stanley was at his wit's end about how blinkered his wife could be when it came to that child and he knew that there was absolutely no point in arguing with her. Bernie thought the sun shone out of the girl and nobody in this house was allowed to even think, let alone say otherwise.

"Well, expect a knock on the door from the police because Geoffrey is fuming, and I don't blame the man. Twice in one week his birds have been killed, someone's got to be bloody responsible, Bernadette."

"Don't swear at me," Bernie said, shocked at how angry her husband must actually be, not only had he raised his voice but he had addressed her by her full name.

"Swear? I'll do worse in a minute. That kid's nothing but a nuisance, Bernie. Look at the state of the house. 'Oh, I accidently dropped some paint... I accidently started a fire in Grandad's shed... I accidently nipped next door and snapped the heads off Geoffrey's precious bloody birds.'" Stanley was shouting. He was sick of having to suppress his feelings when he was with his family, and it was about time that Bernie faced the truth. The kid was troubled.

Bernie rolled her eyes at her husband, whose cheeks were flushing red as his voice increased in decibels with each word. As far as she was concerned, if anyone in this house caused problems it was him. Where was his loyalty? He was no better than their neighbour.

"When will you just admit that there is something not quite right with her, Bernie? Seven years old and killing our neighbour's birds for fun! We ignored all this once before if you remember rightly and look where that bloody got us," Stanley said in despair as he referred to the videos they had found in Jonathan's room years ago, which Bernie had destroyed and refused to talk about ever since. Surely Stanley wasn't the only one that could see that history was once again repeating itself.

"She isn't right in the head, Bernie," Stanley pleaded, hoping that his wife would stop denying what was become clearer with each passing day.

"Problem?" Jonathan had appeared in the hallway.

Stanley's words hung awkwardly in the charged air; he and Bernie had been too engrossed in the argument to realise that their son was standing there listening to the conversation.

"No, darling," Bernie lied. "No problem at all, love, your dad was just ranting about the paint, that's all."

Stanley stared at his wife in disbelief. She was doing what she always did, sweeping all their problems under the paint-stained carpet so that she could pretend that everything was perfect. When the reality was that everything was far from perfect.

Sick to death at the pretence, Stanley glared at his son furiously: this was all his fault. Everything was his bloody fault.

"Do you know what, just forget it. I'm going for a few pints." Grabbing his jacket from the hook behind the front door, Stanley tugged it on while avoiding eye contact with both his wife and son. There was no point in discussing the situation with either of them any further. The pair of them were pig-headed.

Over the years Stanley's dislike of Jonathan had grown so much that he could barely stand to be in the same room as the boy anymore. The fact that Jonathan had never left home made that extremely difficult. Sharing a house with a son that he had never been able to bond with was near-on impossible.

Jonathan may have grown into a handsome man, standing at almost six foot tall with the chiselled looks of a model, but Stanley felt not an ounce of pride in his son. He could see right through Jonathan's carefully groomed exterior and there was a lot more than met the eye with that one.   He couldn't stand the sight of him: not after what he had done. Jonathan had torn the family apart. It was because of him that Tommy had left, and for that Stanley would never forgive him.

"You can't just swan off out, Stanley. What about all this paint?" Bernie looked at the streaks on her pink floral wallpaper. The carpet was ruined, too: caked in the stuff. They would have to get it replaced. Maybe she could use this as the excuse she needed to get the hallway redecorated.

"Well, I'll tell you what, seeing as you two seem to be under the illusion that Rosie is Little Miss Perfect, why don't the pair of you clear up her bloody mess?" And with that Stanley pulled the door shut behind him, so hard that Bernie was surprised that the glass panels didn't shatter.

Chapter Twenty-Three

With every step that she took away from the prison, Sophia waited for euphoria to sweep over her. When she was finally free, she had expected the sensation of liberation to be strong, instant and overwhelming.

It wasn't.

Instead, she had stood petrified behind the prison gate, anxiously awaiting her release while the prison officer took her time in signing her out. She had anticipated feeling scared and apprehensive on leaving, but then for this to be countered by an adrenalin rush of freedom. Instead, she was purely terrified. Standing facing the grey steel doors that gradually slid open she had pressed her clammy hands together, as she suppressed the flutter of panic deep down in the pit of her stomach. She was fighting to hold it together, but she couldn't fool herself. She had heard discussions between other inmates whenever reoffenders were brought back in just days after they had been released. They said that they had been drawn in by the system's regimented routine, institutionalised. Spat out by society only to be sucked back in by Her Majesty's Service. Prison had long ago stopped being a barrier that kept them away from the outside world; it was their world. At some point this had started to apply to her: the prison had become a bubble around her, cocooning her safely inside it. The thought of staying within its walls now suddenly seemed welcoming to her.

The gates finally fully opened, and Officer Morgan gave Sophia's arm an affectionate squeeze to reassure her that she would be okay before wishing her the best of luck. And that was it.

There was no grand exit; no fanfare; no crowd of well-wishers waving her away.

It was over. Eight years and she was out.

Sophia's heart pounded as she focused on placing one foot in front of the other, telling herself repeatedly to keep walking. She was so anxious that her legs trembled; she felt like she was intruding in a world in which she no longer belonged.

As she continued to walk down Camden Road she noticed everyone around her carrying on with their day, just as they had done for all that time that she had been away. It felt surreal. She was free, but she was still just as invisible to the rest of society as she had been when she had been locked away in her cell.

Breathing in the cool September air, Sophia rounded the corner and approached a bus stop. Keeping her head down, to avoid making eye contact with anyone, she stood in a long queue of people. The right bus drew up and stepping onto it, Sophia fished into her pocket for the money that her nan had sent her. Her hands shook so much that she dropped a few of the coins, and as she dropped to the dirty floor to look for them, she had heard impatient tuts from the passengers that she was holding up. Finally, after paying the driver the fare, which was more than she expected it to be, she found herself a seat.

"Oh, excuse me, love." A lady chuckled as she sat next to Sophia. She was severely overweight, her bottom taking up her own as well as some of Sophia's seat. "Public transport don't cater for us real women with all our curves." Sophia shuffled up against the window and diverted her attention to what she could see out of the window so that she wouldn't have to make conversation with the stranger.

She thought of Dolly as the bus pulled away and she caught a glimpse of the prison; she stared at it until it had vanished, silently saying a final goodbye to the place she had called home for the past eight years. "Always look forward, Sophia, never look back." Those had been Dolly's parting words as they had tearfully embraced that morning, and Sophia had a feeling that she would be using that mantra for some time to come.

Dolly had been a godsend for the past two weeks and Sophia was very sad to leave her behind. Having alienated herself so much from the other inmates during her sentence, Sophia wouldn't have had anyone else that she could have talked to about her release fears if it hadn't been for Dolly. They had become great friends. Even last night when she had finally told Dolly about the baby, Dolly hadn't judged or interrupted: she had simply held her hand and listened with genuine compassion.

It had felt so good to finally tell someone. Years of holding everything in had taken their toll. Now she was out, she knew that she was going to have to face her demons.

Sophia reflected that getting sent to prison had been the scariest thing that had ever happened to her. She remembered the dark, rainy night when they had first pulled up at the young offenders' institute and how frightened she had been. She had been so petrified that when the officer had checked her in, she had thrown up all over the desk. Right up until the medical examination, Sophia had believed that the nausea she had been down to the fact that she was stressed and hadn't eaten for days.

"No drugs, that's good," the officer had said as she scanned the results of the blood and urine tests.

"And how far along are you, Sophia?" the officer had asked as she jotted down notes.

"Far along? Do you mean how long's my sentence?"

"No, the baby... How far along are you in your pregnancy?"

"Pregnancy?" Sophia thought that she must have misheard, but the officer nodded. "I'm not pregnant."

The officer just looked at her. Sophia felt the walls closing in on her, her ears ringing.

Jonathan was the only person that she had slept with, and he'd used a condom. Or so he'd said. And even if that wasn't the case, it had only happened once, so she couldn't be pregnant. But she knew she was.

As the officer continued talking about Sophia's options as a pregnant inmate, the reality of Sophia's situation sunk in. She felt so faint and disorientated that she thought she might fall off the grey plastic chair. She could feel bile rising up again.

Up until that moment, she hadn't been able to imagine a worse situation than the one that she was already in: she was being sent to prison for a crime she hadn't committed. But it had just got worse: a lot worse. God really did have a messed-up sense of humour, she thought to herself as sat in stunned silence as the officer continued to talk.

She listened in a daze as she was told that she would be able to keep her baby with her until it was eighteen months old, and that they would both be moved into the mother and baby unit. The officer explained that she would have an easier time in the baby unit too, where she would be surrounded by other expectant and new mothers, rather than if she were placed on the main wing.

"Trust me, love, this baby will keep you so busy that your time in here will just fly by," the officer said, as she passed Sophia a tissue to wipe away the tears streaming down her face.

Sophia continued to stare at the officer blankly as she heard that although having a baby in prison wasn't the ideal start to a young child's life they would make provisions for her, as they did with all pregnant inmates; they did their utmost to help them make the best of the situation they were in and to enable the mother and baby to bond.

Sophia didn't want to bond with her baby, though. She didn't even want it.

As the months went on, Sophia's decision had remained the same. She didn't want the baby. Not now; not ever. Her protruding stomach only made her think about the disgusting seed that Jonathan had planted inside of her. It was a large tumour that wouldn't stop growing, making her sick on a daily basis and sapping her energy. Sophia was so ill throughout her entire pregnancy that she had barely been able to keep any food down; physically weak, as well as depressed, she had spent as much time as she could sleeping.

Even now, all these years later, the memory of her labour haunted her dreams every night. She had dilated so quickly that the medical team had no time get her to the hospital. There was not even time to think about any kind of pain relief. Sophia had been terrified as the agony swept through her body. The baby was coming. Carted off to an empty cell and watched over by the officers, she had screamed until minutes later she pushed the baby out.

When the prison nurse laid the baby girl across Sophia's, sweat-covered T-shirt, encouraging mother and baby to bond, Sophia had screamed at her to take it away.

Severely depressed, Sophia hadn't even wanted to look at the child, let alone be its mother. So they did as she said and took away her baby.

Jonathan and his parents had come to the prison as arranged. Social workers had tried to convince Sophia that she might regret her decision. But she was adamant. When they realised she wouldn't change her mind, they told her that Jonathan's parents had offered to support him while he raised the baby, which he was keen to do. The social workers had spoken to her for hours, explaining the procedure, informing her that her right to change her mind would be void once she signed the paperwork.

Sophia hadn't understood why they were trying to make her keep the child; she had been convicted of a murder and was stuck in prison. Surely they could see that the baby would be better off with Jonathan and his family. At least he had said he wanted to care for it. At least his family could provide for it financially. What could she give it? She could barely wipe her own arse without having to ask for permission. No, even if she had wanted to keep the baby, it was better off without her.

As the bus pulled into its next stop, Sophia shook her head as if to banish the memory from her mind as she realised that she had been crying. Wiping away her tears, she looked around to make sure that no-one had noticed how upset she was. She watched people get on and off the bus, keeping her mind focused on the present as she tried to block out the heartache of the past.

A little boy a few rows down waved at Sophia, and his mum smiled at the cheeky little boy who was already familiar with getting attention from strangers. Sophia wondered what the women would think if she found out that her son was gesturing at a convicted murderer. She would judge her: everyone did. She would probably grab her son protectively by his little hand and take him to sit as far away from Sophia as possible.

Sophia glanced away without returning the child's wave. She didn't have the energy to pretend to be happy. She may be free but she still felt cheated and robbed.

She should have listened to her lawyer all those years ago and pleaded guilty. Everyone, except for her nan had believed in her guilt anyway. If she had listened to the advice she was given, she probably would have only served a few months inside. The lawyer had wanted to lead with mitigating circumstances, adamant that they should build up a case in her defence by telling the court about her father's violence. All she had to do was plead guilty and he would do the rest, he had said. He had done his utmost at the time to reassure her that if he could convince the court that Sophia had acted in self-defence then she was likely to be given a more lenient sentence.

But Sophia hadn't listened. There was no way on Earth that she was going to admit she was guilty of a crime that she hadn't committed. She hadn't murdered her father, and no matter what happened she would not be saying that she had. She was innocent and the jury would see that. As for the case that her solicitor was trying to build, Sophia didn't want anyone to find out the details of her father's abusive behaviour; her mother wouldn't have been able to take it, she had just suffered a nervous breakdown and the family name had been dragged through the media and tarnished enough as it was.

Sophia had been convinced that the truth would come out: the killer would be caught and her name cleared. But she was young and naive and had soon been taught that life wasn't always fair. The Crown Prosecution Service's case had been built upon a trail of evidence that led back to Sophia. Her fingerprints were on the murder weapon, she had been found covered in her father's blood and a witness had overheard her saying that she intended on carrying out the crime just two days prior to the attack.

Sophia had begged and pleaded with the jury to believe that she was innocent, convinced that they would listen and realise she was telling the truth. But they hadn't. Sophia had been convicted of murder and given a ten-year sentence. She had only served eight, but to her it had seemed like forever. And the worst of it was that because she had been convicted of the murder, the case had been closed. No-one had looked for the real killer. Over the last eight years that had been the one thing that she had thought about non-stop. She was serving time, and the real killer was free. They were still out there, carrying on with their life unaffected by their actions. Even now she was out it was on a life-licence. She had years of probation officers breathing down her neck ahead of her, while she asked permission to do what others simply took for granted.

Sophia closed her eyes as the bus slowly continued along its route. It made frequent stops, but she was grateful for its leisurely pace, she was in no great hurry to reach her destination. She knew that once she arrived there she would have to make a start on trying to salvage something from the wreck of her life, and she was dreading it.

When the bus pulled in at her stop, Sophia got off without bothering to look at any of the other passengers or the driver as she exited. She stared at the pavement as she walked, clutching the white plastic carrier bag that held her few worldly possessions tightly against her body, as she made her way back down the old familiar street in which she had grown up. As Sophia walked she imagined the curtains twitching in the houses that she passed, the neighbours all peeping out and having a good old look at the murderer returning to the scene of her horrific crime. She knew that it was just her paranoid mind going into overdrive, the neighbours had probably forgotten about her and even if they hadn't, she had been a child when she had last been here: surely no-one would even recognise her. Concentrating on the cracks in the paving slabs as she walked, Sophia felt her heart beat faster as she neared her destination. Across the road was the house in which her father had been murdered. She couldn't look at it. Her nan had told her that someone had bought it years ago, the new residents completely renovating it after the damage that the fire had caused. Her mother had never gone back there: she was in a residential home, and Sophia's nan had told Sophia that even if she had wanted to go back home, which apparently she didn't, she wouldn't have been capable of looking after herself. Most days she was unable to cope with the simplest tasks: she even needed help getting herself dressed some mornings.

Pushing open her grandmother's little brown gate, Sophia heard the rusty hinges squeak noisily. She was shocked at how overgrown the once tidy and nurtured garden was; she was barely able to see the pathway through the overrun bushes and dense weeds.

Knocking on the door, she waited. She looked at the wooden panels, noticing that the thin strips of paint were cracked in places, flaking and peeling off. Just like the garden, the house looked neglected.

Keys jangled on the other side of the door. It slowly opened and Nessa stood there, leaning on a walking stick.

"Sophia, my love," Nessa cried out, overjoyed. "I've done nothing all day but stare at that bleeding clock, willing the hands to move so that you would get here quicker."

Sophia was shocked at her nan's frail appearance. She knew that she had been ill, as she hadn't been able to visit for the past month, but seeing her with a walking stick made her suddenly look every minute of her age. As frail as she was, she had a big smile plastered across her face. "Come here to your old nan," Nessa said, as she stretched out an arm and pulled her granddaughter in close.

"Nan," Sophia cried, feeling both a belated relief at being home and a great sadness at everything that she had missed wash over her simultaneously. "Oh Nan, Nan... I've missed you so much."

She hugged her nan tightly. Finally, after eight long years, she was home.

Chapter Twenty-Four

"Finish up your vegetables, darling, or you won't grow big and strong." Bernie smiled at her little granddaughter, who had placed her cutlery down on her plate and was using her hands to make faces in the gravy with her peas.

"I don't need vegetables, Granny. I'm already big and strong, aren't I, Daddy?" Rosie said, as she folded her arms in front of her chest, to signify that she wouldn't be eating any more of her granny's horrible dinner.

Jonathan nodded his head; Rosie was a chip off the old block. There was nothing anyone could make the kid say or do if she didn't want to. Jonathan loved that about her.

"Of course you are, darling." Bernie rolled her eyes playfully in her son's direction, amused as always that seven-year-old Rosie was so headstrong.

Stanley continued to eat in silence. Lately, his blood had been boiling at what he had let go on under his own roof. He was furious with himself for going along with everything for so long, complying with his wife just to keep the peace: and for what? So that the golden boy could live with them rent-free under their roof forever, while Bernie fell over herself to accommodate him and his ungrateful child.

Clenching his fists around his cutlery, he was still fuming from what had happened with the paint and the bird the day before. It was yet more mayhem that Rosie had caused that had been once again downplayed, treated as if it was just a joke. But it wasn't funny, not to him. Just because Bernie was now happy that the situation had played out to her advantage, now they had no choice but to get some decorators in and to purchase a new carpet, it was as if everything was fine. It was like Rosie's trashing of their home had done them all some kind of a favour. Once again the child could do no wrong.

"I don't have to eat it if I don't want to, do I, Daddy?" Rosie asked her father, knowing that he would agree with her. Her daddy did that a lot, especially if it was in response to something her granny had suggested. Sometimes Rosie thought that her daddy enjoyed winding her granny up.

"Not if you're full up, Rosie, no," Jonathan said, ignoring his mother's attempt to make eye contact; he knew how much his spoiling of the child irked his mother and father, but he also knew that his mum would never say a word against his parenting skills. She had been made aware long ago that any interfering from her would jeopardise their living arrangements and Bernie loved having her granddaughter and son living with her far too much to risk that.

Stanley continued spooning big mouthfuls of food into his mouth so that he wouldn't have to talk. The atmosphere in the room was so dense that it could have been cut with a knife.

"Grandad, are you still sad about yesterday?" Rosie asked, realising he hadn't said a word to her since then. "I did say I was sorry, didn't I Granny?"

"Of course he's not angry, Rosie darling," Bernie quickly answered, hoping to appease the girl before Stanley kicked off with any of his stubborn opinions again. "Grandad's just got a bit of a headache, that's all. He loves you very much."

Stanley stared at his granddaughter blankly. He had tried so hard to bond with her, but he couldn't do it. Sometimes he felt so guilty about the fact that he didn't even like her, let alone feel any form of love for her, he was convinced he'd be sent straight to hell when he died. She was just a little kid, but no matter how much he tried he just couldn't be happy about her existence. He couldn't see any purity in her, just as he had never been able to see it in Jonathan. The pair of them both knew exactly how to manipulate everyone around them.

"Hmm," Stanley grunted, unconvincingly, when he saw from his family's stares that a reaction was called for.

Rosie knew that her grandad didn't love her; she could tell by the way he looked at her. He wasn't nice to her like Daddy and Granny. She didn't like him much either.

"Poor Grandad," Rosie said. Batting her eyelashes in pretend virtue, she flashed her grandad a smile that didn't reach her eyes.

Grinning at the girl, Bernie glared at her husband who was ignoring the child's kind words. If a seven year old could make an attempt at an apology, then the least he could do was make a bit of effort for once.

Stanley glared back at his wife. Rosie was exactly like her father. The only thing that the child seemed to have inherited from her mother was the red curly hair that swept down past her shoulders. The rest was all Jonathan, from the pale skin that was so clear it was almost translucent to the dark beady eyes. Even the cold personality the child possessed was the same as her father's.

Stanley scraped up the last bits of gravy and mash with his fork, ignoring both his wife's and his grandchild's stares.

"Are you going to work tonight, Daddy?" Rosie asked, after realising that she wasn't going to get the reaction that she had hoped for from her granddad.

"Yes, Rosie, I am," Jonathan said, as he leaned back in the chair and burped loudly.

"Jonathan," Bernie scolded, and then grinned once she saw Rosie laugh at her dad getting told off.

"I've got to leave now, actually. The office called earlier. They want me to get the site ready to go live tonight. Place is manic, so it's probably going to be a late one again. You'll give Rosie her bath and story tonight won't you, Mum?" Jonathan knew the answer. Of course his mother would look after Rosie: she lived for the girl.

"Yes, love, of course." Bernie smiled. Knowing how hard he worked, she was only too happy to help him out. Ever since Rosie had come along, she felt that she and Jonathan had got closer. He didn't say it, but she was sure that he appreciated her helping him to raise his daughter. It was a tough decision that the boy had made when he had found out that he was going to be a father at sixteen years old. But Jonathan had embraced his responsibilities like a man despite all the scandal that surrounded them. Bernie had been beside herself when she had first found out that she was going to be a grandmother at such a young age and she hated the thought of all the local gossips sniggering behind her back at her son becoming a father when he was really still just a child himself. But then she had met her granddaughter. Rosie was a blessing who had brought nothing but joy into her life. Yes she could be naughty from time to time, but what child wasn't? Bernie's only regret was that Tommy hadn't met his niece. The situation with Jonathan and Sophia had left him heartbroken. Bernie knew that Tommy had liked the girl but she hadn't realised just how much; even with the stuff that was being written in the papers about the murder, Tommy wouldn't hear a bad word said against her. He fought tooth and nail to get a visiting order to see her, and had been devastated when she refused his requests. He hadn't been able to understand why she didn't want to see him, but it hadn't taken long for him to find out. When Jonathan was contacted by social services and told that he was a father, hc had admitted to Tommy that he had had a secret relationship with Sophia. The news that they were having a baby left Tommy looking as though he had had the air kicked out of him. He was totally devastated. Jonathan hadn't exactly broken the news to him tactfully either, from what Bernie remembered. Stanley had dragged the two boys apart when they had fought, dragging each other around the lounge as Tommy had so uncharacteristically lashed out at his brother. Tommy had left home that night. Bernie had begged him not to go, he was only sixteen and he had nowhere to live. But he had been resolute, and after packing his bags in complete silence he had left. Bernie had imagined that time would heal the rift between the boys, Sophia was just a girl, and she had played them off against each other. She wasn't worth falling out over: blood was thicker than water. But time hadn't made any difference to the situation. In fact, as the years had passed the rift between the boys had only increased. Tommy had moved down to Brighton and had managed to find himself a job. Bernie had waited for him to come home, but he never had. Over the years, on the occasional times that he rang home the conversations were short and tense and he never once mentioned his brother or Rosie. But Bernie still lived in hope, believing that one day Tommy would see sense and come home, and once he met Rosie he would love her too. She was sure of it.

"Bit late to be going in to the office, isn't it?" Stanley asked, as he glanced at the clock.

"You know I work all hours," Jonathan said. His father was always quizzing him about his job, and Jonathan was bored of him fishing for information.

"Last week he left here at almost midnight, didn't you love," Bernie said, adding: "dedicated to the job, aren't you?"

"Isn't he just," Stanley muttered. Whatever it was that Jonathan did as a job, he'd put money on it that it wasn't IT, as Jonathan had led them to believe. He was so secretive about where he worked that Stanley suspected he was up to no good.

"Can you read me my bedtime story, please, Grandad?" Rosie asked. She saw him tense at her question.

"Yes, go on, Stanley," Bernie encouraged. "Rosie would love a story from her old grandad. I'll make you both some hot chocolate, with marshmallows on top; just how you like it, Rosie..."

"No," Stanley said abruptly. "Granny will have to read it for you tonight, Rosie. Grandad has got work to do out in his shed."

Stanley felt Jonathan's eyes boring into him, but he no longer cared if he pissed off his son, nor his wife. He had finished pretending. He would sooner go and eat worms in the garden than sit with that spoilt little madam and read her anything.

Getting up from his chair, Stanley went to the kitchen, putting his plate loudly on to the worktop. He slammed the cupboards, to let the whole house know that he was thoroughly pissed off. He had had enough of his wife's pandering to their son and granddaughter. Things around here were going to change and he was going to make sure of it. Stanley was the head of this household, and it was about time everyone remembered it.

Chapter Twenty-Five

Tommy's house drew Sophia in like a magnet. Before she knew where she was walking to, she was standing at the entrance of the driveway.

Her nan's friend, Albert, had popped over earlier with a lemon drizzle cake that he had baked to celebrate her release, and after a lovely dinner that Sophia had cooked, using what she had learned on her course in prison, and a big slice of Albert's cake, she had made her excuses and left them alone together. She had felt like she was intruding on their time together. She had listened politely as they had made conversation at the dinner table, but she hadn't known which neighbours, or soap-opera characters, they were talking about. She felt so out of the loop. Her nan hadn't even told her about poor Rascal passing away until now. This past month Sophia had believed her nan when she said that she was too ill to come and see her, but she hadn't been ill. She had been sitting at home, beside herself with grief at the loss of her little companion. Unwilling to upset Sophia so close to her release date, Nessa had waited for the right time to tell her. It was strange to be around people who cared about her so much, yet at the same time, to still feel so alone. Sophia had waited until after the meal and then told them that she needed some fresh air, hoping that pounding the pavement would do her good. But as she had wandered around in what soon felt like circles in the neighbourhood that she had grown up in, she felt more lost and alone than ever. Everything around her was so familiar yet so alien.

Standing on the driveway, she tried to pluck up the courage to walk down it and knock on the door. Just as she was about to she spotted somebody moving around on the other side of the glass panel. Quickly hiding in the perfectly trimmed bushes that lined the garden, she stood as still as a statue and watched.

She was barely able to breathe as the figure closed the door behind him and walked casually up the driveway. Her hope faded as she realised it was Jonathan: he may be Tommy's twin but his steely look and the unchanged irritated expression were the give-away. Sophia hadn't expected Jonathan to have changed so much. She still imagined him to look as he had the last time she had seen him at sixteen: Tommy too. But time would have changed them all: even her, she guessed: especially her.

Sophia felt resentful as she saw him swinging a briefcase, as if he didn't have a care in the world, before getting into a smart-looking Saab. He admired himself in the interior mirror, combing his fingers through his hair.

Despite the years that had passed, even from a distance Sophia saw the same bitter coldness seep out of Jonathan. Her thoughts turned to Tommy, as they did so often. He may look like Jonathan did now; but although his height and good looks may be equal to those of his brother, Tommy would have that twinkle in his eye that she remembered so well. His eyes had sparkled whenever they looked at her, and he had had a softness that Jonathan didn't possess.

Watching as Jonathan pulled out of the driveway, Sophia remained concealed by the foliage. The house looked as immaculate as she remembered. The windows sparkled they were so clean, and the garden had not so much as a blade of grass out of place. Pink and purple flowers filled big tubs outside the front door. And Sophia noted that another expensive-looking car was parked on the driveway.

Maybe it was Tommy's.

She thought about her daughter: was she inside that house at that moment? Whilst incarcerated, the only information on her had been from the social workers. She had been shown photos of the girl when she was a baby but had found it too hard to look at her; the last time she had seen a picture of the child she must have been barely eighteen months old. Rosie, they had called her, named after Jonathan and Tommy's dead grandmother. The social workers said she was doing well, but Sophia had shown no interest and asked no questions. She didn't want to know anything. There was no point, and it would only cause her pain.

Sophia imagined that the little girl would be happy living somewhere like this; she couldn't imagine how any child wouldn't be. She would never have been able to offer her a lifestyle like this, and this was especially the case now. When Rosie was born, all she could have offered was a cot in the baby unit of the prison alongside junkies and murderers. She pitied the poor innocent babies confined inside four walls, with wrought-iron bars on every window separating them from the world outside. Prison was no place for a child.

Wrapping her cardigan around herself as she felt a chill penetrate her, she looked up as a light went on behind the curtains of the bedroom at the front of the house.

***

"And so, the little fairy flew all the way home to tell her friends the exciting news and they all lived happily ever after," Bernie said softly. She had missed out the last few pages of the story, hoping that the child wouldn't notice, before placing the book down gently on the bedside table. The soaps were starting and she couldn't wait to just put her feet up and enjoy a nice cup of tea.

"Can you read it again, Nanny?" Rosie sat bolt upright in her bed, her teddy tucked tightly under her arm. Up until then she had had her eyes tightly closed as she had lulled her gran into the false pretence that she had finally gone to sleep.

"You've had three stories tonight already." Bernie kissed Rosie on the top of her head before standing up. The tiny box room that had used to be Stanley's office had been a perfect nursery. But with the myriad teddies and dollies that had accumulated over the years, mostly bought by Bernie, the room felt cramped. She knew that she was spoiling her granddaughter, but she couldn't help herself. She wanted to give Rosie everything. The poor child had had such an unfortunate start to her life that Bernie found it hard to say no to anything the girl asked for.

"Please, Nanny, just one more," Rosie begged. She was bored of her books, they were the same stories that she had read to her every single night, but as she knew that her granny wanted to go and watch her TV programmes Rosie was doing her utmost to be difficult.

Sighing, Bernie felt that she couldn't refuse the girl. Having bathed her and put her into her pink striped pyjamas, with her hair in bunches, Rosie looked so angelic lying there cuddling her teddy. And she probably missed her dad too, Bernie thought; one more story wouldn't hurt.

Settling back on the bed, Bernie smiled.

"Just one more, though, and then Granny is going to go downstairs," Bernie said, hoping that this last story would succeed in making the child sleep.

"Thank you, Granny," Rosie said sweetly.

The doorbell chimed, interrupting Bernie while she was on the first page of the book.

"Stanley, get that," Bernie called, hoping that her husband could hear her over the TV. She would swear he was going deaf the way he had it blaring lately. And she wouldn't mind but half the time it was when he was watching football. She didn't see the point of all that noise just to watch a bunch of men running around on a pitch kicking a ball. "If that's Shirley, tell her that the Avon catalogue is out on the side by the kettle. I'll be down in a minute."

Downstairs, Stanley grabbed the catalogue from the kitchen and went to open the door. His wife's best friend Shirley was a pain in the arse. Thinking nothing of imposing herself on them whenever it suited her, she often popped in unannounced for a quick cup of tea whilst out on her Avon rounds. Often a 'quick' cup of tea, which she would ask for as she came into the house, was code for staying the whole evening and offloading her problems on to Bernie while she drank copious amounts of tea and helped herself to Stanley's favourite biscuits: as this took place in the living room, he couldn't even watch football at the same time.

Well, it wasn't bloody well happening tonight. If Shirley thought for a second that he was going to invite her in at just gone nine o'clock in the evening, she could bloody well think again, he thought to himself. Like everyone else round here, she was going to get a wakeup call.

Pulling open the door, Stanley prepared himself to be assertive and tell the impertinent woman exactly where to go.

"Hello, Mr Jenkins," Sophia said timidly. As soon as her eyes locked with Tommy's dad's she felt like crying. Stanley had been ever so nice to her all those years ago, and Tommy loved him dearly. It pained her to think that Stanley probably hated the sight of her now.

Staring back at the beautiful girl standing on his doorstep, Stanley took a deep breath. It was a shock to see her. Her bright red hair and perfect skin were exactly the same. Sophia O'Hagan may have spent the past eight years locked away in prison, but time had barely changed her appearance, whatever it had done to her mind. "What are you doing here?" Stanley whispered, as he tried to gather himself. If Bernie knew that Sophia was on their doorstep she would hit the roof at the girl's audacity. As far as he was aware no-one knew that Sophia was out, or at least no-one had mentioned it to him. "You're out already?"

Ever since they had gained full custody of Rosie, the girl's mother hadn't been mentioned again in his house, let alone been given another thought by Stanley. Sophia nodded, overwhelmed by emotions. "I'm sorry; I don't know why I came here. I guess I just thought that Tommy..." she was unable to finish her sentence.

Just looking at Stanley's face and seeing the hate and fear in his eyes made Sophia feel even worse that she had done before she left her nan's house that evening. And she couldn't blame him. Like everyone else around in their area, he would have believed everything that he had read in the papers about her murdering her father. The dislike that he felt for her was all too plain to see. Mr Jenkins was a good man, and Sophia wanted more than anything to explain her innocence to him, so that he would be able to convince Tommy, but she had a feeling that he wouldn't believe her even if she did try.

"I'm sorry. I shouldn't have come here," Sophia said again.

"No, you shouldn't have," Stanley said quietly. He couldn't understand how this girl had so cold-heartedly murdered her own father. She has seemed such a nice, decent girl when she had been going out with Tommy.

"I just wanted to see Tommy," Sophia said, feeling foolish. It had been years since she had last seen him, yet she thought of him all the time. Apart from her nan, Tommy was what got her through each day. She just wanted the chance to explain.

"Tommy's gone. You and Jonathan destroyed that boy: broke his heart. He left because he found out about Rosie."

Sophia stared at Stanley; she was unsure of what he meant. Surely none of them blamed her for what Jonathan had done to her?

"Now if you don't mind, I'd be grateful if you left. We don't want you coming here again," Stanley said forcefully as he began to close the door in Sophia's face.

"Wait." Sophia put her hand out, stopping the door from closing. "Please... I know I should have explained to him myself, but it was all too raw. I knew he'd be hurt, but I didn't think he'd blame me..."

Sophia knew that Tommy wouldn't have believed that she had murdered her father. But finding out about the baby would have been too much for him, she more than anyone could understand that.

Losing Tommy was her biggest regret. She should have seen him when he had made one of his visiting requests. She had wanted to explain, to tell him what had happened, but it had been so painful, and after they took Rosie away Sophia had felt too detached from other people to try to make a connection: no-one seemed able to empathise with her, or believe what she said, and reaching out was too difficult.

"Why wouldn't he blame you? You cheated on him with his own brother behind his back: Jonathan told us all about it. I have to say, I expect that kind of thing from him, but you seemed like such a nice girl. But then I guess nice girls don't cheat on their boyfriends, nor murder their fathers in cold blood." Stanley remembered how devastated Tommy had been when Jonathan had told him that he had been having a relationship with Sophia behind his back. "The boy was beside himself when Jonathan told him. How could you?"

"What? That isn't..." Sophia stuttered.

Stanley clenched his fists as he relived the scene in his mind: it felt like it had happened yesterday. "You both broke Tommy's heart."

Sophia was silent for a few seconds while she tried to take in what she was hearing.

"Jonathan was lying. I promise you, I would never have done anything to hurt Tommy."

"Oh please, Sophia." Stanley waved his hand as if to shut Sophia up.

"I swear, Mr Jenkins, on my nan's life. I never even so much as looked at Jonathan that way, ever!" Sophia felt her body shake; she could only imagine the hurt that Jonathan had caused Tommy to feel if that was what he truly believed.

"So where did Rosie come from then?" Stanley asked, his voice rising in anger. Sophia must think he was born yesterday. "Dropped from a bloody stork, was she?"

"Please, Mr Jenkins, I know you won't believe me but please listen. Jonathan tricked me. The night of my party, I was drunk and Jonathan pretended that he was Tommy... I didn't know that it was him that I slept with... I don't know how he could have done it, but I know that Jonathan hated me and Tommy being together. I know he's your son, but he was jealous of us. He tore us apart." Sophia needed Stanley to believe her, in the past eight years everything in her life had been built around lies. Even she was having trouble knowing what was real, but she had no doubt that everything that Jonathan had told his family was untrue.

"You?" Bernie came hurtling down the stairs, interrupting Sophia's plea. She had recognised the girl's voice and prayed that she was hearing things. But seeing the familiar red hair confirmed what Bernie had been dreading for all these years. Sophia was out: what if she wanted Rosie? Panic spread through her at the thought of their precious Rosie being taken away from them.

"What the hell are you playing at, coming around here?" she asked through gritted teeth, aware that Rosie was awake upstairs in her room. "You have no right coming round here and upsetting everyone. You gave up all your rights years ago: you shouldn't be here."

"I'm so sorry. No, I shouldn't have come. Please forgive me," Sophia said, as tears stung the back of her eyes. She thought about trying to tell the truth again but if Stanley didn't believe her, it seemed unlikely that Bernie would.

Then she remembered why she had come.

"I just wanted to see Tommy." Sophia's voice sounded small.

"Oh, you want Tommy now, do you?" Bernie sneered. "What the hell are you playing at? You need to make your mind up about which one of those boys it is you're after. I should have known that you were nothing but a brazen little hussy, leading both my boys on like that. I should never have let you through my front door, let alone welcomed you and given you a birthday party."

Sophia O'Hagan may have been imprisoned for murder, but Bernie wasn't scared of her. If she thought for one second that she was going to start coming around here and throwing Rosie's life into chaos then she had another think coming. She had spent years sheltering Rosie from the truth about her mother, Jonathan had told the girl on the few occasions that she had asked that her mother wasn't very well and was being looked after very far away in a special place and Bernie couldn't have put it better herself. Sophia was sick. Thankfully, Rosie had just accepted the story while Bernie had eagerly stepped into the role of her mother. It wasn't fair that Sophia had turned up unannounced on the doorstep like this.

"You'd better go," Stanley said coldly, for once agreeing with his wife.

"I'm so sorry; I didn't mean to cause any trouble. I'll go. Can you please just tell him that I came to see him?" Sophia cried. She had only wanted to make it right with Tommy, to explain what had happened. If only she hadn't been so stubborn in refusing his visitation requests all those years ago, she wouldn't be in such a mess. She was sure that if she could speak to him, she could make him understand.

"Tommy's not here," Bernie shouted, incredulous at the boldness of the girl who was standing there sobbing. Bernie had heard enough. "You heard my husband, now bugger off. You're nothing but a filthy little whore."

Bernie picked up Stanley's large golfing umbrella from behind the door and swung it at Sophia, stabbing the air and causing her to leap backwards. Sophia ducked to avoid getting hit, and losing her footing tripped over. Landing on the block paving, she felt humiliated as Tommy's parents stood over her like she was vermin.

"Granny," called a small voice from the stairway behind Stanley, "why are you shouting?"

Rosie came down the stairs to see her grandparents standing on the doorstep and looking at the woman picking herself up off the ground in front of the porch. Seeing the confused look on the young girl's face broke Bernie's heart in two.

"Go back to bed, darling; Granny will be up in a minute. I'll read you another story."

Seeing Rosie ignoring her and making her way to the doorway Bernie lowered the umbrella and turned back to Sophia, begging her this time, "Please just go."

But it was too late. Rosie had locked eyes with Sophia.

"Please go," Bernie pleaded again. Jonathan would go berserk if he found out that Sophia had come to the house and seen Rosie. If Sophia went away now, then Bernie could try and make something up so that Rosie wouldn't find out the truth.

Sophia picked herself up off the ground, panicking about the situation she had caused. Her being here would probably cause a lot of upset for her daughter. Stunned, as she stared at the girl, she couldn't help but drink in her features: the mass of curly red hair was so like hers whereas the cold steely eyes that stared back at her were Jonathan's.

"Are you my mummy? I've seen your picture in the newspapers that my daddy keeps in his drawer. He said that you're not well. Am I going to live in the hospital with you?" Rosie asked innocently, as she looked the woman before her up and down curiously.

"Go back inside, Rosie, it's late and you should be in bed. Go on: now," Bernie said.

Sophia rubbed her palms to rid them of the grit embedded in the flesh. "I'm so sorry; I shouldn't have come here.... I'm so sorry."

She scuttled away. She couldn't get away quickly enough from the child's accusing eyes, and the questions that she didn't know how to answer. Tears blurring her vision, she ran home.

Chapter Twenty-Six

"Well, I must say, Sophia, this doesn't look too bad, does it?" Andrea Parks smiled enthusiastically as she glanced around the small bedroom in the hostel as she tried to encourage Sophia that she would be making a good decision if she accepted it.

The room was far from a palace. The brown wallpaper had peeled off in places and the cream carpet had a large brown stain: God knows what had been spilled on it. However, although it wasn't somewhere she would personally want to live, Andrea knew of much worse places that ex-offenders had stayed upon their release.

"It's not so bad, I suppose." Sophia shrugged. She noted that the tiny room had about the same dimensions as the prison cell that she had just vacated, but it was only temporary. Just a place to lay her head and get her paperwork sent while she got back on her feet. Andrea was right: it would do.

Relieved that Sophia seemed to have accepted the room, Andrea opened up the wardrobe doors to check that nothing had been left by the previous tenant. Sophia seemed like a sweet girl and despite the report that Andrea had read on the young woman's list of convictions, she couldn't help but find herself liking her. Her crime seemed beyond what she was capable of, but then Andrea had reasoned to herself that you never really knew what went on in people's heads or what had happened to them in the past. In her line of work she had seen all sorts. But nevertheless, on the few occasions that they had met so far Sophia had always treated her with the utmost respect, and even more importantly than that the girl seemed to have self-respect: which in Andrea's job was a very rare trait to find in a service user. She could tell that Sophia wanted to turn her life around, and because of that she was happy to assist her. She felt drawn to the girl, almost to the point of going above and beyond her duties to make sure that she could help Sophia to get the best start possible for herself.

This place had become available last night, and with Andrea's contacts she had been able to get Sophia in and show her around before anyone else was able to look at it.

Sophia watched her parole officer pull open each drawer in the large chest of drawers. Sophia wasn't bothered about the amount of storage the place had. As long as she had a bed to lie down in each night, she would be happy. She didn't intend on spending much quality time here, that was for sure.

It was nice that Andrea cared about where Sophia lived, though. She had come up trumps for her so far. She also seemed nice enough, but Sophia was still having a hard time trusting anyone. She had learned during her time in prison to be cynical of everyone in a position of power: the mentality was very much authority versus us. The system had wronged her, and she would be a fool to let her guard down. So no matter how many times Andrea told her she had her best interests at heart, Sophia just couldn't let herself entirely believe it. It would have been a lot easier not to like the woman if she hadn't turned out to be so damn nice, Sophia thought to herself.

Andrea's gentle nature and soft voice had thrown Sophia off guard when she had met her last week on the first home visit. Sophia had felt nervous as she had sat with her nan and awaited her parole officer's arrival. Expecting to meet some disciplinarian sent by the prison service to come marching in, enforcing their many rules and regulations, while looking at her like she was worthless scum,

Sophia had been totally thrown by Andrea's easy-going and supportive nature. Seemingly eager to help Sophia get back on her feet, Andrea seemed genuine with her offer of support and had won Sophia's nan over in seconds, which was no mean feat.

And now, just a week later, Andrea had shown to her that she meant it when she had promised to help her. This place was proof of that.

"And the best part is you're close to your nan's house," Andrea said, knowing that Sophia's main priority was to be near Nessa; it had been clear from the very start that she meant the world to her. "I know it's only about five minutes' walk if I go via the old footbridge over the Lea."

Sophia would have stayed at her nan's house permanently if she had had the choice and Nessa would have been only too happy to have the girl do so. But there was only one bedroom, and Sophia hadn't wanted to impose any more than she already had. This was the second-best option. This place was perfect, really, and being only a few streets away from her nan meant that she could still pop round each day and check on her.

"And remember, it's not forever, is it," Andrea said animatedly, making notes on a pad. "At least now you have an address, you can start looking for a job. This is a great opportunity, Sophia. I just hope you won't get too lonely, but you don't seem the type."

Sophia nodded in agreement. She was glad of the solitude that the room would provide. She was used to being on her own, and the noise in the outside world – the traffic, the people – seemed over-loud. Prison had left her feeling isolated but it was what she had become used to. At least now she would have somewhere to go to on her own if things got too tough for her.

"So will one be checking in, madam?" Andrea laughed as she watched Sophia sit on the bed and bounce up and down, testing the mattress.

"I think this place will do me nicely."

"Right then, let's go and get this paperwork sorted out and get you the keys." Andrea grinned to herself as she led the way, pleased that Sophia seemed happy. Everyone had the right to a new start, but Andrea had a feeling that Sophia deserved it more than most people.

Chapter Twenty-Seven

"Are you sure you don't want to come in with me, Nan?" Sophia asked, secretly hoping that her nan would change her mind. She felt suddenly nervous at the thought of seeing her mother again after all this time.

Sandie, her mother's care-worker, had already informed Sophia of her mother's fragile state of mind when she had arrived for the visit. Kaitlin suffered from chronic depression, although there were good days and bad days. Sitting here now in the day room with her nan as she waited to go through to see her mother after all this time, Sophia prayed that today would be one of the good ones.

Her nan had finally come clean to her last night, as with the imminent visit Nessa knew that she couldn't go on lying to Sophia. Kaitlin was a lot worse than Sophia had been led to believe when she was in prison.

Sophia had known that her mother was unwell; her nan had told her a number of times that her mother was too ill to visit the prison. Suffering with her nerves, her nan had said at the time. Knowing the trauma that her mother had experienced, Sophia could understand that.

But last night Nessa had told Sophia the truth, that her mother had suffered a nervous breakdown. Sophia wasn't angry; she knew that her nan had not wanted to worry her. It wasn't as if she had lied, because Sophia had known that her mum was ill, it was just that her nan had played down just how ill she really was.

Looking at some of the other residents who were sitting on the opposite side of the room, staring vacantly at the TV screen, one of them being spoon-fed by a carer, it dawned on Sophia how unwell her mum actually was to be here.

"Oh no, my dearie." Nessa squeezed Sophia's hand reassuringly before sitting on a sofa. "You go and see your mum on your own. It's been a long time; you two have a lot of catching up to do. Besides, I see her so often that she's probably sick to death at looking at my wrinkly old face."

Nessa busied herself with the magazines that were on a nearby table. She knew that Sophia wanted her for moral support but she really felt the girl needed to face her mother on her own. It had been years since Kaitlin had seen her daughter. And Nessa prayed to God that at least now, in her own safe environment, Kaitlin might be at last able to handle seeing Sophia without it tipping her over the edge.

"Come on, Sophia, follow me. You'll be just fine." Sandie spoke in a gentle manner and flashed Sophia an encouraging smile as she led the way down the hallway.

The place seemed nice, much warmer and friendlier than Sophia had imagined. She could see that the place was taken care of: vases of flowers were placed on the windowsills and everywhere smelled fresh and clean.

Reaching the door of Kaitlin's room Sandie turned and faced Sophia, her voice almost a whisper as she said: "Remember what we spoke about; try to keep the conversation light for today, and let's just see how she reacts to your first visit before we push her. There'll be plenty of time to talk things through properly later. She's still very fragile."

Sophia nodded in agreement, but Sandie's words stung. As tactful as she was being, Sophia picked up on the hint that her presence might affect her mum in a negative way. Again she questioned whether she would be welcome, whether she should have come, but there was no time to change her mind now.

Knocking on the door before opening it and putting her head around it, Sandie announced: "Hello, Kaitlin, your daughter's here to see you. Remember I told you earlier that she was coming? Would you like me to get you some tea?"

Sophia walked in behind Sandie and tried to hide her shock. Her mother was sitting in one of the chairs by the window. Sophia walked slowly across, trying not to stare as she took in her mother's emaciated physique. There was nothing to her, she was skin and bones. She was wearing an ill-fitting floral dress that swamped her frame and sat just below her knees, failing to disguise the bones that were jutting out of her, protruding through her pale skin.

"Yes, thanks, some tea would be nice," Sophia answered, feeling embarrassed that her mother had ignored the question. She just sat there staring blankly at Sophia.

Sophia wasn't sure what she had expected: a hug, some tears maybe... but there was nothing. No reaction whatsoever.

"Oh, Mum, it's so good to see you," Sophia said, as she sat in the chair opposite her mum. She could feel her mum's eyes burning through her as she quickly picked up on her negative vibes. Her mum seemed cold towards her. "It looks nice here, Mum, and Sandie seems like a lovely lady. Are you being well looked after?"

Sophia babbled away without a clue as to what she was going to say next. There was so much that she wanted to discuss, so many words that had been left unspoken for so long, but Sophia knew that now wasn't the right time for her to say them. Sandie had told her that had mum had been making great progress, and Sophia didn't want to jeopardise all the hard work by saying something that would affect her mum's fragile state. Kaitlin continued to stare without responding. Sophia frowned, she had heard of places that dosed their patients up with so many medications that they didn't know what month it was, let alone what day. Sophia glanced nervously around the small room. It was cold and clinical and gave no indication of the personality of its occupant. The only thing that broke up the stark whiteness was the brightly coloured pieces of paper that had been stuck on the walls above her mother's bed, all featuring the same abstract red and yellow designs; they looked the kind of thing that a primary-school child may produce.

"Did you do those, Mum?" Sophia asked, pointing at the pictures. Her mother nodded, but her eyes remained glazed.

"They're lovely. Do you do a lot of art here?" Sophia was desperately trying to get her mum to engage in a conversation with her. "We did art classes in pris... when I was away."

Sophia was finding it hard to keep the conversation light: how could she be expected to sit here and pretend that nothing had happened? Both their lives had been ripped apart. Her mother was mentally ill, and she had spent eight years locked up for a crime that she didn't commit. There was so much that needed to be said.

"When you were away?" Kaitlin asked, in a deadpan tone, as she finally found her voice. "Oh yes, that's right, how was your holiday?"

Sophia shuffled in her seat. Holiday? Is that what her mother told herself to help her deal with it? Or was that what someone had told her? "It was... great, Mum; just great."

Sophia wasn't sure she could do this. She felt a hard lump forming in the back of her throat. All she wanted to do was pull her mother close and shake her. She wanted to beg and plead with her to believe in her innocence. She hadn't killed her father, and she wanted more than anything else on Earth for her mother to acknowledge that.

The door opened and Sandie came in.

"Here we go, ladies, got a nice pot of tea here for you. Even threw in some of your favourite bickies, Kaitlin: some of those Garibaldis you like; I find them a bit dry myself."

Sandie beamed as she placed the tray on the table that sat between mother and daughter. Pleased that Kaitlin seemed to be coping okay with her visitor and was not obviously distressed, Sandie nodded to Sophia to check that she was okay before she left the two women alone once more.

Sophia struggled to control her shaking hands as she poured the tea into the cups. Her mother hadn't taken her eyes off her since she had walked in.

"You look different," Kaitlin said. Sophia was still young and beautiful. But the child that had left her was now a woman, and Kaitlin could see the hardened look in her eyes.

"Well, a lot of time has passed, Mum," Sophia said, smiling now that her mother seemed to be finally responding to her. She wanted to say that her mother looked well, but that would have been a lie.

"I told them all about you," Kaitlin said suddenly. "I spoke about nothing else but you when I first got brought in here. The counsellors told me that time would heal. That's a joke, isn't it? Look at the state of me. Picture of tranquillity, aren't I?"

Sophia froze.

"I didn't love Jamesie at the end, did you know that? I didn't need therapy to help me realise that, let me tell you. He treated me so badly, and then you. Is that why you did it?"

"Did what, Mum?" Sophia asked

"Murdered him."

Sophia felt her heart thumping in her chest. "Mum, I'm not sure we should speak about this: not now. There'll be time later..."

"Oh, really? And why's that; because it might upset me?" Kaitlin was whispering, leaning forward in her chair. "My husband was stabbed and left to bleed to death by my daughter, but oh no, don't speak about it. That's why I paint, you see. I can paint whatever I like and no-one can stop me. Beautiful, aren't they." Kaitlin nodded up to the red and yellow abstract streaks that boldly filled the numerous sheets of paper. "That's what I look at every-day, the flickering flames and Jamesie's blood."

Kaitlin began scratching her arms. Big red welts formed as she dug her nails in harder and deeper as she spoke.

"Please Mum..." Sophia tried to calm her mother.

"Please Mum? Don't you dare! Your father may have been many things, Sophia, but no-one deserves to die like that. Every time I close my eyes I see that man: every single time. He's haunting me. That's what you've done, Sophia, you've left me with a bloody ghost who won't leave me alone. He just sits here with me all day long, tormenting me with his sneering face."

Kaitlin began tapping her foot.

"They don't believe I can see him. They think I'm mad. But I'm not. He's here. Can't you see him, Sophia? He's right beside you." Kaitlin pointed to the air next to Sophia.

"There's no-one else here, Mum, it's just me and you."

"Oh, did they tell you to say that? Of course they did. They want me to think that I'm crazy. But I'm not, Sophia. I see him... I always see him. Look what you did to him, Sophia."

Kaitlin stared into space.

"Mum, I swear to you, I didn't do it. You have to believe me. On my life... on Nan's life."

"Stop lying to me; stop bloody lying." Leaping up, Kaitlin swept the tray that had held the tea and biscuits to the floor, sending boiling hot tea everywhere. Hot liquid splashed her legs, but Kaitlin couldn't feel the pain as the water scalded her. She hadn't been able to feel anything for a long time.

"Mum, please... just listen to me..." Sophia grabbed some napkins from the tray and awkwardly dabbed at the liquid on her mum's legs.

"Get out, get out," Kaitlin screamed as she pulled at her hair, ripping a clump out from the roots.

Sophia stared at her mum helplessly until Sandie came running through the door, just in time to stop Kaitlin from doing any further damage.

"You need to leave," Sandie ordered Sophia, as she stood between Sophia and Kaitlin. Holding Kaitlin's arms down by her side, Sandie tried to get Kaitlin to focus on her. Seeing the stern look on Sandie's face, Sophia did as she was told. Her legs felt like jelly as she walked away. Sobbing, she made her way back to the day room and ran into her nan's arms. Nessa soothed her granddaughter, telling her again and again that it was alright.

Sophia appreciated the words, but she knew that they weren't true. She should never have come. Her mother hated her: how was that alright?

Chapter Twenty-Eight

Whistling as he walked, Roache made his way to Dolly's cell. It was her last night so he wanted to ensure that she ended her stay with one great big bang.

Roache had thoroughly enjoyed the time that he had spent supervising Dolly's wing, taking his opportunity to have sex with the girl morning, noon and night. Dolly had been an exceptional fuck. Her tiny twenty-three year old body was tight and perky in all the right places, which made a nice change from the usual frumpy bitches that took residence here in Holloway. Dolly was definitely the cream of the crop in comparison to the other women he had had in here with their jellified bodies, poor hygiene and personalities that would give some of the roughest men he knew a run for their money. Dolly, however, was sweet.

Checking the corridor before he entered her cell, Roache felt himself getting hard at the thought of her hot little lips around his cock.

"You alright, Doll?" Roache locked the door behind him and pulled out three miniature bottles of vodka and a bar of Galaxy chocolate. Slinging them down on to the bed next to Dolly, he grinned as if he had presented her with winnings from the National Lottery.

"Thought you might like a treat tonight, celebrate the end of our beautiful friendship," Roache leered as he looked Dolly up and down. With her hair in plaits and no make-up on she looked ridiculously young and vulnerable. The stiffness in his trousers was becoming uncomfortable. He unzipped his fly, before picking up one of the bottles.

"Here, get that down you," he said, as he unscrewed the lid and passed her the tiny bottle. "You need to loosen up a bit, girl. I wouldn't have guessed by that look on your moosh that you were getting out of here tomorrow. What's the matter with you?"

Roache knew what the matter was: Dolly hated that he had made her satisfy him one way or another every single day that he had been on shift ever since they had started this little arrangement. Whenever she got a bit gobby about it or refused to go along with what he wanted, he threatened her with telling Trevor. She did as she was told once she was reminded of the life that was waiting for her outside. Once a whore, always a whore, Roache thought. Getting into trouble with Trevor was more than her life was worth.

Smiling again, he watched her ignore his question as she obediently tipped her head back. She swallowed one of the vodka miniatures in one big gulp. As she did so, her small but perfectly rounded breasts jiggled beneath her grey T-shirt. Feeling his cock stir for her once more as he realised she had no bra on, he started his usual routine of playing with himself before thrusting himself into her mouth. Dolly moved her lips move expertly up and down the shaft, just getting on with it instead of making her usual show of resistance. It didn't bother him either way. If she started making any noise about his advances it just added to his pleasure when he finally forced her to do what he wanted. He got off on making her sore, enjoying that he could be so rough with the girl. Sometimes the little bitches needed reminding who was in control.

Grabbing Dolly's head, he considered that it was a shame that her sentence had been so short, he was going to miss her. This was a new feeling for him, as he usually felt nothing but contempt for the women in prison; he used them for his own pleasure but they left him feeling dirty, mainly because if they were on the outside he wouldn't have looked at them twice. Dolly was different, she was lovely to look at and not only was she able to satisfy him in just minutes, but she always left him wanting more.

Feeling his loins tingle, he tried not to come as he wanted her to pleasure him for as long as possible. He wanted her to work at it tonight; a few more minutes of this and he was going to flip her over and give her the hardest fuck of her life.

God, he loved his job.

Looking up at him with her puppy-dog eyes, Dolly stopped what she was doing and asked him in a girly voice if it was okay. Hearing this eagerness, Roache almost lost control.

"Yeah... Keep going, suck me harder."

Dolly obliged. She had been waiting all day for Roache's visit. He had said that he wanted to make her last night special, and she was in no doubt that was exactly what it was going to be. Only it was her that was going to make it special for him.

Earlier today she had plucked up the courage to call Trevor; she knew he was going to go ape-shit on for her not phoning sooner, being the control freak that he was, but she was so angry that he had set up this arrangement with Roache that she had wanted to leave him to stew. Three weeks of avoiding all contact with him was stupid, though; he was going to be furious when he saw her tomorrow, and she had hoped that the fact that she had phoned him in the end might soften the blow somehow.

"Three fucking weeks, Dolly, in which I ain't heard jack shit from you," he had bellowed at the other end of the line as Dolly stood out in the main corridor with a row of prisoners lined up behind her as they waited their turn for the phone. "You think that just cos you're inside, you can ignore me? Do you think I'm some sort of a cunt? I've told you before: if you ain't with me, you call me. Every single fucking day. You belong to me."

"I haven't been ignoring you, Trevor; I had no money for a poxy phone-card, did I?"

They both knew Dolly's excuse was bullshit; she could have got some money to buy a phone-card from one of the other girls if she had really wanted to. And Dolly had only so boldly avoided him because she knew there was nothing he would be able to do about it. Trevor refused to go anywhere near prisons: he hated the places. The only time he came anywhere near was when he had to pick one of his girls up from the gate on her release, and even that was too close for comfort for him.

"Don't play games with me, girl," Trevor warned. "You've been taking the piss. What did you think, huh? That you were owed a fucking holiday or something?"

"Oh, please. It was hardly a holiday, was it, Trevor. You've had that bloody Roache up me like a frigging ferret every five minutes since I got here. I'll need a holiday when I get out."

"What the fuck are you talking about?"

"Oh cut the crap, Trevor. Roache said you owed him big time and I've spent the past three weeks paying your debt with fucking interest." Dolly had stopped caring if Trevor was angry: she had a grievance too. The last three weeks had been a nightmare. She had needed a few weeks away from her world, a few weeks of respite, before she got out and had to do it all over again: the same men, the same dirty fantasies, the same never-ending regime. But she couldn't even have that. Even in here, Trevor had seen to it that she paid her way. Roache had been a constant threat. And tomorrow, when she got out, Trevor was going to continue to be a complete arsehole too.

"Dolly darling, I don't know what the fuck you're talking about." Trevor racked his brains. "I don't know anyone by the name of Roache, let alone owe the fucker any debt."

Dolly felt her cheeks burn at the realisation that Roache had been having her over. She had endured three weeks of torment because of that man; three fucking weeks.

"What's his first name?" Trevor asked. His voice had turned cold again and Dolly recognised his mind reverting to business mode. Trevor was a nutcase, but a shrewd one. If Roache had set her up Trevor would see to it that, one way or another, he would pay.

"I only know him as Officer Roache; everyone in here calls him Cockroach."

"Well, do me, and yourself, a favour, yeah? Next time that cunt comes sniffing around tell him from me that he's in my fucking debt now. Tell him I charge a grand a week for your exclusivity, and I'll be adding a premium for his blatant fucking piss-taking. I ain't having no bent fucking screw trying to have one over on me. And I'll be seeing you at the gate tomorrow, so no funny business, you hear? You've got some making up to do."

Long after Trevor had put down the phone, Dolly stood holding it and thinking about what he had said, as the girls standing in the queue behind her shouted at her to let them have their turn. When Roache had mentioned Trevor's name, Dolly hadn't thought to question him. Why would she? Lots of people knew Trevor, and Roache was obviously bent. She had then done everything that man had made her do.

It was typical that Trevor considered that he was the one that had been made a fool of. Just the thought of all those things that she had done with Roache made her feel angry. She wasn't going to let him get away with it.

Now, Dolly had Roache where she wanted him, standing in her cell with his pants around his ankles, as she brought him to the height of pleasure. Dolly knew that she was giving him the best blow job of his life. She wanted him to remember it forever. Just a few moments of him letting her take control was all she needed.

Roache gripped Dolly harder. He wouldn't last more than a few more minutes if she carried on doing that with her mouth. He leaned his head back in ecstasy.

That was when Dolly bit down on his cock as hard as she could. He screamed in agony. Dolly clamped her teeth down harder, paying no heed to the popping sound that his penis made as it crunched between her teeth.

"You fucking bitch," he shouted, as he managed to throw Dolly off him with the little strength that he had left; in agony, he fell to the floor.

His last thought before he blacked out was that the fucking bitch had found out that he had lied to her about Trevor. However, Roache hadn't completely lied. He did know Trevor: everyone did. The way he lorded it above everyone at his local pub, it was difficult not to know who he was. Roache often went for a pint down at The Western Arms after he finished his shift. After a hard day's graft, it was often needed. He had been doing exactly that a few weeks ago, minding his own business as he had downed his well-earned pint. That was where he had first become aware of Trevor. It was hard to miss him: the guy wore so much jewellery, he looked like he had run through Goldsmiths and been hit by every cabinet. The bloke spoke loudly, too, putting on a show for everyone around him. When Trevor had piped up about some bird of his being holed up at Holloway, Roache had decided to get himself another drink while he listened in. Half-cut, Trevor spouted off to his cronies that he was narked because his best girl had been banged up for a few weeks and he was going to lose a shitload of money.

As soon as he mentioned Dolly's name Roache's ears had pricked up, remembering the new bird knocking about with old snooty knickers O'Hagan. Pretty little thing she was too, he recalled, as he sat at the end of the bar, staring at a newspaper, pretending to be absorbed in the news but taking in everything that was being said.

Trevor was a knob, as far as Roache was concerned. Cocky as you like, he was forever flashing his money about as if he was loaded; even if he was just getting a round in he would make a point of paying with a big wedge of notes from his back pocket, waving it around so that everyone knew how well he was doing. And he clearly was doing well, so little Dolly must be raking it in for him, Roache had thought. His best girl, was she? Roache had felt himself getting a boner just thinking about the power he would have over the dirty little mare if he could make her believe that Trevor had set up an arrangement whereby she would keep him satisfied during her stay. It would certainly make a nice change from getting noshed off by the usual munters in there.

It had been easy. He had a long, elaborate story all planned out, but as soon as he had mentioned Trevor's name to Dolly she had believed his words without so much as a question of doubt. All beauty and no brains, it turned out.

Now, as Roache rolled around the floor in pain, he wondered if it had been worth the agro: the stupid bitch had proved to be more trouble than she was worth.

Seeing Dolly make a run for the door, frantically twisting the key that was still sitting in the lock, Roache grabbed at her foot. She tripped and lost her balance, falling with an almighty thud. Whacking her face on the floor, she tasted blood as one of her front teeth pierced her lip. Feeling Roache twist the fabric of her jogging bottoms, as he grabbed onto her to stop her from escaping, she winced in pain as she tried to squirm out of his tight grip. Kicking out at him in a rage she managed to hit him straight in the face with the heel of her trainer.

Struggling to stand, Dolly dashed to the door as she wiped off the blood that spurted down her chin from the deep gouge in her throbbing lip, she glanced back at Roache to make sure he wasn't behind her.

As she watched the pained expression deepen on his face, and the blood all over the hand that was now covering his wounded manhood, Dolly was delighted. She hoped that after the weeks of torment that he had put her through that he hurt like a bitch.

"How's that for paying off a debt?" she asked, with feigned innocence. "Trevor says hi, by the way and I'm sure by now you've worked out that you're in a whole world of shit when he gets hold of you."

Dolly smiled sweetly before pressing the alarm on the cell wall and slamming the door shut as she left. Leaving him to squirm alone in agony, she prepared her tears for when the other officers came running. Roache had already made a name for himself as a bully and a womaniser. It wouldn't be the first time Cockroach had tried it on with one of the girls in here, but she was determined to make sure it was his last. Going by the state of him lying on the cell floor with his bleeding cock in his hand, there was no way that other officers would be able to turn a blind eye to his antics now.

Chapter Twenty-Nine

"Get in," Trevor growled, as he flung the back door open after watching Dolly totter over to the car in the same black lace top and miniskirt that she had worn when she had entered the prison.

Dolly sank into the back seat. She waited for Trevor to dish out an earful once more about her ignoring him.

"You look like a right fucking mess," Jono, Trevor's driver, said, as he glanced at Dolly's face in the rear-view mirror before revving the engine and pulling away from the prison gates.

"Oh, do I? Maybe I should write a letter of complaint, see if I can get a refund on all those fucking spa treatments. And I seriously do not recommend the lip fillers..." Dolly couldn't stand Jono. Jono had been Trevor's driver for a couple of years, and Dolly knew that the pair of them were shagging. Why they tried to keep their relationship secret she had no idea, but Dolly played along pretending she knew nothing.

Of course she looked a mess: had they expected her to rock up looking rested and raring to go? She just spent three weeks holed up in a fucking shithole being pestered constantly by a perverted prison officer. She was knackered, and she needed a bath. It didn't help that she had been made to put back on the same clobber she had worn going in. She felt, and knew she looked, dirty.

"What the fuck happened to your face?" Trevor asked.

"I did what you said, didn't I. Told Roache he was in the shit with you, and this is what I got for it. My lip's so swollen I could give Mick Jagger a run for his money. Mind you, I ain't joking when I say you should see the state of Roache. He won't be sticking his todger anywhere for a while, I can tell you. Carted him off to hospital to sew it back on, last I heard," Dolly said.

Trevor smirked: he had missed Dolly's banter. He didn't know any other girl that could dish it out as well as her. Then he remembered that he was still annoyed about Dolly's lack of contact. "You poor bitch, my heart bleeds for you. Prison not quite the holiday you expected it to be?"

Dolly shrugged; prison had certainly been anything but a holiday. "I just need to get home and get a bath. Then I'll be fine."

There was no response. Dolly sighed, knowing that Trevor had no sympathy for her so there was no point in playing on the fact that she felt like a bag of hot shit.

"Oh no, Dolly my darling. We ain't got time for that this morning. You have places you need to be, my girl." Trevor smiled nastily, as Dolly realised what he was getting at.

Trevor thought about the money that Dolly would earn for him. Her punters had been gagging for her release. "Your three weeks off has left some of your customers feeling very unsatisfied, Dolly. Poor buggers can't wait to get their nuts in. You're going to be a very busy girl over the next few days."

Dolly leaned her head back against the seat. It would be more agro than it was worth to argue with Trevor in the mood that he was clearly in. He had said that he was going to make sure that she was taught a lesson for avoiding him while she was inside, so she had been expecting him to do something like this. He was a man of his word, if nothing else.

They drove for fifteen minutes in silence; then Jono pulled into a lay-by at the back of an industrial estate and said: "This is it, isn't it?"

"How long will you be?" Trevor asked, as Jono got out of the car.

"If all goes to plan, twenty minutes max," Jono said through the open driver's window, as he felt for his flick-knife in his pocket.

"Good. Me and Dolly will have that chat while you're gone," Trevor replied, as he took the car keys from Jono in case they had to make a move in a hurry. You never knew when a pig car would turn up, and Trevor always liked to be prepared.

"Now then, time for you to make amends, Dolly darling," Trevor said, as he locked the car doors and ordered Dolly to undress. Tipping a line of cocaine onto his hand, he watched as Dolly did as she was told.

Trevor had spent the past three weeks listening to all of Dolly's regular punters bang on about her being the best shag they had ever had and Trevor had started to wonder about having a go himself. Trevor had a fondness for Dolly, partly because she had turned out to be a little money-making machine, raking in quadruple what the other girls earned each day, but there was also something about her that he really liked. Unlike the other girls, Dolly wasn't afraid to speak her mind. But though she got away with a lot more than most would, she always seemed to know when to shut up and do as she was told. It had been years since he and Dolly had been near each other, though. The last time he had fucked her had been when he had groomed her to work with him, eight years ago. It was the way he lured all of his girls, until he got them under his spell. He thought that was why he usually preferred men. Women had lost their appeal and his respect. They were far too gullible, and far too easy.

No one knew that he preferred men to women. He liked to keep his private business exactly that. And with all those girls on tap, people were never suspicious of his sexual predilections.

Her breasts exposed, Dolly stared blankly at Trevor as he snorted the coke. She refused the line he offered her, so Trevor had both.

"Now, Dolly, you've a lot of making up to do to me," Trevor said, as he placed her hand on his crotch and let her do what she apparently did best. Closing his eyes, he smiled to himself. Dolly had no idea how busy she was going to be today. After she had satisfied him, and he was by no means going to make that an easy task, he had arranged ten calls for her. He had booked her up all day.

Sex wasn't always about gratification: sometimes it was about power. The cheeky little mare wouldn't be so quick to ignore him next time.

Chapter Thirty

Jono cut through the long alleyway, his fists clenched at the thought of Trevor alone with Dolly. Dolly was a mouthy little trollop; Jono had no time for the girl. He couldn't understand why Trevor stuck up for the little bitch.

He tried to banish the thoughts of the two people that he had left in the car, and what they were doing in his absence from his mind as he psyched himself up for his task. It was early in the morning and therefore still quiet, so he could see, as he drew nearer, that the man he was looking for was asleep in his usual spot. Despite being so het up, Jono was impressed that the man had survived another night on London's bitter streets.

Timing was crucial to this mission. Jono tiptoed so as not to disturb the sleeping man, moving in closer so that he could get a better look at him. He spotted the half-empty bottle of whiskey that lay discarded on the ground next to him. Even in his obviously heavily intoxicated state after gulping down half the bottle, he had still padded out his clothing with sheets of screwed-up newspaper before drifting off. Dodge, he was known as, due to spending every waking minute avoiding those he owed money to. And that was pretty much everyone he came in contact with these days, seeing as he clearly didn't have a pot to piss in anymore.

Staring down at him in the cardboard den that he had built, Jono was finding it hard to believe that this pitiable man had even worked for Trevor let alone been one of his busiest and most reputable dealers. He was in a sorry state now, unrecognisable from the man he had once been. His facial hair had grown unruly, making him look fifty rather than thirty.

Wrinkling his nose up at the strong stench of piss, Jono tried not to gag. The man's demise was a waste but Jono couldn't allow himself to feel any sympathy, his downfall had been all his own doing. Dodge had committed the ultimate fuck-up as a dealer by dabbling in his own goods. His addiction had quickly grown and it hadn't taken him long to leave himself wide open to not only his punters and also his suppliers. The more stoned he became, the less enthusiastic people were about doing business with him and the slacker he got at collecting his money. Dodge had become desperate as word got out he was a junkie himself, no longer the threat he once had been, his clients stopped paying him. It wasn't long before Dodge wasn't able to score himself a fix, let alone pay his debts, and when he heard that Trevor Creevy had a price on his head he had been left with no choice but to go on the run. Everyone knew that Trevor was a nutcase, and the word lenient wasn't in the man's vocabulary. Now, living on the streets and begging for loose change to fund his new addiction to alcohol Dodge spent his days drinking whatever he could get his hands on before pissing it all away again.

Jono had been tipped off that Dodge was hiding away in this secluded patch of wasteland at the back of the industrial estate. The man must have stupidly thought that he would be safer out here.

Jono picked up the whiskey bottle that had been cast aside onto the grass next to the man's plot, and inhaled the fumes. Cheap and nasty, but strong enough to leave Dodge sparko, Jono thought to himself as he carefully tipped the remnants of booze into the box; no wonder the man was comatose.

Dodge snored loudly. He was entombed under numerous layers of clothes and newspapers, so padded out that he looked like the Michelin Man. This was a real social outcast, Jono thought. No-one would care, or notice if he no longer roamed the neighbourhoods at night.

Jono took a few minutes to enjoy the man's peaceful and oblivious expression. Then he pulled out a box of matches, leaving his knife in his pocket: this way, his hands didn't need to get dirty.

This was his favourite part of his job. He loved the power that just one strike of a match gave him, whilst putting men like this at his mercy.

Watching the flame sparkle on the end of the match until it had burned right down to his fingers Jono finally tossed it into the box. Small flames flickered at first but they became bigger as they met the alcohol, as he had expected. Jono, a pyromaniac, stood mesmerised as the blaze engulfed the cardboard.

Dodge woke when the flames reached his clothes. Desperately trying to pat them out, he let out a panicked scream and rolled around in agony as the fire lapped up around him.

"Did you think that you were invisible, Dodge?" Jono tutted, "Did you think Trevor was just going to scrub out a thirty grand debt?"

The odour of burning flesh filled Jono's nostrils; he moved further away, in case he was seen by anyone alerted by the smell.

Screaming for help as he realised Jono wasn't going to let him live, Dodge howled in pain.

"Don't mind if I smoke, do you?" Jono lit up a cigarette and enjoyed the show.

Chapter Thirty-One

Dolly felt emotionally and physically drained. The last bloke had been a nightmare. He had been so fat that Dolly was surprised he could even find his cock, let alone muster up the energy to use it. That heavy load pumping on top of her for fifteen minutes solid had been hard going. Still, she thought, as she walked to the car, her day must be almost over. She prayed that now Trevor had dragged her halfway round the houses he would let her go home and have a rest. It had been a long day.

"Money," Trevor demanded, twisting around to face her from the passenger seat, holding out his hand for the cash that she had earned.

Dolly placed the notes in his hand, before sinking back against the cool leather of the back seat. Jono started the car. No one spoke.

"What's up with you two?" she asked.

She could feel she had interrupted an argument: Trevor's lips were pursed and Jono was glaring. She should be the one with the hump after what she had been through today. They had obviously just had a lover's tiff, she thought to herself; they were always bickering like an old married couple. It was hilarious that Trevor thought that no-one knew about his relationship with Jono. She didn't know why he was so insistent on hiding the fact that he swung both ways, most people in this day and age didn't really care what sexual preference you had. If Trevor didn't want to draw attention to his sexuality he was going about it the wrong way. The more he tried to hide it, the more he got people's tongues wagging.

"Mind your own business," Jono sneered and shot Trevor a dirty look.

Dolly guessed that Jono was annoyed about what Trevor had made her do to him that morning. Jono was the possessive type, and there was no way he would have been happy with Trevor's idea of punishment. She wasn't too pleased about it, either. She had been shocked when Trevor had told her to take her clothes off, but as always had done as she was told. She hadn't slept with him since they had first met. Not once, in all the eight years, had he so much as looked at her as if he wanted a repeat performance. And he had seen her in all sorts of compromising positions.

Today, he had taken her roughly and quickly. Grabbing her from behind he had panted for a few minutes but Dolly could tell that he hadn't been enjoying it. It was like he was forcing himself to touch her. It had only lasted a few minutes and she could tell by the way that Trevor hadn't said a word to her about it afterwards, that he had probably found their encounter just as peculiar as she had.

Dolly thought it was amusing that the punishment Trevor thought he was dishing out to her had clearly backfired. She was almost certain that Trevor hadn't reached an orgasm, let alone enjoyed the sex. He had obviously just been on a power trip and had had to be coked-up in order to do it too. She knew that he had only fucked her to put her in her place and remind her who was boss. But Dolly had a feeling that she hadn't been the only one who had been taught a lesson. And as for Jono, she couldn't help but feel smug if she had made him jealous. If they wanted to play their little game of make believe, who was she to call them on it?

Shrugging, she rested her head back against the seat, tempted to close her eyes. However, she knew that if she did fall asleep now she wouldn't wake for hours.

"Where are we going?" Dolly recognised the familiar streets. Trevor's house was around the corner, and Dolly imagined getting into a hot bath, putting some clean underwear on and getting into her own bed. She hadn't been home for three weeks: it felt like an eternity.

Trevor being a complete and utter control freak, with a very acute dose of OCD thrown in for good measure, he would no doubt have kept the house spotless while she had been away. As homes went, this place was one of the nicest places she had lived. Her room was her very own sanctuary; somewhere she could go to get away from everyone.

"Jono's dropping us home," Trevor said, as he counted the pile of money that Dolly had earned him. "But he's picking you up first thing tomorrow. He's got one last bit of business to attend to in the morning and you're going with him."

Dolly nodded. The last thing she wanted to do was spend any time alone with Jono, especially in the mood he was in. She saw the way that he looked at her, making no attempt to disguise the fact that he hated her, and the feeling was mutual: Dolly couldn't stand the man. Dolly had always considered Trevor was a force to be reckoned with, but since Jono had come on the scene Dolly had realised that in comparison Trevor was a pussy cat. Dolly would never let on that she was scared of him though. She did as she always did and hid her fear with humour and sarcasm. Trevor would never let Jono do anything to hurt her anyway.

Jono was Trevor's wing man. He was his minder as well as his driver, and if Trevor needed any form of problem sorted Jono was only too happy to oblige. Dolly hated the rare times that she was alone with him. Trevor often instructed him to drop Dolly off with punters and to wait outside until she had finished; Jono would drive her in silence and when she came out she was usually met with a contemptuous stare.

The car stopped outside Trevor's house. It didn't look anything special outside, just an average two-bedroom house. The paintwork looked tired and the blinds were nearly always drawn, but that was where Trevor was smart. The outside was just a front. Inside was a different story. Trevor's house was immaculate. Never shit on your own doorstep was a phrase he lived by. He paid every single bill up front, he kept himself to himself in regard to the neighbours, and he never had any punters back at his house.

"Right, we'll see you nice and early. You make sure you sort him out good and proper, okay," Trevor warned Jono, before getting out of the car.

Following behind Trevor as he made his way up the front path, Dolly wondered who they had been talking about. Whoever it was sounded like they were in deep shit. Dolly had witnessed first-hand how dangerous Jono could be on more than a few occasions over the years and if Trevor had sent him to sort someone out, then that is exactly what he would do. Dolly had seen how the man had ruthlessly inflicted pain on others. A couple of times Jono's vicious temperament and willingness to do anything had actually saved her life, not that she liked to admit that very often. Jono had only ever done what he was paid to do; it wasn't as if he had protected her as a personal favour. The worst incident, which was always in the back of her mind, was the night some nutter had locked her inside his flat. The punter had been a friend of one of her regulars, and Dolly had been happy to oblige when the man had offered her a ridiculous sum of money to sleep with him. Clearly, with no idea how the game worked, the man had been oblivious to the fact that Jono was sitting outside waiting for Dolly the entire time. Thinking back now Dolly felt that he must have been off his head on something with what he had in store for her: either that or he was a psycho. Dolly never got to find out which. The last thing that she remembered was the thudding pain on one side of her head as he punched her, knocking her off her feet. When she regained consciousness, she found herself tied to a chair in his kitchen. As she looked around the room for some way of escaping, her eyes rested on a brown leather bag open to display shiny and sharp implements inside. She had known instantly by the evil look on the man's face as he stood over her that he intended to use his collection of tools on her to get his kicks. Dolly had tried to scream, but the man had covered her mouth with duct tape and her wrists were strapped so tightly to the arms of the chair that she was unable to get away. Trapped, she imagined dying in the flat without anyone realising. Then she remembered that Jono was outside. Looking up at a clock on the wall, she saw that she had already been here longer than she would normally spend with a punter. Forty-five minutes was the maximum time allowed and most of her punters barely needed half of that. Jono would have known that too: that was his job. Where the fuck was he?

She didn't have to wait long. As if on cue, as she sat there with tears trickling down her face while she silently prayed for Jono to save her, he did. After a few unanswered knocks on the front door, he kicked it in. Jono had then grabbed the man by his throat and swung him forwards before proceeding to beat the man's head repeatedly off the exposed brick wall until all that remained of his face was a bloody pulp of flesh. He then untied Dolly, and she had grabbed her clothes and fled to the car. Jono had remained in the flat for another ten minutes, and Dolly had been too scared to ask him what he had done to the man when he finally returned covered in blood. The smoke that she saw billowing from the building as they drove off gave her a good indication that she wouldn't be seeing that man again. Jono had never mentioned the attack since; neither had Dolly. She felt a shiver down her spine at the thought of what would have happened if he hadn't been there.

But Dolly remembered feeling something apart from gratitude. She had recognised the look in Jono's eyes: it mirrored what she had seen in the nutter's. Jono had scared the life out of her since then.

Trying not to think about him, she waited while Trevor opened the front door to the house. "Here we go, Dolly darling; welcome home."

Chapter Thirty-Two

"Do you fancy some scrambled eggs and bacon, love?" Bernie asked, as she poured out a mug of coffee.

Her son looked tired, sitting at the dining table in his jogging bottoms and vest as he listened to the radio as if in a trance. She hoped there was nothing wrong that a large coffee and one of her nice big cooked breakfasts couldn't sort out.

Jonathan had been working harder than ever lately, and although Bernie was proud of how well her son was doing at the company he worked for – he always had money in his pocket and his car was top of the range – she thought that he was doing too much. He seemed constantly tired.

"Nasty business that, isn't it?" Bernie nodded at the radio, as the news reporter talked about the badly burnt body of, they thought, a local homeless man. "Jesus Christ, as if that poor bugger wasn't already down on his luck. What sort of sick individual would do such a thing?"

Bernie shook her head. Thanking her lucky stars that her world felt like a million miles away from such sickening acts, she switched off the radio. Every single day, the news was plagued by acts of violence and negativity and listening to the horrendous stories each morning was enough to leave her feeling depressed.

"Hey, I was listening to that," Jonathan protested.

"You don't want that sort of thing on when little Rosie comes down," Bernie said softly. "Poor girl doesn't want to hear something like that. So, you didn't answer my question: do you want something to eat?"

"No, but I'll have another coffee," Jonathan said, as he took a large gulp.

Stanley came into the dining room and sat at the table. Bernie glared at her husband, but Stanley ignored her. She knew what he was going to say. He looked like he couldn't wait to break the news about Sophia's visit to Jonathan.

"We need to talk, Jonathan," Stanley said, in a matter-of-fact tone, as his son stared at him over the rim of his mug, bracing himself for another of his father's rants about something Rosie had said or done that his old man didn't approve of. He always had to moan about something, and Jonathan was getting bored of the sound of his pathetic voice. "Sophia came to the house last night. She saw Rosie."

"Stanley!" Bernie reprimanded her husband, as Jonathan choked on a mouthful of his drink. Tact wasn't her husband's strong point and Bernie was hoping that she would have been able to gently break the news to Jonathan before Stanley had got up.

"You what? She's out? What do you mean she came here?" Jonathan demanded. "What the hell were you doing letting that cunt come into this house to see Rosie?"

Jonathan rose to his feet, seething. What the hell did they think they were playing at? "That fucking bitch can't just turn up here without warning. She lost her rights when she gave Rosie away like she was a broken fucking toy."

Jonathan was so angry that he felt breathless. Sophia giving up their baby had been the ultimate insult, as far as he was concerned. For her to hate him so much that she treated their baby like she was nothing was unforgiveable. And if that bitch thought that she was going to swan back in here and see Rosie, she had another think coming.

"Calm down, love," Bernie said. Even though it hadn't been the way she would have broken the news to him, at least Rosie was upstairs out of the way;

they may as well have this conversation with Jonathan now while she was out of earshot. Last night had been distressing enough for the girl having her mother turn up out of the blue. Bernie had spent at least an hour stroking the poor mite's head as she soothed her off to sleep. The last thing Rosie needed right now was to hear her father going off on one and shouting obscenities. "We didn't let her do anything, Jonathan, I promise. She just turned up. We told her that she wasn't welcome here and to sling her hook. Rosie heard the commotion and came down to see what was going on. She knew who Sophia was straight away."

"She is the image of her," Stanley added, "and whatever you feel about her, Jonathan, she has got rights."

Stanley liked the fact that Jonathan appeared rattled; for once, he was showing some emotion. Normally nothing fazed him: clearly Sophia's release had.

"She hasn't got any fucking rights. She's a murderer. Is that what you want, is it? Give Rosie to some fucking psycho for weekly outings? Maybe she will be the one who ends up with a knife sticking out of her chest next, huh?" Jonathan banged his fists on the table. He could tell by the look on his dad's face that he was enjoying every moment of this. Well, no-one was getting their hands on his Rosie. She belonged to him, and there was no way Sophia was going to worm her way in and start playing mummy now after all these years. "Bet you'd be over the fucking moon, wouldn't you, Dad, if I just palmed your grandchild off on to her? You've never had any time for her, have you? You haven't for me, either."

"Do you know what, Jonathan, you are absolutely right," Stanley shouted back. Jonathan didn't care how anyone else felt, and Stanley would put money on the fact that the only reason he was playing the 'poor me' card now was to get sympathy from Bernie. Stanley, as always, could see right through him. He had had enough of his son's games. "I can't stand the bloody sight of you. You've always been a horrible little shit. Even when you were a small boy you knew exactly how to manipulate everyone around you with your nasty bullying ways. Your mother is blinded by your bullshit, but I'm not."

Stanley felt liberated as he said everything that he had been thinking for so long. He continued, "And to top it all off, you drove my Tommy away with all your deceit. Sleeping with his girlfriend and then rubbing his nose in it when you found out that she was pregnant... I spoke to Sophia. She told me what you did to her. I'd bet my life on the fact that you filled Tommy's head with bullshit too. Could you not stand to see your brother happy?"

"What are you talking about?" Bernie demanded.

"Sophia told me that you tricked her, Jonathan. She thought you were Tommy that night at the party. You broke your brother's heart."

"She's lying," Jonathan said.

"I don't believe you. You tricked that poor girl; you got her pregnant and you drove Tommy away. I'd swap a million of you for just one of our Tommy, do you know that? He's a good boy, a decent boy. And I'll tell you something else, Rosie's just like you: I can see it in her eyes."

Jonathan's hands gripped Stanley's throat. He slammed his dad into the wall, knocking one of Bernie's framed photos onto the floor with a crash as he did so. Stanley reacted instantly, grabbing Jonathan, pushing him with all of his might so that he would release his grip.

"Stop it, please. Think about Rosie," Bernie implored, aware that at any moment the child could walk in and witness her father and grandad literally at each other's throats.

The two men stared at each other as they gripped each other's bodies, their faces so close that they could feel each other's breath as they panted. Jonathan was the first to let go. Then Stanley did the same. Rubbing his throat, he watched Jonathan pacing the room.

Bernie slumped down on her chair and held her head in her hands. Her husband and son's feud had been a long-drawn-out battle over the years, and she had felt like she was forever in the middle of them. But it had gone way too far this time.

"Please, this has got to stop, both of you," Bernie begged, then began to cry.

"Yeah, you're right, Mum, it does. And if that's the way he feels, then me and Rosie will be moving out. We ain't staying where we're not wanted," Jonathan said quietly. His blood boiled in anger as his dislike for his father grew even greater than normal.

"No, darling, you can't leave," Bernie pleaded, just as he had known that she would. His mother would be heartbroken if they left, and she would make his dad's life hell: that seemed the perfect solution for the miserable old fucker.

"Tell that to him. He's as good as admitted that he hates our little Rosie," Jonathan sneered. "What sort of a man says shit like that about their own granddaughter?"

Jonathan shook his head in disgust. He was sowing enough seeds in his mother's mind to make her crucify his old man.

"Your dad doesn't mean it; do you, Stanley?" Bernie pleaded with her husband. She couldn't let Jonathan and Rosie leave: not like this. "Tell him you don't mean it, Stanley."

Stanley stared at his wife. Her tear-filled eyes were wide open, desperate and beseeching. "No. I can't tell him that because I did mean it: I meant every damn word. Your son is sick in the head, Bernie. We should have taken him to a shrink when we found those videos of him torturing those animals. But no, you made up excuses for him, just like you've done ever since. And now look… look where denial's got you. You're breeding another one upstairs."

Stanley was shaking. "How can you stand by him and pretend that he didn't drive Tommy away? I believe Sophia."

"Stanley, you can't really believe that girl over your own son. She's nothing but a brazen little hussy. Jonathan's told us she's lying," Bernie shouted.

"Oh, I know what Jonathan told us." Stanley glared at his son, who smiled at him. "Well, I don't believe him. Do you know why? Because he could never stand that his brother was everything that he would never be. Go on, admit it, Jonathan. You were jealous that your brother and Sophia were together, weren't you? You always wanted what other people had. And if you couldn't have it, you went out of your way to destroy it. Is that what happened, Jonathan? You were jealous that your brother wasn't a bloody crackpot like you are?"

Stanley realised by his son's facial expression that he had hit the nail on the head. "What, were you frightened that if Tommy had a girlfriend he would leave you behind? It wasn't like you had any friends of your own, did you?"

"Shut up," Jonathan shouted. How dare his father speak to him like this?

"Your mother thinks the sun shines out of your arse, boy. Proud as punch you are, aren't you, Bernie, that Jonathan has such a great job? What is it again, Jonathan? This high-flying job of yours?"

"I said shut up." Jonathan was seething. Whatever his current thoughts, his father had no idea what he was capable of. If he kept pushing him he would find out.

"No, I won't shut up. I'm done with pretending. And you, Bernie; your obsession with keeping up appearances for your ignorant bloody friends' benefits is a joke. That boy there is nothing but a thug. I've seen it with my own eyes. He works for some lowlife scumbag who rents out girls as whores. Isn't that right, Jonathan?" Stanley had made it his mission to find out what Jonathan did on the nights he had told them he was at work in an office. "I followed you Jonathan. Working in an office, my arse! Some of those girls you and that other thug were dragging around London and pimping out looked like school kids. You have a daughter yourself, how the fuck could you, Jonathan?"

Bernie shook her head. "Stanley, why are you saying this?"

Jonathan was high up in his company; he had a nice car, he earned a good wage. He had nothing to do with prostitutes.

Stanley looked at Jonathan, who stood there snarling like a dog. Then he looked at his wife as she stood there frowning at him like he was crazy. "Go on, Jonathan, admit it. Tell your mother how you make your money. How the local hookers fund Rosie's dresses and toys."

"Fuck you," Jonathan said.

"You can't deny it, can you?" Stanley got up. "As for moving out, good idea. I want you gone today."

Chapter Thirty-Three

The couple who lived next door to Sophia had been arguing for almost two hours. She had heard heavy footsteps and shouted abuse. It was the same most nights, alcohol-fuelled rows that continued into the early hours until the fiery couple had burned themselves out. Sophia had no idea what they were rowing about tonight, but whatever it was their argument was probably keeping half the street awake too. She was surprised that no-one had called the police. Then again, the police were less welcome around here than rats; this place was crawling with ex-offenders.

Wrapping the pillow tighter around her head in a vain attempt to block out the noise, she felt the room start spinning again. The bottle of vodka she had drunk earlier was lying empty on the floor next to the bed. She regretted her binge.

Drinking it had helped at first, numbing the sting of the prior day's meeting with the social worker. Sophia had glugged the bottle as she tried to dull out the noise of the woman's harsh words which echoed in her head, taunting her.

"Rosie has been in Jonathan's sole care since birth. Frankly, with your criminal record, the chances of you getting any kind of custody are very slim."

Sophia had cringed at the social worker's bluntness. The hope that she had felt since she had first set eyes on Rosie: that she would be able to get to know her, vanished.

The social worker was a complete jobs-worth. From the second Sophia had entered her office she had known she was fighting a losing battle. Looking down her nose at Sophia, she kept banging on about was the way the system worked. From what Sophia could gather from reading between the lines of what the woman was saying, the system was full of do-gooders who were so busy focusing their time on people like Sophia that they managed to let the real dregs of society slip through the net and get away with all sorts.

The woman had spoken to her slowly, emphasising words as if Sophia was foreign or simple. Afterwards, she just wanted to get drunk and forget it. But despite her inebriation, the woman's words continued to swim around her mind. "And even if we could come to an arrangement with Mr Jenkins, what you're asking for wouldn't happen overnight. It's a very long, slow and drawn-out process and the courts will need to see you settled and in a permanent home and employment before you'd be considered for any kind of access. At the moment supervised visitation is your only option, and even that will be a battle if Mr Jenkins disputes it."

Sophia had gone back to her room at the hostel with a heavy heart, cursing the system that had caused her so much grief. The rules and regulations had stripped her of her innocence and freedom, and now the same system was stopping her from seeing her child. Never had she felt so lost and alone. Sitting on the floor, drunk and in tears, she couldn't shake the thought that there must be another way.

She regretted going to the Jenkins' house. They thought that she was heartless; a cold, unloving and un-maternal girl who had given away her baby. They couldn't understand how scared and confused she had been: still a child herself. But seeing Rosie had stirred up feelings inside her that she never knew she had. As soon as she saw Rosie's innocent little face, she felt something deep within her heart stir. Her little girl had looked so perfect. She must have been out of her mind to have given her away to someone as disgusting as Jonathan, but back then she had just wanted everyone and everything to disappear.

There was no point dragging up the past now. None of them would believe that Jonathan had forced himself upon her, tricking her into having sex with him, and accomplishing his wish of splitting up her and Tommy. God knows what Jonathan had told him, but whatever it was it had worked: Tommy had gone. She remembered how worried Bernie had looked as she had hurtled down the stairs in a blind panic on hearing Sophia at her front door after all these years. She had probably thought that she had gone there to take Rosie. But that had never been Sophia's intention when she found herself at the house: she had only wanted Tommy. Seeing Rosie, with her red curls and her face that was like looking into a mirror, had been a punch in the stomach for Sophia; she had been winded by the sudden connection that she felt with her own flesh and blood.

Now, Sophia couldn't close her eyes without seeing her; Rosie was all she could think about. It was so unexpected. For years the thought of the child, Jonathan's child, was only a painful reminder of what Jonathan had done to her.

Rosie had stared through her with the same cold eyes as her father. But whereas he made Sophia feel angry, when she looked at her daughter she only felt heart-sorry for what she had done. She had made a dreadful mistake in giving Rosie up.

With thoughts of her daughter swimming around her head Sophia must have finally drifted off, because when she next glanced at the small alarm clock on her dresser she saw that it was five am.

Getting out of bed, unsteady on her feet after the alcohol, she grabbed her robe and wrapped it tightly around her body before making her way to the balcony to get some fresh air. The crisp, cool air that hit her felt refreshing after being in her room all night. The sun peeped through the gaps of the buildings, beguiling her with its false promise of a brighter day. She stared out into the distance taking in the view of the rich green mosaic of the Marshes, a stark contrast to the grey mass of rundown tower blocks that stood in between. She exhaled loudly as the brightness of the sun blinded her for a split second, leaving her squinting. She much preferred dismal rainy days to the brighter sunny ones like this: as at least they mirrored her mood perfectly.

Staring down at the balcony beneath hers, she looked at the washing that was strewn on any available space, including the backs of chairs and the bars of an old rusty bike. The washing swung aimlessly in the breeze above pots filled with dead or wilting plants.

She tried to take her mind off her current situation, and thought about getting dressed. She had wanted to get over to her nan's early that morning and do her a nice cooked breakfast. She hadn't been eating properly and Sophia was worried. Albert continued to make her lovely meals, but her nan never seemed to have an appetite for them or anything else.

Sophia tried to gather some energy; even just the thought of cooking a breakfast with the mother of all hangovers was making her feel queasy. Running her hand along the banister, she flicked a tiny purple flower that lay flaccidly on the metal railing. The dot of colour floated gracefully down to the road below.

It was then that she saw him. He was standing at the end of the street, leaning against a fence, watching her.

For a second she thought that the tall dark figure was Tommy and automatically her heart raced. Then she saw iciness of his stare and realised her mistake.

Obviously unfazed at being visible Jonathan lit a cigarette, his eyes never leaving Sophia. He was trying to frighten her, she realised. It worked. Sophia ran from the balcony and into her room, her heart beating hard in her chest. How did he know where to find her, and what did he want? She had known that Bernie and

Stanley would have told him of her visit by now and he wouldn't have been happy about her seeing Rosie.

Waiting a few minutes, she peeped out from behind her curtain to check if he was still there, still watching. But he had gone. Feeling her heart rate slow, her panic turned to anger. What did he think: that he could warn her off? That she was going to do just as she always had and not fight back?

Everything, and everyone, in her life had changed over the past eight years. Her father was dead; her mother a shadow of her former self; Tommy was gone. All she had left was her nan, who seemed to be getting frailer by the day. And then there was little Rosie.

As she tugged on her jeans, Sophia's mind was all over the place. For years, Jonathan had been in the back of her mind confusing and scaring her. Everything had worked out fine for him. He had it all. He had destroyed her and Tommy's relationship, and as a reward he been given a daughter. And it wasn't enough: now he was trying to intimidate her. Well, Sophia had had enough of being intimidated. If Jonathan was worried about her trying to make contact with her child, then so he bloody well should be she thought. Rosie was her daughter, and she was going to get her back.

Chapter Thirty-Four

Paranoid that she was being followed, Sophia walked faster. Unable to shake the unsettled feeling in the pit of her stomach, she just wanted to get to her nan's house. Jonathan knew where she lived; he had been watching her.

Turning into the street where she had been brought up, Sophia couldn't bear to look at her old house. The memories were too painful. Quickly she made her way down her nan's garden path.

When she saw that the front door was ajar, Sophia knew something bad had happened. Following a spate of burglaries in the area, her nan locked up the house as if it was Fort Knox. Sophia's hands trembled as she pushed the door open and stepped inside.

"Nan?"

Sophia gave a gasp as she saw that the house had been ransacked. Her nan's belongings were strewn on the floor, many of them broken.

Stepping carefully over the broken pieces of Nessa's favourite vase, Sophia knew she would have to call the police; but first she needed to find her nan.

In the kitchen, the cupboards had been emptied and their contents were on the floor. The fridge had been upturned with food spilling out. Four chairs had been broken and her nan's finest china smashed into smithereens.

Sophia couldn't believe how much stuff had been destroyed.

"Nan?" Sophia called again as she climbed the stairs. If someone had caused this much carnage, they were capable of hurting a vulnerable old lady. And her nan wouldn't have taken this attack lying down. She had a fighting spirit, and if someone had broken into her home to rob her, she would have fought tooth and nail on principle. Sophia knew only too well just from being locked up with crackheads when she was in prison that you couldn't be like that anymore. She had met people so twisted they would think nothing of bumping you off for their next fix of drugs. One nutcase that had been in the cell next door had beaten someone to death for a tenner... ten pounds for a life.

Reaching her nan's bedroom, Sophia felt so scared at what she might find that she could barely open the door.

"Oh Nan, thank God," Sophia said, relief spreading through her. Her nan was cowering in the chair in the corner of the room, shaking like a leaf and clutching her chest with trembling hands. "Are you hurt, Nan?"

"Has he gone?" Nessa whispered.

"I think so," Sophia knelt at her nan's feet, reaching for her hands.

"I've had a bit of an accident," Nessa admitted.

Nessa had always prided herself in the fact that even in her eighties and with a bad hip she was always in full control of her faculties, unlike some of her friends that were of a similar age, and Sophia knew that she would be mortified that she had wet herself.

"Forget about that, Nan," Sophia said quietly as she ignored the dark patch of urine on her nan's nightdress. It was the least of their worries right now.

"He came here," Nessa said, in a strained voice.

"Who?"

"That Jonathan," Nessa cried. "He broke in a couple of hours ago. He said that you're to take this as a warning to leave Rosie alone."

As she relayed the message, she wheezed as she fought against the increasing pain in her chest.

"Oh my God, Nan, I'm so sorry." Sophia felt sick with guilt. This was all her fault. Her nan's house had been smashed up and she had been left in this terrified state because of her. Sophia constantly brought pain and trouble to her nan's life.

"I only went to their house to see Tommy, but he wasn't there. I didn't mean for Rosie to see me, but she did. It's all such a mess, Nan... I'm so sorry." Sophia started to cry. Everything backfired on her. She had only ever had good intentions, but she was always being punished for what she did. "Nan, we have to call the police. We can't let him get away with this."

"No... no police. He said he'll kill you if you cause him any trouble, and I think he really meant it. You didn't see him, he looked crazy..."

Nessa keeled over.

"Nan," Sophia screamed.

Her nan lay motionless at her feet. Sophia used the phone on the dresser to call an ambulance.

"Please help, it's my nan, she's unconscious." As she begged for help, the woman at the other end of the phone told her to remain calm. Remain calm? Her nan was lying unresponsive on the floor. How could anyone be calm at a time like this?

"Please, just hurry," Sophia cried. "I think she's had a heart attack. Please..."

Sophia couldn't lose her nan: not now. She had only just got her back.

Chapter Thirty-Five

As the car pulled up in a narrow street, Dolly looked at the row of terraced houses in confusion. She didn't think she had any punters around there. Jono got out of the car and opened the passenger door.

"Where are we, then?" Dolly asked as Jono led her across the road to a pathway. Dolly had had the best night's sleep in ages last night at home in her own bed. However, she had woken up dreading going back out with Jono. She couldn't face another punter. Not after all the work she had put in the previous day.

Tottering behind him on her heels as he strode in front of her, his six-foot frame towering above her and his long leather jacket swishing around him, she was knackered but she tried her hardest to keep up.

As they reached the front of the hospital Dolly realised that this must be their destination, but knowing better than to keep asking Jono questions she just followed without saying a word. Envisaging that she would probably have to give some bed-bound old codger a blowie, she just hoped that whatever they were there for was over quickly so she could get home and get some more well-earned sleep.

They went into the hospital and Jono pressed the lift button. Waiting for it to come, Dolly tried to ignore the stares that she was receiving from the old grannies sitting in a cluster just outside the little tea kiosk. She could tell that they were talking about her. Dolly guessed her black PVC playsuit and red six-inch heels were bound to draw attention: after all that's exactly why she wore them. Except at this time of day and in this kind of environment it was the wrong kind of attention. It didn't help that Jono was standing next to her, and with his towering frame giving him the look of her minder they both stuck out a mile.

"Would you look at the state of that one? She's leaving nothing to the imagination," one of the old dears with a sour pout and a disapproving stare said loudly. The other ladies were listening intently, taking in the old bag's words as if they were gospel. "Her clothes are so skimpy you can almost see her religion."

The other women sniggered.

"My religion?" Dolly smiled at the woman who had spoken. "Oh, I've never heard anyone call it that before. I just call it my cunt."

Dolly winked and blew the old lady a kiss as the lift door closed on her and Jono. Smiling to herself about putting the miserable cow in her place, Dolly turned to see that Jono was glaring at her.

"Did you have to do that?" he demanded.

"What?" Dolly feigned innocence. "You have to admit, it was funny. Never mind choking on her tea, that old dear almost choked on her false gnashers."

"Just keep your head down and stop drawing attention to us," Jono warned.

"You are joking, aren't you?" Dolly scoffed. She looked at them both in the mirrored wall. "You have seen what we look like, haven't you? I'm trussed up in my streetwalking finest, and you look like something that's just stepped out of the bloody Matrix."

Jono didn't reply: he was in one of his humourless moods again. Dolly changed the subject. "So, what are we here for then?"

"You'll see," Jono said bluntly, as the lift doors opened. "Now no more of your bloody lip, okay, just follow me."

Jono was having second thoughts about bringing Dolly with him; working alone was always easier. The girl was a bleeding liability.

***

Maria Byrnes had worked as a nurse at Homerton University Hospital for a year, but every single day had the freshness and excitement of her first. She enjoyed everything about her job: the buzz, the busy atmosphere, the other staff and the patients. She didn't care about the debt that she had accumulated to get there nor did the thought of the endless nights where she had stay up into the early hours almost pulling her hair out in frustration as she studied for her exams bother her anymore. Every bit of effort she had put in had been worth it, as far as she was concerned. She had worked so hard to get to where she was, and now at twenty-seven years old she was living her dream.

As she stared down at her patient's flaccid penis, with its torn skin and jagged stitches, she tried to remind herself of all of the above.

"Christ al-fucking-mighty, will you please be a little more careful, my nads are bloody killing me," Roache screamed, as Maria reapplied the dressing around his crotch area. Gripping the bed sheets until his knuckles went white, Roache grimaced. The nurse was pretty, albeit a bit chubby, and on a normal day Roache would have been only too pleased to have her playing with his todger but right now he was in so much agony that all he wanted was some strong painkillers and then to get the hell out of there. He hated hospitals.

"I'm very sorry, Mr Roache; I know it must be ever so sore." Maria tried to sympathise with the man who had been brought in with a severed penis, but holding on to it as she spoke was making her blush. Apparently he was a prison officer who had been assaulted by one of his female prisoners. Maria couldn't imagine what sort of woman would have inflicted such a wound. She had been horrified when she had seen his injury, but now with her senior nurse standing behind her and monitoring her every move Maria was carrying out her patient's care with the utmost professionalism, treating his injury just as she would any other.

"That's it, Nurse Byrnes, wrap it round once more and then check his medication sheet," the sister said, standing behind Maria and making notes on the staff nurse's progress. Mr Roache's injury had been the perfect opportunity to put the girl to the test and Sister Croft was pleased with the young nurse's conduct in dealing with the delicate situation so far. Sister Croft had seen it all in her time as a nurse; the predicaments some patients got themselves into had long since stopped shocking her, but it was different for the younger ones.

"I need some more pills, the pain is too fucking much, and something to help me sleep too," Roache groaned, his cock throbbing from all the stitches that he had received on a penis that had swollen to almost triple its normal size. Pain was an understatement.

Maria did as she was told and checked Roache's medical notes. Scanning the numerous notes she bit the end of her pen thoughtfully.

"I'm afraid you're not due any more painkillers for at least another two hours," Maria said, offering a sympathetic smile as soon as she saw Mr Roache's face redden in annoyance.

"Two fucking hours? Are you having a laugh?" Roache felt like crying; ever since that bitch Dolly had sunk her teeth into his manhood, his whole world had been turned upside down. Not only was he in a lot of pain, he had suffered the humiliation of his governor visiting him. And now Roache's head was swirling with the news he had been given. Suspended pending investigation, the governor had said, without an ounce of compassion or commiseration. Due to the high number of complaints that he had received, the governor could no longer turn a blind eye to the allegations that had been made against him. As much as Roache had denied the misdemeanours, the governor was having none of it. So much for being friends, Roache had thought miserably to himself. Now this blithering nurse, having just tinkered with his bits and made his pecker even more sore, was refusing him any more medication.

"I've had enough of this shit. I'm going home." Roache tried to swing his legs around to get off the bed, but the raw pain in his groin made him fall back. "Argh," he spat, as he realised he wasn't even able to stand without making the pain worse.

"I'm afraid that you can't go home until the doctor has examined you. He is doing his rounds shortly," Maria told him.

"For fucks sake. Unless the doctor is going to stand there and physically rub my dick better what's can he bloody do for me? I'm in pain and I want to go home."

"Mr Roache," Sister Croft reprimanded.

Then after waiting for him to lie back down, Maria continued: "Get some rest and I'll be back later with some more medication for you, and we can see how you're getting on. Once the doctor has been, we can look into discharging you."

Maria spoke more confidently than she felt, as she waited for yet another tirade of abuse from the man. She was so glad that Mr Roache's bed was next to a patient that had been sent off for a morning of physio. She would have been mortified if any of the other patients could hear the despicable way he was talking to her. Most of the patients in here were fine, but this one had tested her to her limit with his attitude.

Smiling at Maria for doing such an excellent job, Nurse Croft opened the curtain to let the flustered nurse out before her.

"We'll close this for you, Mr Roache, to give you a bit of privacy," Nurse Croft said, as she pulled the curtain around Roache's bed.

Winking at Maria, the senior nurse whispered: "See no gob-shite, hear no gob-shite."

Maria giggled at her manager's sense of humour and smiled in agreement. Mr Roache had been her most challenging patient to date.

***

Jono scanned the whiteboard behind the unattended nurse's station, looking for Roache's name. His informant had told him that Roache would be in here for at least two days and Trevor had reckoned a friendly little visit from Jono was just what the sly fucker needed. Finding what he was looking for, he nodded to Dolly to follow him down the corridor.

Reaching the ward, Jono saw the cubicle he was looking for was at the far end of the corridor. Walking towards it, he opened the curtains to check that Roache was alone.

"What now?" Roache asked grumpily, as he sensed someone coming into his cubicle. He was lying on his side facing the wall, hoping that the pressure around his groin would ease up so that he could finally get some sleep. And now he was being disturbed yet again. "For fuck's sake, I've already had my dressing done, what does a man have to do around here to get a bit of shut eye?"

Roache turned to see who was disturbing him. However, instead of being met by the plump nurse he encountered Dolly and a man he didn't recognise.

"Is this the piss-taking bent screw you told us about?" Jono asked Dolly, as she took in the big bandage around Roache's penis that covered up the damage she had inflicted.

Nodding at Jono, Dolly grinned as she realised that she didn't feel an ounce of remorse.

Before Roache knew what was happening, Jono had smashed his fist into his face. Feeling several of his teeth loosen inside his mouth, Roache went to call out for help but Jono was too quick. Clamping his hand over Roache's mouth, Jono grabbed him by the back of his neck with his other hand and hoisted him into a sitting position. He was in no fit state to fight back; even moving on the bed hurt his groin.

Jono bent down, his voice low, sounding more menacing than if he had shouted. "See that girl there? I hear you've been having a few freebies with her."

Roache shook his head, trying to protest, but the man's hand was clamped so tightly over his mouth that all he managed to do was make muffled groans. Staring at Dolly, Roache felt sick to his stomach. He had a severed penis, no job and now this thug on his back. No girl was worth this amount of grief.

"Well, let me tell you now, nothing in this life is free, mate; you always pay the price in the end. Trevor Creevy owns that girl, and now you owe him for her. Five grand for her, another three for the fucking liberty you took." Jono tightened his grip, as he listened to the man whimper in pain. "I'll be seeing you, and that eight grand, again very soon."

Jono took his hand off Roache's mouth and put his finger to his own lips.

Roache did as he was told and didn't speak. All he wanted was for Dolly and her psychotic companion to leave.

Leaning his head back against his pillow when they had gone, Roache could taste blood and felt a tooth under his tongue. Again, he fought the urge to cry. He wished more than anything that he had never laid eyes on Dolly.

Chapter Thirty-Six

Stanley felt a twinge of guilt as his dishevelled wife walked past him to get a drink of water. In the three days since Rosie and Jonathan had been gone, Bernie had done nothing but look miserable. She hadn't uttered a word and had barely eaten a thing. Stanley watched as she drank the water. She had big dark circles under her eyes, her hair was lank and greasy and she had been wearing her dressing gown for the past three days. In all the years that they had been married Bernie hadn't been able to so much as leave the bedroom without making sure she was immaculately turned out.

"Do you fancy a brew?" Stanley asked, hoping to break the ice a little.

Shaking her head, she didn't even bother to answer.

"Look, love, we can't go on like this, can we?" Stanley said. Trust Bernie to over-dramatize things. The way she was behaving you would think Jonathan and Rosie had died, not just moved into their own place. He knew that she was upset about Rosie going more than anything, but this was the way it was supposed to be.

Stanley had spent the days relaxing, drinking tea and reading the newspapers, thoroughly enjoying the fact that he no longer felt like an unwanted guest in his own home. No noise; no sneers. As far as he was concerned, Jonathan moving out was the best thing that had happened in years. "Come on, love; this is stupid. Jonathan is twenty-three: he wasn't going to live at home forever."

Slamming her glass down on the worktop, Bernie swung around to face her husband.

"Stupid?" Bernie shouted. "I'll tell you what stupid is, shall I? Stupid is driving your own son and granddaughter out of their home. Stupid is you and your bloody tantrums. Rosie is the daughter I never had, Stanley; don't you see that? I'm the closest thing that little girl has to a mother."

Bernie was so angry with her husband it was all she could do not to smash the glass of water over his head.

"She has a mother, Bernie," Stanley said quietly, bowing his head. He knew that Bernie wouldn't want to hear this but it needed to be said. From the moment that Jonathan had brought that baby home, Bernie had devoted her life to her care. She had raised her as if she was her own and Jonathan had let her because it suited him. He had been able to go off and work unsociable hours, every time he had been called in with a minute's notice. Jonathan had taken advantage of his mother's good nature, and the bond that she had formed with Rosie, to get her to do everything that he asked. But she wasn't Rosie's mother, she was her gran.

He knew that his wife was feeling lost without Jonathan and Rosie to molly-coddle and he felt bad about that. His intention had never been to cause her upset. But Jonathan needed to stop using her and stand on his own two feet for a while. And Stanley wasn't going to go back on what he had said and done. Bernie would see in the end that it had been the right thing to do, he was sure.

For years Stanley had only put up with Jonathan to please his wife. He couldn't do it anymore. Now it was Bernie's turn to make some sacrifices.

"You haven't lost them, Bernie, they've just moved out," Stanley reasoned with his wife as her bottom lip trembled and tears rolled down her cheeks. He knew that she was upset but until now he hadn't realised just how much, she was obviously desperately unhappy but he was damned if she thought for a second that she was going to persuade him into changing his mind by putting on the waterworks. Losing his patience, Stanley changed tack.

"That boy has controlled this house for far too long. Why can't you just admit it, Bernie?"

Bernie clamped her hands over her ears, refusing to listen to the words of venom which her husband was spewing out about Jonathan yet again. Stanley had always bullied Jonathan; he had never had a good word to say about him.

"And whether you want to admit it or not, Bernie, Rosie's turning out just like him. She's not right," Stanley said sadly. He had wanted more than anything to love his only grandchild but he had seen right through her, just as he had with Jonathan. The pair of them manipulated everyone. He needed Bernie to acknowledge that she could see it too.

"You know it's true, Bernie; that girl's just as heartless as her father. Do you think Geoffrey next door just came round here shouting the odds all those times for the fun of it? Twenty-five years he's been our neighbour, and we never had a peep of trouble from him. Rosie killed his birds, snapped their necks just like Jonathan did to all those poor bloody animals in those videos. When are you going to face it, Bernie? History's repeating itself; she's cut from the same cloth as her father."

Even after all the years that had elapsed, Bernie still couldn't bring herself to talk about what they had found. Stanley remembered it all so clearly. He had come home from work to find his wife sobbing hysterically as she had played the tapes that she found stashed underneath Jonathan's bed while she had been hoovering. Jonathan had been at school and Bernie had found the camcorder that the boy was obsessed with. Jonathan had a hard time at school; he had no friends and seemed to his teachers like an angry child. Bernie had thought that if she watched the films, saw the secret world that Jonathan had filmed from his angle, they would help her understand him.

Most of the tapes featured tortured animals. He had filmed himself killing defenceless creatures in the vilest of ways. Feeling sick, she had made herself watch every tape as if it was her punishment for not realising what Jonathan had been doing. The worst video had been the one of Tommy. Bernie had sat with her hand placed over her mouth as the camcorder had zoomed in on her Tommy as he struggled to keep his head out of the water, spluttering and coughing as he begged for help.

Bernie had realised that not only had Jonathan stood there and filmed the whole thing, but that he had zoomed in on Tommy's face as if he had been enjoying his brother's panic and distress. At one point the whole screen had been taken up with a close-up of Tommy's eyes. His desperately scared eyes had bored into the lens, behind which Jonathan would have just stared back. By the time that Stanley had got home, Bernie had been so distraught she could barely talk. She had shown him the videos instead, and Stanley had hit the roof.

But Bernie had done her usual thing and begged him not to say anything. She pleaded with him to destroy the tapes, terrified that someone would find them and take Jonathan away from her. She vowed that if he got rid of everything she would speak to Jonathan, properly. Stanley had stuck to his part of the bargain, burning all the evidence of their son's sadistic pastime in the incinerator in the back garden. But Bernie had never stuck to hers. Once the tapes had been destroyed, she refused point blank to discuss what they had both seen. The violence... the blood... she would never really be able to shake off the memory of what she had seen but for her son's sake she had fought to pretend that it hadn't happened. Even now, all these years later, she wouldn't talk about it.

"How dare you say such a thing, Stanley? Rosie is an eight-year-old girl, and you are nothing but a horrible bully. We were a family..." Bernie shouted. Enough was enough for her too. If Stanley thought for one moment that she was going to let him stand there and say such things about poor innocent Rosie then he had another think coming. "Look at us now, Stanley, me and you rattling around in this big empty house on our own. I'll be lucky if Jonathan even lets me visit her... you do know that, don't you? You've ruined everything." Bernie was weeping again as she spoke, but she didn't care. The void inside her was growing bigger with every passing minute that she was away from her precious Rosie.

Stanley sighed, defeated. Bernie would never listen to the truth.

Bernie missed Jonathan as well as Rosie. Of course he had his funny ways; she knew that better than anyone did, but so what? She felt like the whole world was against him sometimes. She remembered the way her friends had looked at him in disgust when he had been a young boy, turning their noses up at the way she 'spoilt' him. She had watched the way her husband had become jealous of the time that they spent together, detest for his own son written all over his face. It had been Bernie that had fought Jonathan's corner every single time when he had been growing up. She had been there for him when the teachers in each of his schools had taken a dislike to him and tried to make out that he was a troublemaker. She had been the one that had tried to speak to him when he had come home from school in tears as a small boy because all of the kids in his class had singled him out, taunting him by calling him nasty names and refusing to play with him. Jonathan had been and was different to most people, yes, but Bernie didn't care. He was her son and, unlike everyone else, she would never turn her back on him.

"You just don't get it, do you, Stanley," Bernie spat. "I don't care if you're here or not. All I care about is Rosie and Jonathan. It was you who had the problem, so you should have been the one who left."

Bernie stood there trembling. She had seen the hurt in Stanley's eyes the second that her words had tumbled out of her mouth. By looking at her husband's expression, she could tell that the truth that had just rolled out of her mouth had smacked him straight in the face.

She meant what she had said, though.

Pushing past Stanley, Bernie felt her head start to pound. She needed to lie down. She just wanted to close her eyes and forget.

Rubbing his head, which was aching, Stanley sighed. Bernie would never change, and nothing he said or did would make her: it was time to give up.

Stanley felt crushed. His wife had made her choice, and she hadn't chosen him. After all these years, after everything, Jonathan had won.

There was one last thing he had to do, though. Taking his phone out of his pocket, Stanley's hand trembled as he pressed a series of buttons. Even if he had lost Bernie, even if Jonathan had ripped them apart, he wasn't prepared to let him do it to other people.

Hearing Tommy's familiar voice on the other end of the line almost tipped Stanley over the edge; shutting his eyes tightly, as if to stop the emotion tumbling out of him, he said: "Son, it's me. It's time we had a little chat."

Chapter Thirty-Seven

Sophia hadn't left her nan's side since she had found her cowering in her bedroom earlier. When Nessa was seen in A&E, the doctor said that she had only fainted but, although he assured Sophia that her nan would be okay, they wanted to keep Nessa in and run some tests due to her high blood pressure. .

"I'm bored out of my blooming tree, Soph... Can't we go for a little wander? I can't sit here all day, not with that view. Look at her over there; she looks like something out of a horror film." Nessa nodded at the cubicle opposite in her usual tactless manner.

"You're supposed to be resting, Nan," Sophia said, then, turning to where her nan was looking, saw in horror that a woman was lying on the bed opposite with her nightdress hitched up around her waist completely exposing herself. Spotting the wheelchair at the other end of the ward she had second thoughts.

"Okay, I'll make a deal with you, Nan. I'll take you outside so that you can sit in the fresh air for a little while if you promise me that when we come back you'll get some rest."

Nessa beamed as Sophia got the chair.

"We're only going out there for five minutes though," Sophia said, as she helped her nan off the bed and to ease her frail body into the chair. "Carefully does it."

"Sophia my dearie, if I had a few feathers stuck to my bottom would that make me a chicken?" Nessa asked.

"What?" replied Sophia, confused by another of her nan's wacky sayings.

"This." Nessa pointed at the wheelchair. "Just because I'm in a wheelchair it doesn't make me an invalid, Sophia, so stop with all your to-do, my girl."

Shaking her head at how strong-spirited her nan was, after everything she had been through that day, Sophia wheeled her out of the ward, shooting the old girl opposite a quick glance as they passed her. "I'll get the nurse to come and help you get more comfortable," Sophia said feeling embarrassed.

They took the lift to the garden area, which had benches. It was a beautiful day, and Sophia thought that a breath of fresh air would do her nan good.

Wheeling the chair next to a bench, Sophia took a seat on it as she watched her nan close her eyes and bask in the glorious sunshine.

"Oh, this is better. I can't bloody stand being inside these places. They're so sterile and cold. The place reeks of death," Nessa said, as she opened one eye and looked at Sophia. "You know, Sophia, I was lucky today but I'm getting on, love. The day's going to come when I'm not going to be here anymore."

"Nan, don't, please..." Sophia shook her head. She didn't want to think that one day she would lose her nan, let alone talk about it. Especially after the shock she had got that morning. At one point, seeing the destruction of her nan's house, Sophia had thought that she would find Nessa in a similar state. It had been a horrible feeling.

"There's no use pretending, sweetheart, my day will come. The only certainty in life is death, you know," Nessa continued, thinking that now was as good a time as any to broach the subject. "I just want to make sure that you're going to be okay, lovey, when I'm no longer here. Your mum isn't much use to you, what with her nerves, but I want you to promise me that you won't give up on her. She is very ill and she has no idea what she's saying. But one thing I know for sure is that if she was in her right mind, she would have never given up on you. Promise me you'll see her again."

Sophia nodded. Of course she would. It didn't matter how long it took, or even if her mother never acknowledged her again, Sophia knew she had to try and get through to her.

Sophia felt a heavy lump form in her throat. Her nan was the only person she really had left now, she couldn't bear the thought of her death. She had always been there for her. She felt closer to her than she did to anyone. She couldn't bear the thought of her death.

"Nan, don't you be worrying about me; I'll be fine. I'm going to get back on my feet, I promise. Once I get myself a job and move into a better place, I'll be able to start seeing Rosie. That's all I want now. I've got a lot of making up to do to her. And as for you..." Sophia said wistfully. "You're not going anywhere. You could give a woman half your age a run for her money. So no more of this morbid talk okay?"

"It's not morbid talk to me. The day I meet my maker will be a happy one because I know that your dear grandad Patrick will be up there waiting for me, along with little Rascal." Nessa smiled though Sophia saw the tears glisten in her eyes as she spoke.

"And as for seeing Rosie, what about Jonathan? He won't let you anywhere near the girl. He was like a man possessed today, Sophia. I've never in all my life seen someone look so capable of... well, murder." Nessa shook as she thought of the damage that man had caused. He had smashed up the place in front of her, and

Nessa had seen the glint in his eye as he enjoyed the fact that he was terrifying her as he did so.

"But that's exactly why I need to see her, Nan. Jonathan is evil. I should never have given her to him. You should see her, Nan, she's like a mini-me: all curly red hair. Dinky, though." Sophia smiled. "But boy is she outspoken. She talked to me with more confidence than I've felt in all my life."

"Don't you be so sure; that'll be another trait she gets from you, I'd put money on it," Nessa insisted. "Don't you ever forget that you, my girl, are strong. Always have been; even as a nipper you'd have talked the hind legs off a donkey. You'd have me and all the ladies down at the social club in fits on a Sunday afternoon with all your stories."

It was true, but prison had changed the girl, knocking her confidence; Nessa hoped in time she would get it back. "You've been through a lot; too much, Sophia. But I have never, not for a second, doubted you. And now you've come out of the other side in one piece, and it's time to start building your life back up. But just be careful, that's all I ask. As my dear old mother used to say, you can't argue with crazy and that Jonathan is a whole load of that."

"I know what you're saying, Nan, but since I saw Rosie it's like I'm possessed. I'm determined to get her back. And if I do it all the right way and get a job then move to a decent place, like the social workers said, then there'll be nothing that he can do to stop me," Sophia said before adding carefully, "are you sure that you're not going to tell the police what happened, Nan? You can't let him get away with it."

Her nan was as stubborn as they came and once she made her mind up about something there was nothing that anyone could say to sway her, but Sophia needed to try.

"No, lovey, its more hassle than it's worth."

***

"Well, looks like those old bags must've got bored and gone to find someone else to cast aspersions on," Dolly said lightly, as they walked back to the hospital's main entrance. She had been practising her most seductive wiggle for them and was disappointed to see that they were no longer there to witness it. Mind you, she thought, it may have been just as well that they had left, the old prudes wouldn't have known where to look once she got going; she would have probably brought on a few heart attacks.

Jono walked on in silence. He hadn't uttered a word since they'd left Roache's cubicle.

Just as they reached the main doors, Dolly heard a familiar giggle. Turning around she saw Sophia, of all people, pushing an elderly lady in a wheelchair into the hospital shop.

"Oh bollocks," Dolly said to Jono. "Can you hang on a second? I've got to go to the toilet. Ladies' business, you know." The type of bloke that Jono was, even hinting about her having a period would make him run a mile.

"Hurry up then," Jono said impatiently. "I'll meet you at the car."

"Which do you fancy, Nan? Gingernuts or Hobnobs?" Sophia scanned the shelves for treats for her nan.

"If they're the chocolate ones, go with the Hobnobs. Gingernuts don't even come close," said a voice from behind her.

"Dolly!" Sophia squealed. "Wow, I nearly didn't recognise you."

Sophia tried to hide her shock as she took in her friend's heavily made-up face and brash clothing. She had only previously seen Dolly in tracksuit bottoms and a T-shirt, and the most the girl had worn on her face had been tinted lip-butter. Sophia had imagined that Dolly was one of those high-class call girls, all designer labels and clients with posh motors. Every time she had told her one of her funny stories about her job, Sophia pictured Dolly's life as full of glamour.

Knowing what Sophia was thinking, Dolly shrugged. "Well, you know I like to stand out from the crowd. My work clobber is a bit in your face, admittedly."

Dolly grinned cheekily. She was what she was; hopefully Sophia's opinion of her wouldn't change now.

"Work uniform? I bet your boss makes you wear that on purpose so he can get a few cheap thrills," Nessa interrupted from her chair. She watched the two girls embrace, guessing that this was the famous Dolly.

Copping an eyeful of Dolly's bum cheeks as they poked out of her black shiny shorts, she added: "I think your boss could probably get done for sexual harassment. You should contact that *Watchdog*. What is it that you do?"

"Dolly works as a..."

Sophia knew that her nan was very open-minded and would always welcome her friends no matter what, but Dolly said before she could finish: "How rude of me, sorry; I'm Dolly; you must be the lovely Nessa. I've heard all about you. I'm an actress. First proper day out and my agent called offering me a part in a TV show, playing the role of a lady of ill-repute. Beggars can't be choosers, and all that."

Dolly bent down and kissed Nessa on the cheek, then winked at Sophia. Sometimes it was nice when people didn't know what she did for a living. It wasn't that she was ashamed, as she had been doing it far too long to let her feelings about it bother her anymore, but this way she felt less judged. And from everything that Sophia had told Dolly about her nan when they had been at

Holloway, Dolly didn't want to give the old dear any reason not to like her. She remembered how highly Sophia had spoken of her nan in prison; she wanted to make a good impression.

"An actress… oh, how lovely." Nessa beamed. "Amazing what they can do these days; those make-up girls are so talented. Is that part of your role too?"

Nessa pointed at Dolly's bulging and puffy lip.

"Did Trevor do that?" Sophia asked.

She knew that Dolly had been dreading her release date; she had told Sophia that she would have to face her pimp again, and he was going to go nuts at her for shunning him while she had been inside. Sophia had tried to persuade Dolly to call him, but Dolly wouldn't listen.

"No, it wasn't Trevor, although trust me he wasn't happy with me. It was handbags at dawn at the gate. It was Roache who did this."

"Oh my God," Sophia said, clapping her hand over her mouth in shock. She had had a feeling that something had been going on between Dolly and Roache, but every time she had quizzed Dolly about, she had strongly denied it.

"It's only a fat lip. Trust me: Cockroach ended up getting a lot worse than I did. He's here, on one of the wards. He got brought in on my last night, problems with his wotsit, I heard," Dolly said quietly, raising her eyebrows.

Sophia, getting the gist of what her friend was saying, giggled. It was about time that slimeball got his comeuppance and, whatever had been going on between her friend and him, Sophia was just glad that it sounded as if Dolly had been the one to get the better of the man.

"Listen, I've got to go, my driver," she emphasised the last two words for Nessa's benefit, "is waiting in the car. Here..."

Dolly took a screwed-up receipt out of her handbag and jotted down her address. "Come over tonight, if you fancy it?"

Dolly had missed her friend and couldn't wait to tell Sophia the details of what she had done to Roache. "Trevor's going out tonight, on a hot date, so I'll be all on my tod. We could get a bottle of wine and a takeaway?"

"Oh, I don't know, I can't really leave Nan. We had a bit of trouble ourselves this morning..." Sophia trailed off, not wanting to bring up what had happened while her nan was there in case it upset her.

"Don't you be silly, girl; you go," Nessa said. "Go and have some fun with your friend. Dolly, can you tell her not to be so daft? I'm only in here tonight so that the doctors can keep an eye on my blood pressure. Sophia keeps acting like I'm on my death bed, insisting that she wheels me about in this poxy thing like I'm some sort of an invalid."

"Nan!" Sophia tapped her on the shoulder playfully. It was true that she hadn't been able to shake off the worry about the way her nan looked just before she keeled over.

Dolly thought that it wasn't Sophia just wanting to look after her nan that was stopping her from coming over. She knew that she was wary about going to her house because of whom she lived with. And Dolly couldn't blame her. She had told Sophia all about Trevor when she had been inside.

"Or I could come to yours? Makes no odds where we are; it'd just be nice to catch up, that's all," Dolly said.

Thinking of her bleak room at the halfway house, Sophia would have been mortified to have Dolly visit her there; it was so small and pokey they would both feel like they were back in their cell. But her nan was right, after she left the hospital, what was she going to do? Going home alone for another depressing night of listening to her neighbours tearing chunks out of each other was the only option if she didn't see Dolly.

"Well, if Trevor's definitely going to be out, I don't see why not. Is about eight okay?"

"Great. He'll definitely be out, so it'll be just you and me. I'd better go now, mustn't keep my chauffeur waiting."

Dolly smiled and hugged Sophia once more, and then looking at Nessa said, "It was lovely to meet you, Nessa. Sophia used to say how brilliant you were all the time. Hope you feel better soon."

Kissing the two women on their cheeks, Dolly strutted out to where Jono would no doubt be impatiently waiting.

"Well, she was rather lovely." Nessa smiled, as they went back to choosing which biscuits to take to the ward. "You didn't say she was an actress."

"Well..." Sophia hated lying to her nan, even if it was only a little white one.

Seeing Sophia's struggle to think of why she had kept her friend's occupation a secret, Nessa giggled. "Oh, you girls... You do know that being eighty years young does mean that I wasn't born yesterday, don't you? I know what she does. God, I'd have to be blind not to realise, the girl looked cheaper than the Pound Shop. I was just being polite and playing along. Your friends are your business, Sophia. She seems genuinely nice, and that's all that matters. Now, on Dolly's recommendation, grab me a packet of those Hobnobs. Here, we should have invited her back to the ward. She'd have given that brazen flasher opposite us a run for her money."

Nessa chuckled to herself as she wheeled over to the till, leaving Sophia speechless.

Chapter Thirty-Eight

Hearing the knock at the door, Dolly gave the room a once-over, checking that everything was spotless, before she went to greet her friend. Suddenly, letting Sophia see her in her own environment made Dolly feel nervous. What if Sophia didn't like what she saw? She took a deep breath and opened the door.

"Ah, Sophia, I'm so glad you came." Dolly hugged her friend. "Come in, come in."

Sophia walked through the hallway and into the lounge, surprised at what she saw. The lounge had white walls and minimal décor; it looked more like a show-home than the stereotypical pimp's den.

"Right, so Trevor has gone on a hot date with his fella, and I've been left holding the baby. Long story short: Trevor's boyfriend, who has a little kid, turned up saying they needed somewhere to stay for a few days, so Trevor has taken him out to wine and dine him and I've been lumbered with babysitting duties." Dolly smiled apologetically. "Hope you don't mind. She's in my bed watching movies that I've bribed her with to make her stay quiet, but I can't promise you that she won't be trouble. Proper little madam she is."

"I don't mind at all," Sophia said. The only thing she cared about was the fact that this Trevor wouldn't be home. Just seeing Dolly again, with her upbeat chatter and her permanent smile, made Sophia feel at ease. Dolly strolled through to the kitchen, indicating that Sophia should follow, and offered her friend a glass of wine. Feeling herself tear up as Dolly handed her a glass, Sophia laughed.

"God, look at me. I'm an emotional wreck. So much has happened, Dolly, and then seeing you today..." she trailed off. "I've missed you so much."

Dolly didn't need Sophia to explain; she knew what she meant. When you had been sharing a cell twenty-four seven, you could quickly get to know someone on a deep level. Dolly knew how Sophia felt about her, and she felt exactly the same about Sophia.

"I know, love, me too; what are we like?" Dolly led the way back into the lounge, sat on one of the sofas and nodded to Sophia to take the opposite one.

"So?" Dolly asked, as she tucked her feet underneath her. "How's your nan?"

Sipping her wine, Sophia sat back on the sofa feeling herself relax for the first time that day. "She is fine, thank God. But it's a long story, so first tell me exactly what the hell happened between you and Cockroach."

The girls spent the next hour telling each other everything that had happened since they had been freed. Dolly admitted to Sophia about what Roache had done, and Sophia told her about Jonathan breaking into her nan's house and smashing up the place. Pouring the last dregs of the wine into the two glasses, Dolly thought how much she was enjoying Sophia's company.

"Wow, how did it get to be so late? I'm starving: bet you are too. Shall we order food?" Dolly asked. It was almost half-past nine, but as Trevor and Jono probably wouldn't be home until at least midnight they should have plenty of time to have dinner so that Sophia could get away without encountering them. "Trevor's been going on all day about this fancy restaurant they're going to; they're having seven courses, the greedy sods. They're probably only just on their second ones by now. Then knowing him they'll go to a few bars afterwards. He's on a proper mission to cheer up his fella. Shall I order us a curry?"

Sophia nodded to indicate that was fine with her.

"I'll have anything as long as it's chicken and spicy," she said as she kicked off her shoes off. She sunk back into the chair and closed her eyes, while Dolly grabbed the phone and went into the kitchen to get the menu and order some food. Sophia smiled to herself as she sat in the blissfully relaxing room, surrounded by the flickering lights of the candles. Tonight was the first time since she had been out that she had felt normal. Dolly was a real tonic; the only person that Sophia knew other than her nan who didn't judge her.

"Dolly," a little voice called from upstairs.

Sophia sat still, not knowing whether to get up and check on the child. Dolly wouldn't be much longer, so it probably wasn't necessary.

"Dolly."

Sophia decided that it wouldn't hurt if she just made sure that the girl was okay. She made her way up the stairs; she would just stick her head around the door and see if the little girl needed anything. Dolly could go up and see to her once she was done.

"Right, chicken madras and a chicken bhuna coming right up... Sophia?" Dolly realised the room was empty. She figured that Sophia was in the toilet.

Dolly opened another bottle of wine and filled up the two glasses. After sitting patiently for a good five minutes, Dolly thought she would go and check. Knowing her luck the kid was up to her tricks again; maybe Sophia was trying to settle her.

"Are you alright in here?" Dolly walked into her bedroom and saw Sophia, tears streaming down her face, sitting on the bed and hugging Rosie tightly.

"What's going on?" At first, Dolly thought that the kid had had a nightmare, but Sophia was holding onto the girl for dear life as she rocked her back and forwards: she looked more distraught than the child she was holding.

"Rosie, what's the matter?" Dolly asked, wondering if she was going to have to get the phone and interrupt Trevor's hot date.

Rosie looked confused, and Sophia was beside herself with tears.

"Soph, I think you'd best go downstairs and leave little Rosie to me."

It must have really screwed Sophia's head up having her baby taken away from her if this was her reaction to every child that she came into contact with.

"Dolly, it's Rosie."

"I know, darling: I told you that. Come on, let's go downstairs." Dolly wondered if Sophia was losing the plot. Rosie was probably petrified that Dolly had let this lunatic in. Sophia was hugging her tightly to her, and Dolly could see that while the girl didn't seem too distressed, she didn't look too comfortable either. Sophia was obviously unstable, and Dolly could have kicked herself for being so gullible. Trust her to finally make a real friend only for her to turn out to be a nut-job.

"No, Dolly." Sophia held Rosie's face in her hands and kissed the girl's forehead. "This is my Rosie. This is my daughter."

Rosie started crying then. It was all too much for her.

"I want my gran," the little girl sobbed.

"Right, Sophia, I think it's time that you left actually," Dolly said, suddenly feeling worried about Sophia's state of mind. She was clearly delusional and the fact that she was gripping Rosie tightly and still rocking her backwards and forwards only added to the madness of the situation. If it got back to Jono that she had let some weirdo touch his child, he would hit the roof.

"She is my mummy, Dolly," Rosie said in a quiet voice.

Dolly frowned. She felt like she had woken up in the middle of a film having slept through the early and crucial scenes.

"You said Trevor has a boyfriend," Sophia said. "His name's Jonathan, isn't it?"

"Well, yeah, It's Jono."

"Rosie, darling, tell Dolly the names of your nanny and granddad, they are called Bernie and Stanley, aren't they?" Sophia asked.

Rosie nodded, really crying now. "I want you to take me to see them. I miss my granny."

"Shush, don't cry, darling." Sophia hugged the girl closer, and Rosie tried to wriggle free from her clasp.

"Bloody hell." Dolly sat on the end of the bed. "I'm sorry, Sophia, for a minute I thought you were tripping out on me. Your daughter... what are the chances, huh?"

Looking at Sophia and Rosie, Dolly could see the truth staring her right in the face. They both had the same pale skin and red curly hair: they were clearly mother and daughter.

"Oh my God, Sophia," Dolly said as she remembered something. Taking a half-eaten packet of Polos out of her pocket, she gave the mints to Rosie to keep her quiet for a few minutes.

"Don't cry, darling," she said softly. "We'll get this all sorted out."

Grabbing her friend by the arm and pulling her over to the bedroom door, Dolly brought her voice down to a whisper so that the child wouldn't overhear.

"Jesus," Dolly said as she shook her head. "If you're Rosie's mum, then... You ain't going to like this, Soph, but I've overheard Jono slagging you off. I've never heard him speak about anyone the way he has done about you, real venom in his voice."

"Go on." Sophia watched Dolly pause, uncertain whether to continue. But Sophia didn't think that things could get any worse, so Dolly may as well come out and say whatever it was that she had heard.

"He said that it was because of him that you'd been sent away."

"What do you mean, he got me sent away? I don't get it. What exactly did he say?" Sophia's brow creased, as she wondered what Jonathan would gain by making something like that up. It didn't make sense.

"God, Soph, it was about two years ago now, I wasn't really paying much attention. Jono was always spouting his mouth off about something to Trevor. I thought he was just trying to impress him, you know. But I remember he told Trevor that you'd been sent down for murder and that Trevor didn't have to worry about you... you were off the scene. Trevor's a jealous fucker, Soph, and I think he was checking where the land lay with you and Jono before he rushed into anything with him. Anyway Trevor had a bee in his bonnet and was convinced that Jono had feelings for you, because he'd got you pregnant. So Jono had told him everything."

Dolly wasn't sure if she could continue, especially with Rosie in the room, but seeing the look on Sophia's face she knew she had to tell her everything. Her voice even quieter now, Dolly continued, "He said he murdered your father, Sophia. He stabbed him and left him to die. And you were done for it. The creepy fucker laughed so hard I think even Trevor was freaked out."

Sophia felt dizzy, but she said: "Go on."

As Dolly was opening her mouth to say more, there was the sound of a key scraping in the front-door lock.

"Hello," Trevor called from downstairs.

"Holy fuck," Dolly said, hearing footsteps wandering around downstairs, and a bunch of keys being thrown down on the table. "They're home early. Something must be up. You're going to have to hide, Soph. If Jono finds you here he'll bloody well string us both up."

Holding Rosie firmly by the shoulders, Sophia spoke as calmly as she could. "Rosie darling, this is really important. I want you to do something for me, okay? I need you to lie down and pretend to be asleep when your daddy comes in."

Jonathan was likely to check on Rosie, and Sophia couldn't risk him staying long enough to find her. Rosie shook her head disobediently, and then surprisingly did as she was asked as she shuffled down the bed and closed her eyes tightly.

"I'll go down and find out what's going on," Dolly said. "You get under the bed till the coast is clear, Sophia."

Dolly switched the main light off and left the room. Making her way downstairs, she put on her biggest smile.

"You two are back early, everything okay?" Dolly could tell that things were anything but: Trevor was sitting on one sofa with his arms folded while Jono, who she now thought of as Jonathan, sat stony-faced on the opposite one.

Seeing Sophia's shoes on the floor, Dolly grabbed them and put them behind a chair, then started tidying the rest of the room. "God, look at me, eh, a right slob, aren't I? I just checked on Rosie, Jono."

Dolly smiled at Jonathan. "Sleeping beauty, she is; been an angel all night. She must have conked out the second you left. So, how was your evening?"

"Oh, you know, mostly shit." Trevor's tone made it clear that he and Jono were doing their usual routine of arguing and sulking, probably over nothing as usual, before they ended up in bed, noisily making it up to each other. They had the most fucked-up relationship Dolly had ever seen, and that was saying something.

"Oh no. Well, I've just ordered a curry, so if you haven't eaten I can plate you some up when it arrives? Think my eyes were bigger than my belly when I ordered."

"Whatever," Trevor said sulkily.

"Perfect timing," Dolly said as the doorbell rang a few minutes later, grateful that it had broken the awkward silence in the room. As she was dishing up the curry onto three plates, Jonathan came out into the kitchen.

"What were you doing while we were out?" He put a piece of chicken into his mouth.

"Oh, just watching a bit of telly and chilling out," Dolly said nervously. Jonathan stared intently at her, like he knew what she was thinking. All those times that Sophia had spoken about the evil Jonathan, and it had been Jono all along: it made sense.

"There's a lot of food here for one person," Jonathan said.

"Think I went a bit overboard?" Dolly continued to spoon the food onto the plates. Her shoulders tensed as she spoke. "This is what eating prison food does to you, been craving this for weeks."

"And the wine?"

"What about it?"

"There are two full glasses." Dolly must think he was stupid. When he grabbed her wrist, she dropped the spoon and curry sauce landed on the worktop.

"Jono, you're hurting me."

Jonathan had always disliked Dolly. He didn't know why Trevor was fond of her: she spoke to him so disrespectfully; if Jonathan had his way she would be down the road living in the brothel with Trevor's other slags.

"Do you think I'm fucking stupid, Dolly? Did you think that I wouldn't find out?"

Jono twisted her arm so hard that Dolly was convinced he was going to break it. "Please, Jono, you're hurting me."

"What the fuck's going on in here?" Trevor had come to see what the commotion was about.

Jonathan squeezed Dolly's skinny wrist tighter before pushing her away. "I know that you're sometimes a bit slow off the mark, Trevor, so let me enlighten you. There's enough curry here to feed about four people, for starters."

"So the girl can put her food away."

"Well, what about that then?" He pointed into the lounge to the two glasses of wine on the coffee table. "She's had someone here."

Trevor stared at Dolly. She knew better than to let anyone come back to the house.

"You got a fella here?" Trevor knew how precious Jono was about his kid; Dolly should have been babysitting, not letting some man get his end away.

"No, course I ain't. What the hell would I want with a fella? I had my bloody fill of them yesterday," Dolly said, cursing herself for not removing Sophia's wine glass.

"Is he still here?" Jonathan remembered Dolly coming downstairs when they had got back; she had looked flustered. "You'd better not have been up there fucking some scroat while you were supposed to be looking after my daughter."

Jonathan made his way to the stairs to investigate. The mood he was in, if he did find some half-clad Casanova up there hiding in a wardrobe then he was going to get great pleasure in kicking the cunt all around the house.

"Honestly, Jono, I ain't had anyone here I swear. I poured a glass of wine out, and completely forgot I already had one sitting there. And as for the food... well, like I said, I'm starving," Dolly shouted up the stairs.

Jonathan knew she was lying. Taking the stairs two at a time, he searched Trevor's room first, checking under the bed and inside the walk-in wardrobe. If the fucker was hiding in here, he may have walked in but he wouldn't be walking back out. The room was empty.

"Jono, calm the fuck down." Running into the room, Trevor tried to restrain Jonathan as he smashed the en-suite door off the wall, before he ripped the shower curtain back. There was no one there either.

The only other place the man could be was in Dolly's room, and if he was then that would mean he was in there with his daughter. If so, Jono would string up the fucker by his balls.

Pushing Trevor away he slowly opened the door, and peered into Dolly's room. The bedside lamp was on, and to his horror the bed was empty.

"Where the fuck is my daughter?" he bellowed at the top of his voice when he realised that not only was the bed empty but the window was open.

Rosie had gone. Jonathan kicked the chest of drawers and wardrobe that stood side by side: Dolly was in a whole world of shit for this.

Chapter Thirty-Nine

Running down the street, Sophia kept stopping to look around in case any of the headlights of the passing traffic belonged to Jonathan. Ducking into yet another front garden, Sophia crouched down behind the hedge as she watched a car pass.

"My daddy isn't going to be very happy with you," Rosie said, as she huddled close to Sophia to keep warm. Sophia put her arm around her and pulled her against her body. She hoped that Rosie wasn't frightened, although the child had every reason to be. As soon as Sophia had heard Jonathan shouting at Dolly downstairs, she guessed that he was on to her. She had no time to think about where she was going to go, she just knew that she had to get out of there quickly. She had opened the bedroom window and on seeing the sturdy-looking conservatory roof just below had told Rosie that they were going to go on a little adventure.

Rosie had once again shaken her head defiantly until Sophia had said the words the girl had been waiting to hear. "If you come with me, I'll take you to your gran's house." She had then lowered Rosie onto the roof, whispering to her to hold on tightly. Hearing feet running up the stairs, Sophia had climbed out backwards and held on to the ledge before dropping down next to Rosie. Then jumping to the ground, she had put her arms out and tried to coax Rosie into jumping down.

"Rosie: jump. I'll catch you."

Rosie had shaken her head, looking scared. Seeing lights go on above them, Sophia knew that if they didn't move soon Jonathan would catch them.

"Rosie, if you want to see Granny you're going to have to be a very brave girl and do as I say. I promise I'll catch you. Now jump."

She watched Rosie hesitate before jumping down safely into her arms. And then, shoeless and sockless, they had run.

"Okay, come on." Sophia checked that the road was clear and indicated to Rosie to get onto her back. She ran as fast as she could, Rosie's hands clamped around her neck, with no idea where she was going. Jonathan would make Dolly tell her that it was her who had been there tonight, and in a car he would reach her place before she could if she tried to go there. The only other option was her nan's house: the next place he would check. She had no-one to help her. What had she been thinking?

"Are we nearly at my granny's, Sophia? I'm cold." Rosie's teeth chattered as she spoke. Sophia hadn't even had time to get the girl a jumper; she must be freezing. What could she do to look after her? And then she realised. Going to the Jenkins' house wasn't such a bad idea; it would certainly be the very last place that Jonathan would look for her. They would have to help her, as she had Rosie with her. And now that she knew that Jonathan had killed her father, they would have to listen.

"Hold on, Munchkin, we're almost there," she said to her daughter.

***

Jonathan slammed Dolly against the wall. "Where the fuck is she?" he bellowed, lifting her up.

Shaking her head, Dolly felt sick: Jonathan was terrifying her.

"Jono, you're going to fucking kill her." Trevor grabbed at Jono's arms, trying to get him to release his grip, as Dolly struggled to breathe.

"That's the fucking idea," Jonathan shouted as he pushed Trevor off him once more. "Where is my fucking daughter, Dolly? Tell me right now or I'm going to throw you out of that window head first onto the fucking concrete below." He meant every word. He wanted his daughter: she was his; she belonged to him.

"I didn't know who she was, Jonathan, I swear; I met her in prison," Dolly whimpered.

"What? Who did you meet?" Jonathan demanded.

"Sophia O'Hagan. We shared a cell."

Letting Dolly drop to the floor, Jonathan stared at her.

"Rosie's mum?" Trevor asked. Jonathan had hardly ever talked to him about Sophia, but on the few occasions that he had Trevor had seen the hate that the girl stirred in him. "I thought she was doing time?"

"She was." Jonathan glared at Dolly, who was shaking. "Oh, I get it. You met up on your stint inside and Sophia filled your head with stories, did she? Brainwashed you? The pair of you thought that you'd fucking stitch me up, did you?" Reaching into his pocket, he felt for his knife.

"No. I swear on Rosie's life, Jono. It wasn't like that... Sophia didn't know that we knew each other. She came here tonight just to see me, we're friends. I didn't even know that she'd gone upstairs and when I found her she was in my room with Rosie, crying and saying that she was her daughter. That's when you came home." Dolly could tell by the look on Jono's face that even though he might believe her story, the fact remained Sophia had taken his child and Dolly hadn't stopped her.

"You stupid fucking bitch." Jonathan lunged at Dolly, striking out with the knife.

Trevor put his body between them. "That's enough, Jono."

"Get out of my way, Trevor, before you end up getting hurt."

At first, Trevor thought he must have heard wrong. Had Jono threatened him? He stared at him, as if seeing him for the very first time.

"I think you're forgetting who you're talking to, Jono. You don't tell me what to do. I run things around here: not you. When I took you on, you were nothing but my lackey." Trevor glared at Jonathan.

"That's where you're wrong, Trevor. I've been running things. I've been creaming off some of your girls since I started. We've a little arrangement. I get a cut of their money before they show you what they've got left. If you weren't so fucking flash, the big 'I am', you'd have realised that. I don't need you anymore."

Jonathan rammed his knife into Trevor's torso. Dolly screamed.

"But you love me," Trevor said, as he felt the blade's sharp steel pierce his skin.

Jonathan's steely eyes bore into him as he spoke in a cool tone. "Love? You were a means to an end."

Taking his weapon out, Jonathan grinned as Trevor slumped to the floor. Blood all over his hands, Jonathan waved the knife in Dolly's direction.

"You're coming with me," he said, as he grabbed her by her hair and frogmarched her out of the house towards his car.

Chapter Forty

"So? Have I done well?" Stanley asked, as his wife filled the kettle to make another round of coffees. It was the first time in a week that he had seen her smiling. He hoped that it heralded a new beginning. They had been ignoring important issues for far too long, and it was time to start dealing with them.

"You've done more than good, Stanley. I still can't believe he's here. How did you manage it?" Earlier, when her husband had said that he had a surprise lined up for her, she had thought it would be something like a meal at their local pub. He had insisted that she get out of her robe and get a shower, and boy was she glad she had.

When the doorbell chimed, Bernie thought that it was a taxi coming to pick them up. Never in a million years had she expected to open the door and be greeted by Tommy.

Looking now at the big bouquet of flowers he had brought her, Bernie felt like crying.

"It was time. Tommy's been gone for too long. I know how you feel about Jonathan, and I accept it, Bernie; God knows, after all these years I'm used to playing second fiddle to that boy. But Tommy is equally your son, and we owe him. We let him down once, and I won't be doing that again."

"I just didn't want Jonathan to feel like I let him down. I just wanted to do everything I could so that I wouldn't feel like such a failure."

Hugging his wife, Stanley whispered: "You didn't fail, Bernie. No-one could have loved that boy more than you. But it's time you admitted to yourself that Jonathan has problems. You know as well as I do that Sophia was telling the truth. Jonathan has lied, cheated and ripped this family apart. We either stop it all right here or..."

"I know, Stan, I know." Bernie hung her head in shame. Finally Bernie was admitting what she had secretly known all along.

"We need to start being honest; we owe it to Tommy."

***

Reaching the Jenkins' front door, Sophia repeatedly rang on the bell. Rosie stood at her side, a big smile on her face now that she was home, despite the fact that she was still shivering.

"Hold your horses," Stanley shouted, as he made his way down the hallway. It was almost half ten, so whoever it was had better have a good reason for interrupting them.

"Sophia?" Stanley was shocked to see the distressed look on the face of the girl standing before him. Then seeing Rosie at her side, he frowned. "What the hell's going on?"

"Is everything okay, Stanley?" Bernie called.

"Granny," Rosie shouted, as she ran into the house and flung her arms around her amazed grandmother.

Bernie felt the child's cold skin. "You're freezing, Rosie." She turned to Sophia. "What are you doing dragging the poor child around at this time of night without so much as shoes and a coat?"

"I'm so sorry," Sophia said, "but I had to get away quickly and I had nowhere else to go. He killed him... he killed my dad."

Tommy recognised the voice of the girl on the doorstep. He stood up slowly. Walking down the hallway, he saw his mum holding a little girl and his dad hugging Sophia.

Even after all this time, when Tommy looked at her, he still felt it.

"Tommy," Sophia gasped. He was taller now, and even more handsome.

"What's happened?" he asked, seeing the child was wearing just her nightie and that she and Sophia had bare feet.

"It's Jonathan; I've just found out that he killed my dad. I took Rosie. He's going to kill me." Sobbing, Sophia fell into Tommy's arms.

Tommy's stiff body relaxed as he hugged her. As he buried his face into her hair and breathed in her smell, the eight years that stood between them melted away.

***

"Think Dolly, she must have mentioned somewhere else. Where's she gone?" Jonathan kicked the side of his car in a rage. That bitch thought that she could steal his daughter from under his nose and get away with it. He was going to kill her when he caught up with her.

Standing outside Sophia's flat, Dolly shivered as she tried to think of where else Jono could look.

"I don't know, Jono, honestly. This place and her nan's are the only ones she has ever spoken of." Dolly's body was shaking in fear.

"You don't know?" he growled. "You lying bitch. You both fucking planned this, didn't you? You better start thinking, Dolly because if you don't come up with something quickly I'm going to start smashing your pretty little face repeatedly on that brick fucking wall." Pacing up and down the path next to the car, Jono was building himself up into a frenzy. Two things he hated more than anything was being mugged off and being mugged off by a woman. Sophia must have a death wish.

"There's nowhere else I can think of, I promise; she hasn't mentioned anywhere else, just here or her nan's. The only other place she said she's been since she got out was your parents' house." Dolly didn't want to mention the hospital, because Jono would have no qualms in going there and causing merry hell for poor old Nessa. "And Rosie did keep mentioning her granny tonight, saying she missed her."

The more that Dolly thought about it, the more she believed that if she could get Jono onto familiar territory, she might have a chance of distracting him so she could get away. Failing that, if they turned up at his home, she might be able to get his parents to talk him down.

Jonathan frowned. "That would be the last place she'd go. She's not welcome there."

"Yes, and she knows that you'll think it's the least likely place, too. Tell you what, you can say a lot about her but Sophia is sharper than a razor," Dolly said, feeling clever; she could see the clogs moving in Jonathan's head as he took her bait. "And that's the only other place she has ever mentioned. But maybe you're right, she wouldn't go there."

"Get in."

Starting the engine, Jonathan thought it wouldn't hurt to take a look. His mum had been warned about letting in Sophia: she wouldn't get over the front step. He wasn't so sure about his dad, the disloyal bastard. He'd take the word of the postman's over the word of his own son.

***

Crouching on the ground, Jonathan crept around the back of the house with his hand against Dolly's mouth. He didn't want the silly bitch to start screaming. The lights in the kitchen were on and he could see movement. He dragged Dolly behind him as he got closer for a better view.

Sitting around the table were his parents, deep in conversation with a young couple. His father was pacing the kitchen. The younger man stretched his arm out and rested it on Stanley's shoulder as he passed him. The younger man was Tommy. He had come home. And Sophia was sitting next to him.

Feeling like he had been punched in the gut, Jonathan struggled to catch his breath. He stood there, taking it all in, gripping Dolly tighter as he felt his anger bubble. Tommy was back, and all was forgiven with Sophia by the looks of it. Yet again Jonathan was on the outside, staring in through the window of a stranger's home; they were so familiar to him but he didn't share any of their warmth. In fact, he despised them all. He particularly despised his dad for being a weak, pathetic excuse of a man. He couldn't stand his mother because of her constant neediness; the way she clung to her kids and granddaughter for dear life because she didn't have a life of her own irritated the hell out of him. He despised Tommy for being everything that he would never be: he had got all the good genes. Tommy was the nice one, the caring one, while all he got all the leftover crap.

Scanning the room for his daughter, Jonathan couldn't see her. He guessed that she would be upstairs, out of the way. It was late and she would be tired.

Dragging Dolly to his dad's shed Jonathan yanked the lock off and opened the door, forcing her inside. Then, he wound a thick roll of masking tape repeatedly around her mouth. Then pushing her down onto his dad's chair by the window he bound her hands and legs.

Dolly winced as he tugged at her skin, pinching her as he ensured that the tape was tight enough. She could see that he was capable of murder. He was an empty shell, void of any feeling such as empathy.

"I'll be back to sort you out properly soon," he whispered in Dolly's ear before shutting her inside the pitch-black shed.

Climbing onto the roof under the bathroom, Jonathan pulled himself across and onto a ledge, crouching under the bedroom window; he made sure that the coast was clear before hoisting himself up and slipping inside. Tiptoeing through his parents' room, he could see the hallway light glowing through the doorway and he could hear faint voices. He couldn't make out what they were saying, but he knew they were talking about him.

Creeping into the hallway, he made his way to Rosie's room and pushed open the door. Rosie was lying in bed, a Disney movie playing quietly in the background. Plaits framed her sleeping face, her closed eyes emphasising her long and perfect eyelashes. Rosie was the only thing in his life that he had done right, and he wasn't going to let anyone take her away from him. Bending down, he gently kissed the top of her head, before sneaking out of the room and down the stairs. Here, the voices were louder.

"We need to call the police," his father said.

"You're right," his mother said, "we have to, for Rosie's sake."

Rosie was the most important person in Bernie's life, and she wasn't going to allow Jonathan to mess her up. When Rosie had flung her arms around Bernie's neck, she had felt every bit the child's mother. Picking up the receiver, she dialled. Not only had Jonathan let Sophia rot away in prison for something she didn't do, her son had murdered in cold blood. Bernie was sickened to her core that she could have birthed someone as heartless.

Opening the kitchen door, Jonathan stood in the doorway. He smiled as he watched the four shocked-looking faces turn to him.

"Put the phone down," he commanded his mother and Bernie, seeing the look in his eyes, did as she was told.

"Well, this all looks very cosy. You're home then, Tommy: lovely." Jonathan nodded at his brother. "And I see you two little lovebirds have made up now."

"Why did you do it Jonathan? Why did you murder my dad?" Sophia asked.

"Oh, Sophia, please. Your father was a waste of space. If I hadn't killed him, it would have only been a matter of time before you did... or the alcohol would have finished him off. Either way it was inevitable: I did you a favour. Are you going to say thank you?"

Tommy clenched his fists. He knew that Jonathan had hated Sophia, but this wasn't normal antipathy. Jonathan was deranged: a psychopath.

"You raped her?" Tommy asked, knowing he wasn't going to like Jonathan's answer.

"Rape is a strong word, Tommy. Especially considering that the stupid bitch was gagging for it. One shag with the lovely Sophia turned me off women for life.' Jonathan laughed. He was enjoying tormenting everyone.

Tommy couldn't listen to any more. He had spent his childhood standing up for Jonathan. And for what? Jonathan had always treated him like he was nothing.

He stood up. "You led me to believe that Sophia had cheated on me... I left, Jonathan. Why? What has happened to you?"

"Oh spare me the dramatics, Tommy," Jonathan mocked. "I'm the same person I've always been. Come on then, what do you want to do? Bear hug me? Give me a couple of bitch slaps? You ain't changed one bit, Tommy; you still couldn't punch your way out of a paper bag. Not as innocent as he'd have you all believe though are you Tommy? Have you told them all that you were there with me the night that Old man O'Hagan met his fate?"

Jonathan grinned now, it was obvious by the look on Sophia's face that she had no idea her precious Tommy had been involved that night.

"I swear Sophia, I didn't know that Jonathan killed your dad. On my life, you have to believe me. We did break in, but only because we wanted to make sure you were okay, and when your dad heard us, he chased us. That was it I promise." Tommy pleaded.

Sophia felt a tear slip down her cheek. How many more lies were there?

"You have to be pretty thick to not add it up Tommy. Didn't you ever suspect that it was me?" Jonathan sneered.

Tommy shook his head. It had briefly crossed his mind but he had known Sophia hated her father, and she had even told him once that she wanted to kill him for what he put her mum through. His mind had been swamped at the time with the evidence that was presented at Sophia's trial, and then when he heard about Rosie, he hadn't known what to believe anymore.

Jonathan laughed, watching his brother as the realisation finally sunk in. All these years and Tommy was only just learning the truth. They all were.

Seeing that Tommy was about to launch himself at him and his father would no doubt help, Jonathan knew he was outnumbered. Deciding to get himself some collateral damage, he grabbed Sophia and hoisted her up off her chair. His pressed his flick knife against her throat just in case anyone had any illusions about how serious he was. Bernie gasped, as she saw the blood smeared along the blade from earlier. Sophia looked like she was scared to breathe.

"One move, Tommy, and I swear to God I will cut her fucking throat."

Reluctantly, Tommy put his hands up, signifying a truce.

"All I've come here for is Rosie," Jonathan said. "I don't want to hurt anyone, I just want my daughter. So Mother, be a dear and go and get her will you?"

"Jonathan, please don't; it's not fair. The girl's been through enough," Bernie begged.

"I ain't asking, Mother, I'm telling, so fucking move!" Jonathan wasn't going to stick around to be handed over to the police, and have his little girl taken away from him.

Bernie ran from the room. Stanley glared at Jonathan, hate radiating out of him in waves. Jonathan saw his look.

"Disappointing, ain't I, Dad? Should have been a do-gooding arse-licker like my brother, shouldn't I?" Jonathan sneered. "Could never match up to Tommy, though, could I? Well, at least you've got good reason to hate me now."

From the looks being exchanged between his dad and Tommy, Jonathan guessed that any minute they were going to try something stupid like making an attempt to ambush him.

Stanley was thinking something different, though. He could see the phone that Bernie had dropped on the table was connected to the caller and hoping that the operator would have contacted the police, he decided to play for time.

"So, how many others have there been, Jonathan?" Stanley demanded. "Go on; tell us; if you were capable of murdering Sophia's dad when you were a kid, then you must've done it again since, right?"

"Too many to count," Jonathan boasted and then, for effect, added: "Actually, it started off out of curiosity; I just wanted to see what death looked like. And then I began to enjoy it. It was a bit of game really. You'd be surprised at the amount of people that cry and beg before they die. You just can never tell what a man – or woman – is made of until those last final moments. Some people have no dignity; it's shameful." Jonathan shook his head in genuine dissatisfaction. Some of his victims really hadn't met his expectations.

Despite the question he had asked, Stanley listened to his son speaking in disbelief. All these years he had known that Jonathan was not all there, but this was a whole other level: it was impossible to comprehend, or to forgive.

Seeing Bernie coming down the hallway holding Rosie's hand to stop the child from running to her father at the sound of his voice, Stanley shook his head at her. Bernie slowly backed away.

"But why, Jonathan? Why take all those lives?" Stanley asked.

"Why? Why not? It makes life exciting... What would have been a crime was if I'd ended up living a boring existence, like you. Look at you. You get up day after day and do the same mind-numbing job, tinkering with the same shitty cars whilst talking to the same dull people. You're the freak, not me. Bring Rosie in here now, Mum. I'm not waiting any longer."

Bernie led the child, a lamb to the slaughter, into the kitchen.

"Daddy, no," Rosie cried, as she saw her dad holding a knife against Sophia's throat. "Leave Sophia alone, Daddy."

"Rosie, be a good girl and open the back door," Jonathan said.

"Put the knife down, Daddy, and then I'll come," Rosie said.

Jonathan was impressed: Rosie was a real chip off the old block. "Okay, but promise me we're going to go then. You're going to get in the car with Daddy, and we're going to leave."

"I promise."

Jonathan lowered the knife and Sophia ran to Tommy, rubbing her throat. Tommy held her close.

"Come on, Rosie, we're going," Jonathan said.

"No, Daddy: I want to stay here with Granny."

When he picked Rosie up, she kicked him in the face. Stanley took his chance and ran at Jonathan, pinning him against the wall. Tommy, aware that Jonathan still had the knife in his hand, tried to help his dad overpower his brother, but Jonathan was too strong and he lashed out kicking and punching then blindly struck out with the knife. It caught Rosie's shoulder, slicing through her robe and into her flesh. She let out a piercing scream.

"Rosie, darling, I didn't mean it; Daddy didn't mean it." Jonathan realised what he had done, reaching out for her. Rosie flinched, clutching her arm, blood trickling through her hands.

Reaching for the saucepan on the stove, Bernie smashed it against Jonathan's head. He slumped on the floor, his blood spilling onto it. Sophia grabbed Rosie and hugged her, shielding the child's eyes as she pressed her closer.

"Call an ambulance Tommy," she cried.

Bernie had lost control, still hitting her son. Stanley tried to grab his wife's hands but she batted his away.

"Bernie, stop," Stanley cried.

There was a gouge in the back of Jonathan's head where his skull had caved in. Still, Bernie continued to beat him with the pan.

"Granny, please stop," Rosie shouted.

Coming to when she heard her granddaughter's plea, Bernie screamed as she realised that Jonathan was lying face down in a pool of blood. He was dead. She had killed him.

Chapter Forty-One

Seeing Tommy sitting on the bench at the back of the garden, Stanley made his way over to join him. The day was gloriously sunny and the barbeque that he was cooking would be fine without him for a few minutes.

"Are you alright, son? Mind if I join you?" he asked, as he sat next to Tommy. His son was staying with them, and Stanley was grateful for his company. It was helping Bernie to cope.

"I was just thinking about him, you know." Tommy's head had been all over the place for the past few weeks. Jonathan had tried to destroy the people Tommy loved. He had lied, cheated, and murdered. But Tommy couldn't find it in himself to feel any hate for him.

"I know, son." Stanley patted Tommy's leg. Jonathan's death had affected every member of the family in one way or another but Tommy had taken it harder than anyone: being his twin gave him a different kind of connection with Jonathan. He had lived with him in the womb, and despite what he had done he would always be part of Tommy.

"He just seemed so lost. It wasn't even like it was him anymore, you know." Tommy deeply regretted staying away for so long. He wondered whether him leaving had made Jonathan worse, maybe if he hadn't things might have turned out differently. Maybe Jonathan wouldn't have felt so alone.

"You could go around in circles for the rest of your life wondering about it, Tommy, but who knows what makes someone behave like that. He's gone now; we can only hope that in death he found some kind of peace."

"Stanley, I can smell burning," Bernie shouted from the patio table.

Stanley laughed. "Your mum still doesn't get the whole barbeque thing, does she? Come on, let's go and get some grub before she gets the bloody fire extinguisher onto it."

Stanley wrapped his arm around Tommy's shoulder as they made their way to where the others were sitting. He sat next to Bernie, who smiled at him. She had been different since Jonathan's death, like a weight had been lifted from her shoulders.

"So what's your news, girls?" Bernie looked from Dolly to Sophia, wondering about the announcement they had said they were going to make.

Bernie had really taken to Sophia over the past few weeks. They had had a heart-to-heart and Sophia had assured her that she had no intention of taking Rosie from her, feeling that Rosie belonged to Bernie; she would love to see her and to build a relationship with her, but she wasn't her mother: Bernie was. Bernie felt that they all owed Sophia for what Jonathan had done to her, and for all that he had taken from her, and she wanted to do her best to make it up. Sophia was part of the family now, and Bernie would make sure that Rosie spent as much time with her biological mum as she could.

"Before you say anything," Nessa interrupted, "I just want to say that if this is what I think it is then you don't have to explain yourselves. It didn't happen much in my day, or if it did then it went on behind closed doors but I have no problem with it."

"What are you talking about, Nan?" Sophia looked at Dolly, who was sitting next to Nessa, clearly trying not to laugh.

"I've had my suspicions," Nessa said.

"Had your suspicions?" Dolly giggled. "About us...?"

"If you two want to dabble in a bit of lesbianism, you have my full approval."

Bernie snorted the mouthful of wine that she was about to swallow back up her nose. She could see by Dolly and Sophia's faces that Nessa had got it wrong.

"We were watching a programme on lesbians the other night," Nessa continued. "Weren't we, Albert? As a bit of research. Very interesting, it was."

"Yes, it was very good." Albert chuckled.

"Nan!" Sophia laughed. "We're not lesbians. Our news is that we've got the flat."

"Ah, that's lovely. I'm so happy for you both." Bernie clapped her hands together.

Sophia and Dolly had been looking at a flat around the corner from the Jenkins' house, a new build. The girls thought that not only would they be good company for each other but if they shared the rent they could afford to undertake further education, with Dolly having decided to train as a counsellor. Trevor's death had hit her harder than she had ever expected, but it had also set her free from her old life. And it meant that now Sophia would be living right between her nan and Rosie, so could split her time between the two; she hoped to train to be a chef.

"What have I missed?" Tommy asked as he returned from the kitchen with a fresh beer for himself and his dad and sat down opposite Sophia.

"My lovely nan here has all but arranged a civil partnership for me and Dolly; think her and Albert are going to want to be bridesmaids." Sophia giggled. "I was just saying that we got the flat."

Tommy beamed. He knew how much getting that flat meant to Sophia. After everything that had happened, she very much deserved a fresh start.

"So I'm afraid, Tommy, that if you want Sophia in the future you'll have to go through me." Dolly winked.

Tommy blushed. He had decided that he wasn't going to go back to his old life. He wanted to move nearer to his parents. After what the family had been through, they had a stronger bond.

He certainly had feelings for Sophia, but it was too soon to make them apparent to her. She had been through so much that he wanted to give her space: one day, who knew. Right now, he just wanted to be her friend.

"Ignore her, Tommy." Sophia smiled. "You'll be one our first guests."

Dolly nudged her friend, smiling.

Laughing, Sophia added, "You can help us with the furniture."

Tommy grinned.

"Right; grub's up." Stanley placed a platter of barbequed food onto the table.

"Where's Rosie?" Bernie asked, as she looked around the garden.

"I know where she is: I'll get her." Stanley was sure that she would be using the new colouring book he had bought her earlier.

Bernie smiled; she appreciated the fact that Stanley was making an effort with Rosie. They were having family counselling sessions, and Bernie hoped that in time they would move on from the events that had taken place. Bernie hadn't been charged for Jonathan's murder. After the police had found Dolly tied up inside the shed and she had told them about Jonathan killing Trevor, along with the little girl's slash wound and the kitchen full of witnesses, there was no question of it.

Bernie didn't need to be punished by the law, though; she would always have to live with the knowledge that she had killed her son. It was a heavy cross to bear, but Bernie was determined she would make it up to Jonathan by looking after his daughter.

"Actually, can I go and find Rosie?" Tommy asked.

Bernie and Stanley looked at each other. It was the first time that Tommy had said anything like that. They knew it was hard for him to accept that Sophia had had a child with Jonathan, especially the way the conception had occurred. But maybe his feelings were starting to change.

Bernie smiled. "Of course you can, love."

***

Rosie was sitting on the edge of her bed when Tommy opened the door. She had her palms in her lap and her head hung down.

"Rosie," Tommy said, "what are you doing in here all on your own?"

"I feel a bit sad today," Rosie said. "I know my daddy was a bad man. But sometimes he was a good man, too, and I miss him."

Tommy sat on the bed next to his niece. Looking at her, he smiled. She had so much of Sophia in her, yet he could see a lot of Jonathan too. Putting his arm around her shoulder, Tommy said to her softly, "You're allowed to miss him, sweetheart. We all do in our own way. Your daddy wasn't bad, he was very poorly, and he lost his way."

"Do you think that he's still lost now, Uncle Tommy?"

"No, darling, I think your daddy is finally at peace," Tommy said, and he hoped to God that he was right. He wished his brother nothing but peace.

"When I get sad I can look at your face, Uncle Tommy, can't I, and then I won't think that he is so far away?"

"Of course you can," Tommy said. A single tear slid down his cheek as he pulled his niece close to him. "Now come on, if we don't get downstairs soon, Granddad will have eaten all the sausages."

Lightning Source UK Ltd.
Milton Keynes UK
UKOW04f1701160915

258730UK00001B/60/P